D0385083

1/8/09

LIVING
THE VIDA
LOLA

LIVING THE VIDA LOLA

A Lola Cruz Mystery

MISA RAMIREZ

 Minotaur Books ✿ New York

Minotaur Books ✿ New York

This is a work of fiction. All of the characters, organizations, and events portrayed in this novel are either products of the author's imagination or are used fictitiously.

A THOMAS DUNNE BOOK FOR MINOTAUR BOOKS.
An imprint of St. Martin's Publishing Group.

www.minotaurbooks.com
www.thomasdunnebooks.com

Library of Congress Cataloging-in-Publication Data

Ramirez, Misa.
    Living the vida Lola : a Lola Cruz mystery / Misa Ramirez.—1st ed.
        p. cm.
    ISBN-13: 978-0-312-38402-9
    ISBN-10: 0-312-38402-5
    1. Women private investigators—California—Sacramento—Fiction.
2. Sacramento (Calif.)—Fiction.   3. Murder—Investigation—Fiction.
I. Title.
    PS3618.A464L58 2009
    813'.6—dc22

                                                        2008030428

First Edition: January 2009

10 9 8 7 6 5 4 3 2 1

To Caleb, Sam, Sophia, AJ, and Jared.
You're pretty decent kids. Okay, great kids.
Seriously, you rock! Don't ever change.

Acknowledgments

It's commonly said that life is about the journey. Ain't that the truth! My writing journey started years ago—as did Lola's journey—and so I'll start there and work my way to the present (as this is my first novel, I have to give props to all!).

Lola was born during Monday night writing sessions with Elena Soto-Chapa. We were both itching to escape home even if it was for just a few hours. Dude, you rock! Thanks to Kim Weber and Cory Hollingsworth, who later joined our Monday nights and saw Lola through the first draft and me through the mechanics of writing a book.

Thanks to Carol McLeroy Loo, through whom I connected with Pat Teal, the first industry person to believe in me and love Lola.

A raucous shout-out goes to the Scarlets: Susan Hatler and Virna de Paul. You two are the best crit partners a writer girl could have and I could not—literally *could not*—have done this without you.

Fellow SVR member Brenda Novak, as well as being an inspiration in writing, has shown me how valuable and supportive the writing community is. Her annual online auction to raise money for research to cure diabetes brought us together. Here's to the forthcoming Texas connection for the auction!

Through Jenny Bent, I was able to make the most valuable and wonderful agent connection with Holly Root. I heartily thank them both for believing in me. Holly has been Lola's champion from the start, and I love her for that and for her enthusiasm.

Of course this leads me to Toni Plummer, my amazing editor at Thomas Dunne Books. I know how difficult it is to make that first sale and how essential it is to have an editor who loves your book and characters. Toni's encouragement, editing, and insight, and love for Lola and her crew is more than I ever dreamed of. She's the best!

The art department has created the most amazing cover for this book, and the behind-the-scenes people at St. Martin's, as well as Eliani Torres, have helped make it what you see here. I am so grateful to them for giving their all to this book.

Without my friends to laugh and cry with, and to have girl time with, life wouldn't be nearly as complete. Here's to Gloria, an inspiration and a more loving sister than any real sister could be; to Paige, the truest best friend and 5:30 A.M. "wogging" buddy a girl could ask for; to Christy, who has taught me so much about myself, fashion, and the appeal of Wal-Mart; to Katie, a future Texan and amazing friend—I wanna dance like you!; to Kim, who makes me try harder, reach deeper for meaning, and gets my sarcasm even when it's about our kids; to Marilyn Bourbon, another future Texan and the person who knows me best and always will, and the best mom a girl can have; again to the Scarlets S and V, who went from writing partners to best friends; and to the Book Babes because y'all are my gals, even from Texas!

Finally, to the family. Unless you're a writer or a creative mind, it's hard to understand the degree of passion we writers often have for our craft. But my husband, Carlos, despite his occasional puzzlement at my obsession, has always cheered me on, reminded me when I'm down that I love writing, and he will always be the one to keep me grounded. To my kids for their understanding when mom just wouldn't get off the computer and for being okay with a "whatever" dinner . . . again. And to mom and dad for their unwavering support and love. You're the best!

Prologue

W hen I was fourteen years old, I snapped pictures of Jack Callaghan doing the horizontal salsa in the backseat of a car with Greta Pritchard. That's when I knew for sure I'd grow up to be a private eye.

I'd stooped to low levels in order to spy on him: disguising myself as a substitute custodian and pushing a mop cart into the boys' locker room as the team dressed for baseball practice; borrowing my uncle's car and following Jack at a safe distance as he went to work at the music store where he gave guitar lessons; and even calling him up, pretending to be a girl he knew, and making a fake date with him at an outdoor café.

I had one goal: to surveil and take photos of Jack for my own personal enjoyment.

It had taken a month of steadfast determination, and at least four rolls of film, before I'd captured images of Jack that were still burned into my memory: him, messing around—no, having sex—with Greta while he was supposedly dating Laura something-or-other. My mother called him *un mujeriego*—a player. I didn't care. I just wanted him to do to me what he'd done to Greta.

Back in high school, Jack and my brother, Antonio, made

their way through the cheerleaders, then the Future Female Leaders of America. But Jack didn't give me, little Lola Cruz, the time of day.

"I'll never get to do that with him!" I'd wailed to my sister, Gracie, when I showed her the pictures I had of him and Greta.

She'd looked longingly at the photos. "Yeah," she sighed heavily. "But at least you can look at him whenever you want and imagine." Then she got serious. "And, more importantly, you discovered what you're good at. Now you won't be stuck working at Abuelita's for the rest of your life."

Gracie was right. If it hadn't been for my relentless pursuit of Jack Callaghan, I might never have discovered my proclivity for surveillance and undercover work.

My favorite picture of Jack, taken that fateful night, still had a place in my dresser drawer, fifteen years later. He stood bare-chested, his business with Greta done, a look of contentment on his face. The edge of his mouth lifted in the smallest smile. He was just seventeen years old, and his smoky blue eyes seemed trained directly on me, as if he were staring straight through the shrubs to where I was hidden.

I was pretty sure Jack Callaghan didn't know I'd been a teenage stalker, and even though I still had a secret longing to feel him pressed against me, my embarrassment at invading his privacy and my anger that I'd never be anything more to him than Antonio's little sister had kept me far, far away from him. I avoided him at all costs so that I wouldn't break down and confess in a moment of guilty Catholic repentance.

I'd been in and out of relationships, but those old photos of Jack reminded me of what I'd lost, even though I'd never had it. Or him. He was still my favorite fantasy, as well as a reminder of how I'd gotten to where I was now.

Still, while Jack—and his untamed libido—had never given me an orgasm (well, at least not person-to-person), he had done something earth-moving for me. I was Dolores Cruz, aka Lola, PI. Thanks to him, I'd answered my calling.

Chapter 1

*C*aliente. Hotter than hell. There's no other way to describe Sacramento summers. I checked my reflection in the window as I approached Camacho and Associates, the small PI firm where I worked. I frowned and flicked at a stringy strand of hair. What the hell. Being a black belt in kung fu did not, apparently, prevent me from completely wilting. Nothing—not my ability to kick ass or even my eighty-five-dollar coppery salon highlights—could withstand triple-digit valley temperatures. And it was barely ten in the morning.

An alarm beeped as I opened the front door. Inside the office, I wiped the dust from a leaf of the sad little artificial palm that sat on the floor against the wall. It looked shabby, which was no small feat for a plant that didn't need sun, water, or tender love and care. After four years, I would have thought my ritualistic token of attention would spruce it up.

It hadn't.

I waved to the camera that was mounted in the ceiling corner. It was no secret that my arrival had been monitored. Neil Lashby was the video go-to guy of the operation. He owned more cameras than I did Victoria's Secret lingerie. Sorta frightening when you thought about it.

I walked through the lobby—which really wasn't a lobby—and passed into the main conference room. Reilly Fuller, our six-hour-a-day secretary and a full-fledged—not to mention full-figured—J. Lo wannabe, had a little table in one corner of the conference room where she spent her time typing reports, transcribing tapes, filing, and doing whatever other menial jobs the associates handed her. Being a licensed PI, I was above her on the food chain. But I liked to type my own reports and do my own filing, and as a result, she liked me. Important, since Neil Lashby, one of the agency's associates, was a nonverbal, ex–football player, ex-cop Neanderthal-type PI; Sadie Metcalf, the second associate, was hot and cold toward me and I hadn't yet figured out a rhyme or reason to her temperature changes; and the boss, Manny Camacho, was, well, he was just plain dangerous—hot in a dark, sinister, attractive-to-every-woman-with-a-pulse kind of way.

Reilly was a good ally.

I raised a questioning eyebrow at her as I passed her desk—as much a reaction to her newly dyed blue hair as to get the scoop on the new case we were meeting about. "Hey, Reilly."

She did a complicated maneuver at me with her own mousy brown brows and mouthed something. I peered at her, but try as I might, I couldn't decipher her silent words.

She bugged her eyes, clamped her mouth shut, and went back to her computer when Manny walked out of his private office. He approached the conference table, a brown file folder clutched to his side. His mouth was drawn into its typical tight line, his square jaw interrupted by a slight vertical cleft. Manny's crew-cut hair was the color of dark roast coffee, which pretty much described his personality, too. He wasn't quite bitter, but he wasn't smooth either. Even the scalp that showed through his close-cut hair was burnished. He was intense and needed a bit of cream to mellow the flavor. Unfortunately, he and his cream had divorced.

And that's all I knew about his personal life.

The associates had already gathered around the conference table. "Morning," I said, nodding to all two of them.

He checked his watch. "Cutting it close, Dolores." His deep voice held the hint of an accent. The way he said my name—low, gravelly long *o* and rolling *r*—made my legs wobble. I couldn't help but wonder what it would sound like if he called me Lola instead.

Breathing deeply and pushing the wayward thought away, I mustered a smile and glanced at the wall clock. The minute hand clicked up to ten o'clock. I felt my eyebrows pull together, and I pressed my fingers to my forehead to smooth the creases away. "Right on time, actually."

His jaw was set, and I could tell he was clenching his teeth, holding his tension deep in his bones. He held out a file folder to me. Something about me bugged him—I just didn't know what.

I took the folder from his grasp and slipped into a vacant chair at the conference table. Truth was, I didn't really want to know.

Sadie sat directly across from me. As usual, her strawberry blond hair was styled to perfection, a precise work of casual messiness. "Dolores," she said. "You really should arrive a few minutes early for meetings."

Okay, so today was a cold day for Sadie. God, she acted like she owned the place. Why did Manny put up with it? I flashed her an *eat shit* smile and then opened my file folder.

The agency's standard information sheet was secured to the folder with metal prongs. I looked at the photo that was clipped to the top and ticked my observations off in my head. Female, mid to late forties, dark brown hair with a tuft of gray springing from her temple, deep eye sockets with nearly

7

translucent irises that hinted at the color of sand, full pink lips, pale skin. Despite her tired look, she was still stunning. Exotic.

Manny sat down and slid a pile of papers to the center of the table. I snatched the last sheet from the table as he said, "Missing person."

I shifted my focus back to the file folder.

"Emily Diggs, age forty-two, mother of three: daughter Allison, twenty-one years; son, Garrett, eighteen; son, Sean, six. Last seen on the morning of August twenty-third."

My heart thumped. A missing mother. Getting emotionally involved in a case was Manny's number-one taboo. It was also the first rule I always broke. After five seconds, this woman was just Emily, no last name needed. Her haunting face burned behind my eyelids.

Neil grunted before asking, "The client? Police?"

He tended not to speak in complete sentences. I'd learned to fill in the blanks in my head. *Who'd hired us, and are the police involved?* Two very good questions. Neil was always on top of things.

Manny gave a succinct nod. He read between the lines, too. "The police are working the case but have zero so far. Their immediate reaction is that she bolted. Walter Diggs, the brother, and our client, has temporary custody of the boy."

Neil shifted his linebacker body in his chair. "Anything else?"

"Mother and son left their P Street rental house around seven A.M. last Tuesday. Kid was stranded after school with no pickup. Emily Diggs never showed for work that day." Manny tapped his index finger against the table, ready to field the next question.

"Kindergarten or first grade?" I asked, wanting to get in the game.

"First." He had no need to double-check the information. He'd already committed it to memory. What a pro.

8

"Maybe drugs—," Sadie began.

I shook my head. She always thought the worst about people.

"Yup, could be into something bad," Neil said.

Okay, maybe thinking the worst came with the profession. I just wasn't jaded yet. Give me another ten years.

"Too soon to tell. Our client says his sister shut everyone out of her life after her youngest son was born. They stayed in contact, but he didn't see her often. She wanted to keep the boy to herself." Manny looked at each of us, pausing for a second when he got to me.

I bristled under his scrutiny and studied the folder more intently. He was waiting for me to make a brilliant comment, I realized. "Have they always lived in Sacramento?"

"According to our client, yes, but they recently moved. The address in the file is the most recent residence."

What would make a woman distance herself from her family? I couldn't, even if I tried. They'd hunt me down. "How old is the photo?"

"Two months," Manny said. "Client said it was taken last time they all went to the zoo."

"She looks sad to me, not addicted."

"Hard to tell from a photo," Sadie said.

I ignored her. "Her kids must be devastated."

No response. I had to stop myself from sliding down in my chair.

"I've broken down assignments," Manny said, pulling out another sheet of paper.

Don't pair me with Sadie, I willed. We'd worked the firm's last surveillance gig together, and I was still decompressing.

"Status quo with our active cases," he continued. "Lashby. Status?"

Neil lifted his head up from his laptop. "Two weeks, sealed tight."

Manny nodded. "Behind the scenes here, as needed."

Neil nodded his square head quickly and just once. "Yup."

Manny looked at Sadie next. "You go undercover tomorrow?"

"Grocery store checker at Laughlin's." She gave him a steely look. "Training's this afternoon." She paused. "Dolores should take it."

No way. I was the only one without an active case. It was my turn. And I'd earned it after my last success. Club Ambrosía was Sacramento's salsa-dancing hot spot. A month ago, the co-owners had hired Camacho and Associates to flush out some women they suspected were using the club as a call girl meet-and-greet. I'd landed the assignment, gone in undercover, gleaned evidence of the prostitution service, and managed to infiltrate. It had taken two weeks, and some close calls, but I'd gotten one of the women to talk about how they ran their business, on tape, and the police had been able to shut them down, though sadly, the madam had escaped. Still, Club Ambrosía was free of prostitution—thanks to me.

Manny narrowed his eyes at her, looked at me, and then back to her. "You stick with Laughlin's. Dolores will be the primary on the Diggs case. We'll shift for backup if needed."

Color rose on Sadie's face like a helium balloon slowly filling. She pressed her palms against the table. "But this is a missing—"

Manny's hand flew up, his palm facing her.

She didn't listen—to the unspoken command or to the hand. "I've done dozens of missing persons—," she started.

"Decision's made," Manny interrupted, his voice tight. Then he scribbled something onto the paper he had in front of him.

Sadie snapped her mouth shut. I could almost see her blood simmering.

"Questions, Dolores?" Manny asked.

I shook my head. "No. I'm clear."

"*Explícamelo*."

I stifled the thread of anger that wound through me. I was a professional. I'd been working my ass off, first as an assistant under his license while I earned the mandatory PI hours for the state of California, and for the last two years as a full-fledged associate. He always questioned everything—with everyone—but at this moment, it irked me. I didn't want to explain myself in front of Sadie. "I'm going to investigate the disappearance of Emily Diggs," I said, sounding a bit too much like a regurgitated line from my worn PI manual.

Sadie leaned back and folded her arms, looking smug. "Right, but what's your first move going to be, Veronica Mars?"

Oooh, she was *ice*-cold today. My left eye started to twitch. I sat up straight in my chair and, making my voice strong and clear, looked straight at Manny. "I believe I'll start with the last known address, talk to some people she knows, and go from there." I wasn't about to give away all my secrets. Anyway, a good part of investigation was intuitive, and I had to see where the clues led.

Sadie frowned. I could tell she wanted to keep me on the hot seat, but Manny said, "Fine. Report directly to me—"

Of course. Who else would I report to? But I looked at him and notched up the corner of my mouth. "*Por supuesto, Manny*," I said, forcing my face to stay impassive when I heard Sadie hiss. She hated when Manny and I spoke Spanish to each other almost as much as I hated her juvenile nicknames for me. But it made the world go round.

"I'll keep you up to date on the police investigation." He gathered up his papers and stood. "That's all."

We were dismissed. The minute hand on the wall clock

clicked up a notch. Ten forty-five. I scooted my chair back and headed out to search for Emily Diggs.

The heat outside pressed against me like a wall of fire. Shimmering panes of glass seemed to stretch across the asphalt, and the air rippled and distorted before my eyes. Flowers in the yard wilted, my hair drooped even more, and sweat dripped from my temples. Another glorious summer day in Sacramento.

I quickly cocooned myself in my car and turned up the Juanes song, *"La Paga,"* until it roared out of my speakers. Dancing. It was at the top of my wish list—with or without a *rico suave* guy to partner with. It was a short drive to downtown, and I spotted Emily's house right away, nestled under a canopy of leafy branches. Even lock-your-car areas of Sac, like this one, had spectacular trees. I found one, parked under it, and turned off my car. Juanes would have to wait.

Emily Diggs's residence blended in with all the others on the block—a little run-down with ancient geraniums sprawled in the border. I picked my way up to the old wooden door and knocked. A moment later, a small arched cutout in the door creaked open and two lifeless eyes stared at me.

"Hi." I held my business card up to the cutout. "My name's Dolores Cruz. I'm investigating the disappearance of Emily Diggs. Do you have a few minutes?"

But the muddy eyes just peered at me, obviously not impressed by my bright professionalism.

I regrouped, smiled, and tried again. "I'm a private investigator. Is there someone here I could talk to about Emily?"

After a few more seconds, the cutout in the door slammed shut. I stood on the stoop, slack-jawed, threw my arms out in disbelief, and stared at a lone snail clinging to the wall. "Great," I said to it. I'd been thwarted already. "So what now?"

The snail didn't move.

"Kick the door open?" I suggested, but then shook my head. I'd worn strappy sandals, and I was pretty sure Camacho's wouldn't cover the damage. "No can do."

Still, the snail didn't budge.

"I know," I admitted, "Kung fu isn't the answer to everything."

The door squeaked open, and my hope returned. A twenty-something black woman stood there looking more refreshed than a person had a right to in this heat. "Can I help you?"

She was not the same person who'd peered at me a minute ago. Their skin had a similar brown tone, but this woman's eyes were bronze, and they sparkled like a tiger's.

Putting my game face back on, I said, "I'm investigating the disappearance of Emily Diggs." I stuck my hand out to her. "My name's Dolores."

The young woman recoiled. Her eyes darted to my hand then back to my face. I wavered, almost pulling it back. Was offering a handshake totally uncool? Had I committed a Generation X (or was it Y?) faux pas? *Dios mío*, at twenty-eight, was it possible that I was no longer hip?

I swallowed and persevered, my hand dangling like a dead fish for what felt like an hour. Finally, she took it in a limp grip, gave it a quick shake, and pulled her arm back to the safety of her own space.

"And you are?" I prompted with a lilt. Ick. I sounded perky, like I was selling magazine subscriptions for the cheerleading squad. *Rein it in, Lola,* I told myself.

"Mary Bonatee," she said with a touch of angst-ridden teenager. *What the hell's it to you?* her tone screamed.

A name to go with the face. It was progress. "Mary, nice to meet you. Do you mind if we step inside? I'm melting out here."

It was no lie. I was on the verge of looking like the Wicked Witch after Dorothy threw water on her. My blouse stuck to my body, my palms were sweaty, and even my sandaled feet were sticky.

I edged forward, hoping to ease into the house, but Mary pulled the door close to her side, blocking my entrance. "I don't know—"

Once again I contemplated kicking the door in, but I wouldn't get very much information if Mary were sprawled out on the floor. I smacked my tongue against the roof of my mouth searching for any sign of moisture. *Nada.* Dry as the desert. I tried another tactic. "I understand Emily has children. They must be terrified."

A flicker of emotion passed over Mary's face, but it was gone so fast that I couldn't be sure it had been there at all. Suddenly, however, she opened the door and let me pass. Relief washed over me the second I hit cool air inside.

I barely resisted the impulse to rush to the nearest sink and start guzzling from the faucet.

"How's that working for you?" Dr. Phil asked from behind curved glass. I didn't see anyone watching the TV, but I felt a lurking presence. I cranked my head around and searched. *Nadie.* No one. Zip.

Mary led me to the kitchen. She was skeletal, but I envied the crispness of her appearance. She filled a glass of water from the tap and handed it to me.

"Thanks," I murmured, my sandpaper-tongue thick. I gulped it down, finally able to shake the wooziness out of my brain and focus on Mary. She stood with her bony arms crossed in front of her and leaned against the kitchen counter. Classic defiance. I went on alert. What did she have to hide?

"Can you tell me anything about Emily? Has she disappeared before?"

14

"The police were already here." She frowned. "Why don't you talk to them?"

"I don't work for the police. I was hired by Emily's brother."

Mary stared out the window and blinked heavily. "Just like I told them," she said. "I don't know anything. She just didn't come home one day."

"Was that unusual for her?"

Mary shrugged her shoulders. "Yes." She shifted her chin, kind of rolling it, as if she were loosening a tight collar around her neck. Guilty behavior. Maybe *she* was involved in Emily's disappearance.

"How long have you known Emily?"

She looked off to the side, as if she was counting back days and hours. "She's lived here a little more than a month and a half," she said after a few seconds. "She moved in right around the Fourth of July."

Not exactly enough time to evaluate patterns of behavior, but it corroborated our client's story. Had something changed in Emily's life that had made her move in here? "Do you have a prior address for her?"

She shrugged again.

I kept trying. "Employment history? Anything that could help?"

She hesitated, and then nodded. "She filled out a rental application." She didn't budge to find it for me.

I gave myself a mental pep talk. Slow and steady won the race. "Does she have any friends? Relatives?" I asked.

"She's always kind of kept to herself." Mary's expression softened. "Never brought people around, even when I pla—" She stopped abruptly, swallowed, and continued. "Even when I told her she could."

A red flag shot up in my mind. Mary had been about to say something else. The question was what?

15

"Have you seen Sean?" she asked.

The youngest son. "Not yet."

The color of her eyes seemed to dull. She leaned forward, looking anxious. "But you know where he is?"

"He's with his uncle." And probably pretty freaked, poor kid.

"She was never mother of the year, but how could Emily leave Sean?" Mary's back straightened, her lips pursing. I could sense her gearing up for a rant. "Why do parents screw with their children—that's what I want to know. If you choose to have kids, you should think about *them* instead of yourself, right? They get divorced, they promise they'll spend time with you, but they don't—" Her eyes bugged. "—and they screw around with your friend's—"

So one of Mary's parents—or maybe both—had done a pretty good number on her when she was younger.

My folks, on the other hand, had done zip to damage me—unless you counted the whole relationship-with-Sergio debacle. And their total lack of support about my career choice. And the guilt. God, *the guilt*. But otherwise . . .

Okay, I gave two points to Mary. Parents could definitely make things difficult. "I'm sorry," I said, pushing my own familial eccentricities aside, "but could we get back to Emily?"

She blinked and snapped back to reality, her eyes returning to normal size. "Sorry. I just don't get it."

"So you really think she could have just up and left Sean?"

"Well, she's not here."

She crossed the room and sank into a chair at the table. Her short black hair had a hint of wave and was parted at the side and slicked across her head. She had one of those faces with perfect cheekbones and flawless skin. Short hair was attractive on her. On me I was pretty sure it would look like a helmet. "Could she be running from someone?" I suggested.

16

She smiled. Sort of. "Who would she run from? It's not like this is a James Bond movie."

No kidding. "So you think she walked out on motherhood," I repeated, going back to Mary's original idea.

Mary ran a hand under her eyes, sweeping away a tear that slipped down. "I'll say it again," she snipped. "Sean's alone. She *did* walk out on him."

"Why are you so sure her disappearance was by choice?" Something inside me screamed foul play. And, no, I hadn't been watching too much *CSI*. My conviction wasn't based on anything, but I wasn't ready to condemn Emily without cause. Call it women's intuition, but she *looked* nice in her photograph.

Mary cocked her head and looked at me. "Maybe she was just tired of being a mother."

"Why would you think that?"

"It happens, right? Sean wasn't planned."

"Did she tell you that?"

Mary shook her head, her perfect hair still in place. "Not in so many words, but I picked up on it."

Apparently I'd been wrong. A month and a half had been plenty of time for Mary to have discerned quite a lot about Emily Diggs and her deep emotional baggage. "Any idea who the father is?"

Her lips were tight, and she shook her head. "No."

This interview was beginning to feel like slow torture, worse than slathering *masa* on a thousand drenched corn husks for tamales. "Even if Sean was unplanned, it's been six years. Why leave now?"

Mary stared at me, unblinking. "Why not? Some people bolt when things get tough."

Rule number one in the PI handbook is to be a good listener—well, after don't get emotionally involved and protect yourself at all costs, but those were throwaways. Mary had her own personal baggage. "What was tough for Emily?"

She continued as if she were in a trance. "You get wrapped up in your own life and forget about how your decisions affect the people around you. Too bad you can't choose your parents," she muttered. "Or trade. My roommate, Joanie, would have taken my dad instead of hers in a second."

Again with the parents. "But what was tough for Emily?"

"Being a mother, I guess."

I didn't want to pour salt on whatever festering wound Mary had involving her parents, so I maneuvered the conversation in a different direction. "Did you see or talk to Emily the day she disappeared?"

"No."

A change in the environment registered in the back of my mind. I turned and looked down the hallway. Something was different. The house was still. Dr. Phil's voice was gone.

After popping out of my chair, I strode to the hall. "Had Emily been upset?" I asked over my shoulder, peering toward the front door.

"She was different than she used—"

I lost the rest of her sentence, focusing instead on the mysterious woman with the dead eyes. Where was she? I walked down the hallway, and not two seconds later, she burst from behind the wall as I turned into the front room.

"Beatrice!" Mary shouted from behind me.

Beatrice. Score. I had another name.

An erratic tremor took hold of Beatrice's head. "You ain't found Emily."

I stared at her. Give a girl a chance. I just started looking for her like twenty minutes ago. "Not yet," I said.

Beatrice tugged her hat down over her forehead, shadowing

her face. She turned and faced the wall, breathing deeply. Self-imposed time-out?

"Beatrice, why don't you go watch your show?" Mary said, her tone placating.

Beatrice slowly turned back to us. Her eyes were crossed and her lips stuck out. She considered Mary. "No. I need to help this girl." She looked at me, and I started. A light had come on behind her eyes. "I have something."

I wondered if Beatrice's elevator made it to the top floor, but I asked the obvious question anyway. "What kind of something?"

She folded her arms and straightened her shoulders. "Emily's journal."

Mary blinked slowly and put her hands on her hips. "Aunt Beatrice," she scolded. "You do not."

"Aunt?" I looked from one woman to the other, noticing a vague resemblance for the first time.

Mary nodded. "She's my mom's sister."

Ah, that explained why Mary would tolerate a potentially crazy woman in the house.

Aunt Bea just nodded. "I do have it."

"Why would Emily give you her journal?" I asked.

"She asked me to hold it for her one day. Important stuff in it, she said. So I kept it, but then she didn't come back."

Mary held her hand out. "Give it to me, Bea."

"Uh-uh." She sounded like a rebellious child.

Mary's face grew stern. "Emily's missing. It should go to the police."

"I said uh-uh." Bea was indignant.

I'd already made up my mind. There was no way I was leaving this house without that journal. "Would it be all right if I take a look at it?" I asked. "It might help me find her."

19

She hesitated, shooting an uncertain glance at Mary. Finally, her eyes cleared. She swung her head and looked pointedly at me. "You think so?"

It was my turn to nod. "You never know what important stuff she may have written."

"Well," she said, still hemming and hawing, "I do want you to find her."

I held my breath as she walked to the couch and pulled a spiral notebook from under a cushion. The edges were worn, and the cover was pulling away from the coil. It wasn't much of a journal, but it had a worn look that told me Emily used it well.

Bea came back toward us and held the journal out. I wrapped my fingers around it, but she didn't let go. My smile strained. She'd better hand it over or I'd bust a move on her. "She'd want me to see it," I said sweetly.

Her hands trembled and she looked nervous, but she finally released it.

"Thank you, Bea," I said. And I meant it. Emily had enlisted one of her roommates to watch over the journal. Surely there would be something useful in it.

Bea gave me a wild look, and then she flicked her eyes at Mary. "She should talk to George," she said hoarsely. Then she repeated to me, "Talk to George."

"Aunt Beatrice!"

But Bea didn't even blink at the indignant tone of Mary's voice. "She should. You know she should."

"Who's George?" I asked, but just as quickly as it had gone on, the light in Bea's eyes suddenly snuffed out. She shuffled over to the TV, pressed a button, and Dr. Phil's voice filled the room again.

I turned to Mary. "Who's George?"

"He's the property manager," Mary said. "And my father."

Muy interesante. "Why does Bea think I should talk to him?"

"He has Emily's application. Really, you should ignore my aunt. She means well, but she doesn't always make sense."

Ignore Bea? Not a chance. She'd given me more information in two minutes than Mary had given me in nearly fifteen. Bea might have a loose grip on reality, but that didn't mean she wasn't perceptive. I studied Mary. "Does your father know Emily's missing?"

She nodded. "He's been out of town, but I e-mailed him."

Sounded like a close father–daughter relationship. "Would you give me his number?"

She hesitated and then disappeared into the kitchen, returning a minute later with a business card. I gave it a quick once-over and tucked it into my purse. Paying a visit to Mr. George Bonatee, attorney-at-law, was at the top of my to-do list. I was really rocking now. A journal *and* a business card. Score.

"I'd like to look at Emily's room," I said.

"I don't know what good it'll do," she said, ushering me ahead of her and up a creaky staircase.

I didn't either. "I'll just have a quick peek." We walked to the end of the long corridor. The room was bare bones. "Not much here."

Mary perched on the edge of the bed with her legs crossed and her hands clasped. "She doesn't have much. Sean has a few more toys and stuff outside."

A few watercolor paintings were taped to the wall at child's height. The papers were crooked, and the pieces of tape were at least three inches long. Sean was obviously a proud artist. I ran my finger over a length of tape stuck to the wall. "What was hanging here?"

"I don't come in here much." Mary paused, thinking. "A

21

photo? Yeah, that's right. The river, I think." She didn't sound like she cared. "Maybe a boat—" She stopped, abruptly looking down, twisting her fingers together. "I don't really remember." The angst returned to her voice. "I just can't believe she left."

After a few more attempts at questions, I gave up. "Anything else you can tell me?"

She shook her head. Her perfectly coiffed hair hadn't budged. I wasn't so lucky. A stray strand was caught on my mouth. I picked it away from what was left of my lipstick and grabbed a stuffed stegosaurus up from the bed. "I'll take this to Sean," I said, thinking Emily's little boy might need some comfort from home—as strange as that home was. Setting up a time to meet with him and his uncle was also on my list of things to do.

"That's a great idea. He loves that dinosaur." Mary led me back downstairs. I thanked her for her time, waved to Bea, who didn't acknowledge my presence again, and escaped into the sweltering heat.

Back at my car, air conditioner at full blast and directed straight at my face, I flipped through the journal. A bunch of scribbles and lists and doodles. It would take time to peruse. Best to do it back at Camacho's. I was about to slap it closed again when my finger brushed over a staple. I opened to the page and saw a business card attached to the top of a sheet of paper.

My heart stopped. The *Sacramento Bee* logo marked the card. And there, in the center, was printed

JACK CALLAGHAN STAFF WRITER / REPORTER

My Jack Callaghan? ¡Ay, *caramba!* I knew he'd been back in Sacramento for six months or so and was working at the newspaper. I'd gone out of my way to avoid him. He and Antonio had seen each other, but Jack hadn't been to our house or to Abuelita's, our family's restaurant. Thank God. I didn't want to rekindle my old fantasy—just to end up invisible to him again.

Jack's name stared at me. Why would Emily Diggs have Jack's business card in her notebook? Had he spoken to her? Did he have information on her disappearance? Oh God, I was going to have to call him.

I tried to calm my racing heart. *Dios mío.* After fifteen years, it looked like I wasn't going to be able to avoid Jack Callaghan any longer.

Chapter 2

The minute I pulled into Camacho's parking lot, the smell of hot oil and fried food carved through the heavy air and seemed to land smack on my thighs. If I were a bear, I'd be ripping off car doors to get to the nearest ice chest, I was *that* hungry.

I followed my nose into Szechwan House, greeted Helen at the front counter, and ordered my usual, to go. Popping open a fortune cookie (I'm a firm believer in dessert *before* a meal, especially when the answer to my latest problem might be found on the fortune inside the cookie), I looked hopefully at the slip of white paper that fluttered onto the counter. YOUR LOVE LIFE WILL BE HAPPY AND HARMONIOUS.

Yeah, right. I'd been single for so long that I'd pretty much given up on having a happy and harmonious love life. And now I had to phone up Jack Callaghan and quiz him on why a missing person I was investigating had *his* card in her notebook and all I could think about was what he'd done to Greta Pritchard way back when and how I still wanted him to do it to me. I felt myself blush. Talking to him again after so long was going to be torture.

A few minutes later, I walked into Camacho's with my box

of mapo tofu. "Smells *fabuloso*," Reilly said from her tidy little corner.

I cracked a smile at her use of my native language. She sometimes added a Spanish word—with a heavy American accent—into our conversations just for flavor. She was a wannabe Latina—only with her ever-changing hair color, fair Irish skin, and spattering of freckles, there wasn't a chance in hell she'd ever be mistaken for one.

"*Gracias, amiga*," I said, feeding her fantasy. Camaraderie in the workplace was important, and I liked Reilly. The office was like a tomb. As usual the associates had scattered like cockroaches in the light. They all had places to be, people to see, crimes to solve. They were like smoke. I, on the other hand, was more like fog, a little less vapory and I tended to hang around. But I got the job done. I headed for the conference table to eat my lunch and peruse Emily Diggs's notebook to see what clues I could find. And to put off calling Jack. "How's it going?" I asked Reilly.

She spun her chair around, draped her arm across the back, and notched her chin down. "*El bosso* is in a foul mood, Lola. Something's up."

I looked around in case *el bosso*, aka Manny, was here and Reilly had lost her mind.

She read my thoughts. "He's out front somewhere. Stormed out in a serious huff."

I sat down and lowered my voice. "Why?"

She snapped her eyes from left to right before looking at me again. "I don't know," she whispered.

Gossip was number one on Reilly's agenda, but it looked like she'd drawn a blank this time. "Okay." I opened my box of tofu, inhaling the delicious steam that wafted out. "Let me know when you have the scoop."

She did her sneaky glance around again. "I'm actively

25

investigating. Something about his—" She paused and looked around again. "—ex."

I did a silent gasp. His ex? As in wife? *Muy interesante.* I'd always been curious as hell to see what kind of woman Manny had married—and later divorced. "How do you know?"

She narrowed her eyes at me. "He was talking to her on the phone, and I think he was e-mailing her, too."

I arched a brow back at her. "But how do you *know* it was his ex-wife?"

"I eavesdropped. They were talking about their divided assets, and he told her that if she did what she was threatening to do, he'd take her to court and finish her."

Didn't sound amicable.

"Get this." Reilly lowered her voice to a harsh whisper and looked conspiratorial. "He came in with a woman earlier today. Gorgeous. Very *Tomb Raider,* if you catch my meaning."

"No!" I'd never known Manny to mix business with pleasure. And he'd certainly never brought a woman to the office. I waited for more.

She nodded. "Tall. Gorgeous. Perfect hair, perfect body, perfect lips, perfect everything." She stuck out her tongue and slapped her thighs. "Makes the rest of us look frumpy. It's so unfair."

"Hey."

Reilly gave a sheepish grin. "Sorry." She looked me over. "You're not a frump."

"Thank you. And neither are you. No one does rainbow hair better than you. And rainbow hair is *not* frumpy." I tried to fluff my own flat hair. Pointless. "I wonder why he brought her here."

Reilly's eyes turned to saucers, and she opened her mouth to dish—but snapped it closed again when the alarm beeped. Three seconds later, Manny came around the corner into the main conference room.

26

He looked from me to Reilly and peered at us as if he knew exactly what we'd been talking about. Ex-wives and girlfriends—well, what did he expect? Whatever the 411 was, Reilly would get the scoop and then she'd share it. Surely Mr. Superstar PI knew that about his office assistant.

He passed us by and went straight into his office, but damn it if he didn't end our *chisme* session by leaving the door wide open.

I looked back at Reilly and whispered, "Drinks later?"

She nodded, whispering back, "You got it." She blocked her mouth with the back of her hand and tilted her head toward me. "Oh, and watch out for Sadie. She's on a rampage today. Blasted me for having coffee near the precious computer."

I'd always suspected Sadie harbored secret lust for Manny. An ex-wife and *Tomb Raider* girl—all in one day—would definitely cramp her style.

I thanked Reilly for the heads-up and began flipping through Emily's notebook until I found Jack's card. A few moments later I was scarfing food and lost in my own thoughts. What was I going to say when I called him?

A hand came down on my shoulder.

Shit! I jumped, inhaling a soft glob of tofu. Slamming my palm against my chest, I coughed until my throat was clear and then gulped down more than half my water. So much for Manny's *always be prepared* mantra.

"Are you all right, Dolores?"

I seethed. Sadie. Oh, if only I could meet her alone in a dark alley.

I jerked my shoulder from her icy touch, but she sat down next to me. Reilly stared at her computer, her body completely frozen. Wise girl.

Sadie was dressed in black slacks and a green collared shirt with a Laughlin's Grocer emblem sewn on the front. Her short hair was brushed back and clipped with a silver barrette just past the forehead, and she wore a pair of wire-framed glasses. I cocked an eyebrow at her, holding in my laugh. "Nice outfit."

Her left eye pinched. "I'd take the Diggs case right away from you if . . ."

"If what? Manny gave it to me."

Her pencil-thin eyebrows arched toward her forehead. "His mistake."

"No, his decision."

She flipped a ruffle on the V-neck of my blouse with her red-painted fingernails. "This is not appropriate dress for the workplace, Dolores."

My jaw went slack. I'd had just about enough of Sadie Metcalf. "Who died and made you the clothes police?"

"Food, while you're working around a case file and evidence? Not good." Her voice rose. "There should be rules around here."

Before I knew what was happening, her hand shot out like a claw and knocked over my carton. Tofu cubes and thick brown sauce oozed onto the table.

"Shit!" I jumped up before it spilled onto my lap. "What's your problem?"

But I couldn't wait for her answer. I raced to the bathroom for paper towels, hurrying back to mop up the mess.

When I looked up, Sadie was sashaying toward the lobby, Emily's notebook clenched in her hand. "I'll help you out with this," she said to me over her shoulder.

No. Way. I didn't know if knocking over my food container had been an accident or a planned distraction, but either way, Sadie was diabolical.

Throwing down the soggy paper towel, I charged after her. "You cannot take my evidence!" I grabbed her arm and whirled her.

"What's going on?"

It was Manny. I released my grip and stepped back. He looked from Sadie to me and back. His dark eyes narrowed. "Well?"

I reached for the notebook that Sadie held against her chest. She gripped it tight, scowling at Manny. He held his hand out and gave her a piercing look. Their eyes locked for a long second; then she gave a bitter snort and slapped it onto his open palm.

Wagging an acrylic fingernail at him, she said, "Do I need to remind you, I have every right to—"

"Not another word." Manny's eyes turned to slits.

I shrank back toward the little artificial plant, wishing I could disappear and leave them to their fight. Miraculously, Sadie shut her mouth.

Manny's jaw pulsed as he flipped through the notebook, stopping at a page here and there, glancing at Jack Callaghan's card stapled to one of the pages. My stomach clenched. This was my case. I was following up on the clues. Especially that one, I thought, realizing that I wanted to call the man.

Sadie piped up with a commentary, her voice measured. "It's a compilation of notes, doodles, lists, and who knows what else—"

"Which is why I was studying it." I felt the wrinkles etching into my face. Working in this wacko place was going to make me age prematurely—and I was way too young for anti-wrinkle cream. "Don't you have some *robbers* to catch at the *grocery store?*"

I could see her struggling to keep her tongue under control. Manny and I both brought out the worst in Sadie Metcalf. "As a matter of fact, I do." She ran her fingernails lightly up his arm. "But we need to talk later, Manny," she said with mock sweetness. Then she sidestepped him, glared at me, and plowed out the door.

Manny face was rigid as he watched her.

"*Cabróna*," I muttered as the door swung closed.

He turned and frowned at me. "Dolores."

I jabbed my finger toward the parking lot. "She had no right—"

"Maybe."

"Maybe?" He had to be kidding.

He handed me Emily's journal, and I clutched it protectively. "Make a copy," he said. "I'll need to turn the original over to the police."

I stood rooted to the spot, my heart pounding. Whether it was from Manny's disapproval or from the run-in with Sadie, I wasn't sure. Either way, I didn't like the feeling.

I went back to the conference table, finished cleaning up the tofu mess, and spent the next forty-five minutes photocopying Emily's spiral journal in the tiny back workroom. Maybe I didn't owe that much thanks to Jack Callaghan after all. At least not today. Today there was no glamour in being a PI.

Manny came in just as I pressed COPY for the last time. He stood back and waited while I used our massive stapler to secure the copied pile of sheets before handing him the original notebook.

"Come into my office," he said.

I followed him, regretting that I'd called Sadie a bitch. I hated being reprimanded. I focused on his slight limp and wondered, not for the first time, what had caused it. The unsolved mysteries around this place were monumental—and growing.

"What's your first impression of the case?" he asked when we were in his office.

I breathed a relieved sigh. This was check-for-understanding time. I forgot about Sadie. A few minutes later, I'd finished telling him about Emily's last residence. "I left a message on the landlord's voice mail. He's a lawyer," I added. "And there's a, um, newspaper reporter I need to contact."

Manny gave a final succinct nod with just the hint of a smile pulling up one side of his lips. "Keep your reports up to date, and document your time for billing. And keep me posted," he added as I stood up.

It wasn't even close to unqualified praise, but an approving nod from Manny was huge—the equivalent of a normal boss saying, "Superb! Fantastic job! Keep up the good work!" I took it happily. My goal in life, at least occasionally, was to get him to praise me fully.

I spent the next hour marking key words and phrases from my copy of Emily's notebook with a bright pink highlighter.

- *call A*
- *ask about regulations*
- *zoo with S—call to arrange*
- *my lie*
- *Just Because*

None of it made much sense, but I committed every name I came across to memory, jotting them down in my own notebook just in case my brain failed. I knew clues would unravel as I investigated and Emily's story would start to piece together, but right now I had a bad feeling. Question after question zoomed into my mind—like a damn popcorn maker going wacky.

- *Who are these people Emily wrote about in her book?*
- *Is she a committed mother, or did she abandon her youngest son?*
- *What do Emily's other kids, Garrett and Allison, think happened to their mother?*

- *Where and who is the father of the kids?*
- *Why oh why did Jack Callaghan have to be part of this?*

Ugh. Too much to think about and not enough functioning gray matter. My mind drifted to the photos of Jack that were tucked safely in my dresser drawer. My body suddenly tingled, and heat rose to my cheeks. I'd seen him naked fifteen years ago, and suddenly that image was plastered in my mind. Too bad for me and my pent-up desire. If he looked anything like the photos I had of him, I was sure his bed was rarely empty.

I went from hot to cold in two seconds flat. My bed was *always* empty. Only my boxer, Salsa, kept me warm, and I didn't really love it when she wanted on my bed. I pretty firmly believed that a dog does not take the place of a man.

The wall clock ticked in time with the pounding in my head. I glanced over—six-twenty. Already? I could see Manny hunkered down in front of his computer, no end in sight to his evening. Was he going home alone? And where was home, anyway? Did he and Lara Croft share a tomb together somewhere?

I frowned. *I* was going home alone—to the flat above my parents' house. The flat I shared with my brother, Antonio. Kind of pathetic, when I thought about it, which I tried not to. I wasn't still twenty-three and trying to make it in the big, bad world.

I thumped my forehead. Twenty-eight years old. It was high time I got my own place away from *la familia*. And even higher time for my brother. But we were both saving for our own houses, paying cheap rent and living above our parents in the meantime. We were both kind of stuck.

I shook away my discouragement and packed up my stuff. Reilly and I had a date for drinks at the Forty-niner, a little hole-in-the-wall bar on the edge of midtown. I needed some downtime, and the queen of gossip had some dirt to sprinkle around.

On the way, I finally bit the bullet and dialed the number for the *Sacramento Bee* that was on Jack's business card. A series of instructions led me to Callaghan's voice mail. My heart did a little pitter-patter at the sound of his low, sexy voice.

"Jack," I said after the recording started. "This is, uh, Lola. Cruz. Antonio's sister." I cringed. Real smooth. Not at all breathy and sexy. "Uh, I'd like to talk to you about a case I'm working on." I paused, realizing he probably didn't know what I did for a living. "I'm, um, a private investigator." *Thanks to you, big boy.* "Give me a call. Please. Thanks." I rattled off my cell number and hung up, immediately wishing I could hit ERASE and start the message again. I'd exhibited zero personality, and that fact, I'm sure, had come across loud and clear. I banged my palm against the steering wheel. Damn, damn, damn.

I'd have to rehearse what I was going to say to him when he called me back. *If* he called me back. I frowned at my phone. He better call me back.

The Forty-niner was a dive, but it was clean, cheap, and not usually crowded. Gold rush memorabilia decorated the place, and crooked pictures of Sutter's Fort and Old Sacramento hung on the walls. Inside, I spotted Reilly immediately. She sat at a lacquered table and looked nervous and out of place with her Crayola-colored blue hair.

"Spill it," I said to her after a quick hello and some small talk. I wanted to go home and crawl into bed. Maybe with an old picture or two under my pillow. "What's the lowdown?"

She leaned forward, her slightly chubby hands curved around a tall drink. "First of all, her name's Isabel."

Huh, not Lara Croft. Isabel. I rolled the name around with my tongue, saying it as I knew Manny would: Isa-*bel* with the *I* sounding like a long *e*. I hadn't laid eyes on the woman, but somehow the name fit. I couldn't see Manny with anyone less than perfect.

"So, what do you have on her? Are they serious?"

Her eyes widened and she ran her words together in speed-talk. "I couldn't tell exactly, but she walked into his office like she owned the place, and then he hurried up and shut the door. I could sorta hear them talking, but I couldn't hear what they were saying. It was all very double-oh-seven. Maybe you need to help me investigate them. You might be able to find out more scoop—" She refilled her lungs and took a drink before zipping on. "—Then I didn't hear anything at all for *six minutes*. Six whole minutes."

What was she getting at? *"Okay."*

"That's a long time for total and complete silence. Then—" She clapped her hands and I jumped. "—a crash! I think they were, you know—" She leaned forward. "—*doing it*."

I slapped my hand over my mouth. Not Manny. Not in his office. "No. I don't believe it."

Reilly gaped again. "I totally can! He's a take-charge, throw-a-girl-on-the-desk kind of man. Every morning when I see him, that's the first thing I think about. I wonder what it would be like. What *he'd* be like." She fanned herself with her hand. "Is it hot in here?"

Roasting. I took her Long Island iced tea and gulped down a long drink. "I don't think they were doing it."

She looked at me funny. "What world do you live in? People do that sort of stuff." She leaned closer again. "Sadie's done it."

My mouth dropped open. "You're kidding. You saw her?"

Reilly shook her blue head. "I heard her. Moaning and stuff." She scrunched her eyes like she was trying to block it out. "I had to leave. Just got up and walked out."

"When was this?"

34

"Oh, gosh." She tapped her finger against her pudgy cheek. "A good month—maybe six weeks ago."

I flattened my palms against the table and stared at her. "And you're just now telling me? How is that possible? You can't *keep* secrets."

She lifted an eyebrow. "I was too weirded out."

I was speechless. "I just can't picture it," I said after a minute of silence. "Who was she with? What man in his right mind would—?"

Reilly darted her gaze around as if she were at the office and someone was lurking around the corner. "I think it was Neil," she finally said. "They were in the Lair."

"Neil's Lair? As in the tech room? Are you *serious?*"

She nodded. "Totally serious, *amiga.*"

Amiga. Dios mío. I jumped again when she blurted, "Lola, please set me up with your brother!"

I choked and spewed my mouthful of alcohol. "What?"

"Your brother." She ran a napkin over the mess I'd made on the table and looked at me like I was mentally deficient. She slowed her speech. "Your brother that stopped by the office last week. I want you to set me up with him." She leaned across the table, her enthusiasm catching up with her again. "Does he like Jennifer Lopez?"

It was my turn to stare. "Why?"

She pshawed and waved her hand at me. " 'Cause I look just like her, *loca.*"

Loca. Ha! I was so *not* the crazy one if she thought she looked like J.Lo. But I played along. "You do?"

"Of course." She ran her hand over her hair. "In a slightly frumpier way."

Actually, I was a much better approximation of Mrs. Marc Anthony—minus the ass—than Reilly Fuller. "Um, doesn't Jennifer Lopez have brown hair and olive skin?"

35

"Like I couldn't have brown hair if I wanted it."

"Yeah, but she pretty much keeps hers brown, and while I'm sure you *could* have yours brown, I've never actually seen you with hair remotely resembling the color of a tree trunk."

She ignored this obvious point and started rambling. "Lola, your brother's totally hot. But not scary like the boss." Her eyes grew concerned. "Would he go out with me? Your brother, I mean. Not the—how do you say boss in Spanish?"

She was so random. *"Jefe."*

"Would your brother—what's his name?"

I held in a laugh. I'd worked with her since she'd been hired, two years now; she thought my brother was hot and wanted to go out with him, but she didn't remember his name? "Antonio?" I said, my voice lifting at the end. *Like, hello?*

"Right. So would Antonio go out with me?"

I tapped my finger on my chin to buy time. It would be a really tough sell. Reilly wasn't Antonio's type—although he wasn't one to turn down an opportunity for fun. "I don't know—"

"Come on, Lola. I gotta have him."

What did *that* mean? "Have him how?" I couldn't, in good conscience, set Reilly up with Antonio knowing he might take advantage of her. I didn't want her to get hurt, and I knew my brother. But then again, if Antonio was going to be stalked, even by Reilly, I wasn't sure how I felt about *that*, either. After all, I was a reformed stalker, and living the life wasn't pretty, forget about the invasion of privacy to the target.

"I'm not going to sleep with him right away, if that's what you're worried about. Give me some credit, Lola. I'm not a Friends With Benefits kind of person. I just know what kind of man I want."

Well, knowing what kind of man she wanted was more than I could say about myself. "What's right away? One date? Two dates?"

"When the time's right. If we like each other. I'm a con-senting adult."

I wasn't convinced that Reilly wouldn't turn from con-senting adult to blathering child the second she laid eyes on Antonio again. "I guess I can try," I finally said, knowing it'd take some serious bargaining on my part to make a date be-tween Reilly and Antonio happen.

"Yeah?" She slapped her thighs. "He won't think I'm too chunky?"

He might. And her extra curves might help keep her out of his bed. But I smiled brightly—I didn't want to hurt her feel-ings. "More to love—that's always been my motto."

She grinned. "Excellent motto. When will the date be? I'll have to get a new outfit. Will you come, too? Just to, you know, break the ice. I don't think I want to be alone with him at the beginning. We can have a code word, something like, I don't know, *macaroni*. So if I say *macaroni*, you know things are going great and you can leave. But if I say—" She paused for a sec-ond. "—*penne*, then you know I don't want you to leave."

She wanted me there, which was good. I could keep Anto-nio in line. And it'd be fascinating to see how she was going to work the words *macaroni* or *penne* into normal conversation. If anybody could do it, I thought, it'd be Reilly. "Tuesday is Club Ambrosía's salsa night. We can go there and try it out." Now that they were prostitute-free, thanks to me.

"I'll come with you." A stringy-haired guy that had been sit-ting a few tables away pulled up a chair next to me and plopped down, knees flopping open, a smarmy grin on his face.

Oh, brother. This guy was not what I wanted to deal with right now. "You'll come where?"

He made disgusting smoochy sounds with his lips jutting out a solid half inch. "I'll come anywhere with you."

Jeez. Was this guy serious? "Really? Anywhere?" Like to

visit my grandmother where he'd be tortured by her saying one hundred rosaries, all ten decades, slowly, and in Spanish?

The creep leaned toward me and winked. "Where d'ya wanna go, baby? My car's right outside."

Like I'd get into his car without a gun pointed at my head. I let a slow irritated smile slide onto my face before I took another healthy gulp of Reilly's Long Island. Then I made my voice icy as I stood up, menacing in my pink sandals and ruffled blouse. "Forget it, dude."

"I'm never going to forget you, baby. We'll have fun."

Baby? All he needed was a giant *L* tattooed on his forehead. This guy was no George Clooney. Oh God, maybe I needed the *L* on my forehead. Did losers attract losers?

Reilly's gaze traveled over my shoulder. "Oh my gosh, Lola," she said. "Maybe your brother's not for me. I kinda want *that* one."

I felt someone's presence behind me, and then I heard a man's voice say, "Problem here?" My knees went rubbery. I *knew* that voice. That voice, and the man who it belonged to, lived and breathed in my dreams.

The loser in front of me glared. "No problem, man. Butt the hell out."

Feeling like I was moving in slow motion, I turned and looked into the smokiest blue eyes I'd ever seen, and promptly lurched backwards. "Jack Callaghan," I breathed.

His mouth twitched on one side and lifted into a grin, and damn it if that same tiny little dimple he'd had in high school didn't embed itself into his cheek. It had given him a mischievous edge back then. Now it was just tauntingly, dangerously magnetic. "Lola," he said, all postcoital-like. "Been a long time."

"Yep, long time," I agreed, managing to straighten up, but I backed into loser dude, who promptly wrapped an arm around my waist and pulled me in tight.

"I knew you'd come around, *mamacita*."

He butchered the word with his pathetic Spanish accent. I bristled. "Excuse me?" I said, my fingers clawing at his arms. I was nobody's *mamacita*.

Jack's dimple vanished. "Let go of her, man."

I cocked an eyebrow at him. What, did he suddenly think he was my knight in shining armor? "I can handle this," I said.

Jack folded his arms across his chest, all *machismo*-like. "Oh, you can? Like you handled Megan Crabtree?"

"Megan Crabtree?"

He gave me a *gimme a break* look. "Yes, Megan Crabtree. You put *chile* or something in her soup at your folks' restaurant."

I did a mental head-thump. "Oh," I said, trying to hide the small grin that quirked the corner of my mouth. But it hadn't been malicious. I mean, Jack had brought Megan Crabtree to Abuelita's a measly week after he'd been with Greta Pritchard. And he'd supposedly been dating Laura whatever-the-hell-her-name-was. I'd spiced up Megan's soup for her own good. I'd saved the girl's reputation, for goodness' sakes. "I forgot about that."

Loser dude tightened his arm around me. "You're spunky. I like that."

Ick. Enough was enough. I hauled my knee up, then slammed the heel of my shoe down on his foot. He howled, loosened his grip, and I took the opening to grab his wrist and yank it down and around until I had his arm cocked behind his back and he was doubled over. "Are you done now?" I said. "Ready to take a hike, Romeo?"

He groaned. "Yeah."

I released and pushed the guy away. "Good," I said, and then I turned back to Jack Callaghan, giving an acknowledgment wave and smile to the women in the bar who clapped for me.

The dimple was back on Jack's cheek. He gave me a good

long look before bringing his gaze to Reilly. Her mouth hung open, her double chin in full form. "Hi," Jack said, and he held out his hand to her.

Reilly slammed her teeth together and slid back into her chair. "Hi."

The years fell away, and all the old indignation I'd felt in high school from Jack's indifference toward me—and girls in general—surfaced. Of course, all the old lust was front and center, too. "Jack Callaghan, Reilly Fuller," I said.

"Reilly Fuller," Jack said, shaking her limp hand. "Any friend of Lola's is a friend of mine." He sat down opposite her, and she gulped. "Nice to meet you," he said.

Reilly stammered. "Yeah, n-nice to m-meet you, t-too." I wondered if she'd ever wash that hand again.

"You're looking great, Lola. I was surprised to hear from you." He looked up at me and raised his eyebrows. "Little Lola's a detective. Interesting job choice."

I bristled. *Little Lola, my ass.* I was more woman than he could handle. I eyed him. "How'd you find me?"

"I'm a reporter—"

"So—"

He grinned. "I have my sources."

Well, it hadn't taken him long. "I don't like being watched." And I didn't. Made me *un poquito* uncomfortable. Now, when I was the one doing the watching . . .

"I'll keep that in mind." He gestured toward the chair next to him. "What did you want to talk to me about?"

I sat down—in the chair next to Reilly. "I'm investigating a missing woman, and I found your business card in with some of her things."

He cocked his head and knitted his eyebrows together. "Who?" he asked after a beat.

"Emily Diggs." I watched him, gauging his reaction. It had

40

been years and years since I'd laid eyes on the man. For all I knew, he could be a serial killer.

His eyes didn't change. "Doesn't sound familiar." He leaned forward, forearms folded on the table, and a lock of his cinnamon-colored hair falling over his forehead. No receding hairline for Jack Callaghan. No receding anything. He had a harder edge about him, wary eyes, and a magnetic draw that had me reeling. "She's missing?" he said, and it felt like there was no one else in the bar.

I leaned forward, my body's reaction to him palpable. Our eyes locked. "How would she have gotten your card if you never met her?"

"Yeah," Reilly said. "That's weird."

I'd almost forgotten she was there. I nodded, hardly daring to blink for fear of breaking the connection between Jack and me. "A little *too* weird."

Jack pulled back. "What, do you think I kidnapped her or something, and conveniently dropped my card as I left the scene?"

No, the thought had never *seriously* crossed my mind. "Did you?"

He shook his head matter-of-factly. "If I was a kidnapper, I'd be a hell of a lot smarter than *that*."

"So, Emily's not, say, in the back of your car? Like Greta?"

He looked at me like I was crazy. "Like Greta? What?"

"Nothing," I said quickly, chastising myself and my mouth for spitting out the words before my good sense could kick in. "Never mind."

"So what do you know about your missing woman?"

"Not much so far, but I'm a private investigator. I'm paid to ferret out the truth."

"So you said on your message. Lola, PI. Catchy."

It was more seductive than catchy, coming from his mouth.

"I go by Dolores at work." Can't imagine why I needed to clarify that, but I wanted him to take me seriously, and my name somehow factored into that.

"Dolores," he muttered, my name rolling off his tongue. But he gave his head a little shake and said, "Can't do it. You'll always be Lola to me."

My palms grew clammy. Would I always be Lola, as in his buddy's little sister, or could I be Lola, the woman who haunted his dreams the way he'd haunted mine all these years?

He tapped two fingertips against the table, his gaze unwavering. "So, how's Sergio, Lola?"

"History," I said, bristling at the change of subject. "Ancient."

He nodded and looked satisfied. "Ferreted out the truth about him. Glad to hear it."

Reilly cleared her throat. "So, I take it you two know each other."

"That's right," Jack said, his lips curving up. "We go way back. High school."

I was lost in his brown hair, those amazing eyes, his swarthy Irish complexion. I suddenly questioned my motives for sabotaging Megan Crabtree's soup. Maybe I'd wanted Jack for myself after he'd dumped Greta Pritchard.

I swallowed, tamped down my wandering thoughts, and forced myself back to business. "So you're telling me that you don't remember talking to Emily Diggs?"

He shook his head. Was it my imagination, or did he look a little apologetic? "I didn't talk to her, but I'll look into it from my end."

I just nodded. What else could I say? *Are you dating anyone? Still single? Wanna have your way with me?* I had lots of questions for him, but not many were related to my case.

He smiled at me as if he knew just what I was thinking.

42

Reilly gathered up her purse. "Um, I gotta go."

Jack notched his chin up. "Nice meeting you, Reilly." Then he looked at me again, a little too intently.

I gulped. "Okay," I said, standing up. Time to end this little reunion. "It's been a blast from the past. Thanks for stopping by, Jack."

"How's Antonio?" he asked, rising and walking by my side toward the door.

Reilly jerked to a halt. "Antonio? You know him?" She slapped her thigh. "Of course you know him. High school buddies, right?"

Jack nodded.

"I'm going out with him, you know. Lola's setting it up." She threw her arms up and shimmied. "Salsa dancing."

Jack's smile deepened and spread to his eyes. He looked back to me. "Is that right?"

"Antonio's fine," I said, going back to his question. "He basically runs the restaurant now."

"I keep meaning to stop by. I'll give him a call."

"Yeah, you do that," I said, heading down the stairs behind Reilly. "See you around, Callaghan."

"You can bet on it, Cruz," he said, and I gulped.

When I glanced over my shoulder, he was watching me, that cockeyed grin still on his face.

Chapter 3

When I tiptoed into my mother's kitchen a short time later, she was sifting through dried pinto beans, her back to me, completely absorbed in her task. Antonio and I shared the flat upstairs, but Mami's kitchen was always my first stop. She was separating the good beans from the bad, pulling out any dirt clods and tiny rocks. See, our purposes in life weren't actually so different. I just worked on helping good people stay away from bad people. For Mami, it was separating good beans from rocks.

I watched as she grew still and seemed to sniff the air. For the millionth time in my life, I wondered if she was a *curandera* or if she really did have eyes buried under her dark brown hair like she'd always told us. Even though I knew it was coming, when she whipped her head around to face me in a full-on ambush, I yelped. "I hate it when you do that!"

Her thick Spanish accent colored her speech. "You are late tonight, *mi'ja*. I thought maybe you were dead."

My grandfather ambled into the kitchen before I could answer, the clip-clap of his cane hitting the linoleum at regular intervals. We were a multigenerational family living under one roof. But constant company—despite an endless supply of food—was getting old.

I kissed Abuelo's cheek before turning back toward the door to head upstairs. Turns out I didn't want Cruz companionship or food tonight.

"*Mi'ja*," he greeted in a whispery tone. All he needed was cotton stuffed in his cheeks like Marlon Brando, and the *Godfather* image would be complete.

"Dolores," Mami said, gearing up for her nightly rant. "I do not like this job you do. You come home so late—"

I filled a glass with ice and topped it off with water. "Mami, it's my job—"

"You will get pneumonia drinking such cold water." She jabbed a finger in the air, targeting the glass in my hand. "That is too much ice. Too much."

That sounded more like a curse than a prediction. I stared at her in awe. She had a knack for beginning one conversation and switching topics midway.

I downed my ice water. If I could handle her, I could surely handle pneumonia.

She rolled her eyes to the ceiling and turned to finish sorting the beans. A moment later she was facing me again. "We have to work on Chely's *quinceañera*. Tía Marina is panicking. She tells me Chely won't agree on anything."

¡Ay, caramba! I'd forgotten. My cousin's fifteenth birthday party was only a week away now. The *quinceañera* was supposed to symbolize Chely entering womanhood, but the planning had her acting like a six-year-old, and that's just how my aunt treated her most of the time. And so the plans were falling apart.

They both wanted the coming-of-age party to be perfect, but Tía Marina's idea of perfect (baby pink, hearts and butterflies) was *un poquito diferente* from Chely's idea of perfect (a hip-hop extravaganza with henna tattoos and classic Run DMC from the DJ).

My head started pounding. I had to learn to say no. "I have a new case. A missing person."

Mami pointed her wooden spoon at me. "You are a missing person—from this family."

Oh boy, the guilt was thick today. "No, Mami, I'm not."

She rolled her eyes again. "*¿Por qué quieres ser una detectiva?*"

Why do I want to be a detective? Was she kidding? "Mami, it's all I've ever wanted. You know that." I mean really, she asked the same question nearly every day.

"*Yo sé, yo sé.* It has been your dream since you were fourteen." She jabbed her wooden spoon at me. "I paid for all the—" She made a face. "—kung fu. *Pero,* why can't you be a teacher? Like Gracie? Then you would be married instead of chasing bad men all over town, and you could help with Abuelita's." She waved her spoon around. "You are *una mujer.* A woman. This is not a job for a woman."

Ay, *ay, ay.* I made the sign of the cross. God, give me strength. Mami's male-dominated view of the world made me crazy. And her memory was conveniently spotty. "First of all, Mami, I've always paid for my own kung fu training. And second, this is what I want to do. I don't need to troll for a husband. *¿Entiendes?*"

"*¡No! ¡No entiendo!*" She looked up to the ceiling, waving her spoon at God. "Ay, this one will send me to an early grave. Why does my daughter torment me?"

She jabbed a fistful of dried pintos at me. "No man wants his woman to be a—" She made another face. "—detective. *No es apropiado.*"

It wasn't appropriate to her. To me, it was essential. But I frowned anyway. Maybe she was right. Men probably didn't want someone who could kick ass. If I had to choose between being a detective and being married, which would I pick?

Tough one, although I didn't buy my mother's theory that the two were mutually exclusive. Still, the question stumped me. I suspected a man like Jack Callaghan would want a Cinderella chick, one he could love and leave easily.

But who knows. Maybe I was wrong. Maybe he craved a warrior princess. And here I was: Xena, in the flesh.

I held my palm up to my mother, not willing to let her guilt me into doubting my career choice. "Mami, *es mi vida*." Then I chugged another glass of ice water. It *was* my life. And I could drink ice water if I wanted to.

So there. I know, so mature.

"*Sí, sí.* It is *your* life. *Pero*, you came from my womb."

Oh, no. I sighed. I couldn't argue with her about the womb.

She dropped the beans and moved to the stove, flinging her hand back and forth in the air as if shooing away a fly. "We are running out of time on the *quinceañera*."

My shoulders slumped. "I know. I'll talk to Chely."

"Hey." Antonio sauntered in from the back door. Mami's kitchen was always his first stop, too—mainly because he lacked the grocery-shopping gene and needed to fill his belly before he went upstairs to our sparse refrigerator.

Why was it men seemed inherently unable to stock a refrigerator? Antonio was genetically incapable of shopping for anything except beer or stuff for the restaurant. Aside from the fact that Abuelita's was his passion, I still hadn't figured out how he managed the place without running out of food.

He crunched on a *chicharrón*, grabbing a second piece of crispy pork skin before planting a kiss on my mother's cheek.

Abuelo popped them into his mouth one after another, stopping only when Antonio leaned in to give him a hug.

My mother finally noticed. "*¡No más, Papá!*" she said, slapping his hand. "Leave some for the rest of us."

Abuelo stamped his cane on the floor. "*Tu no eres mi madre, Magdalena.*" He reached around her and snatched another *chicharrón* before she could slap his hand away again. Then he raised his lip in a victorious smile.

They began a tug-of-war over the bowl, and I seized the opportunity to start backing out of the kitchen. Mami was in a foul mood. Definitely time to escape.

I turned the handle on the utility room door, ready to make a dash for the back door. Slowly. Quietly. I was almost through when she flung her arm out and pointed at me. "*¡Basta!*"

I stopped short. "I'm tired."

"We are not finished talking." She poured the beans into a pot, added water, threw in half an onion, a few cloves of garlic, and turned on the stove. "*Abrazo, mi'jo,*" she crooned to Antonio.

Sure, I got lectured and he got hugs. She could overlook the string of vapid women that paraded through his life, as long as she came first in his eyes. I shook my head and tapped my foot impatiently.

Antonio gave her a quick hug back before crunching another *chicharrón*.

"You look terrible with that goatee, you know," she said. "It is not a surprise no respectable girl wants you." She reached up and squeezed his cheeks together, softening the criticism.

"Drop it, Mami. I'm not shaving."

She shook her head and went back to her pintos, pouring salt into her palm and then adding it to the pot. Enough said for today, but we all knew the topic of Tonio's goatee was far from dead. His goatee, my career—she'd rant for the rest of

48

her life and never give up the fight. Only Gracie was safe, bless her perfect heart.

"Hey, Lola." Antonio grinned at me.

That Cheshire cat smile. Oooh, I knew immediately that he was up to something. "Hey," I said.

I picked up my bag and started to back out again—for real, this time. My mother could lecture me about my career and my cousin's *quinceañera* tomorrow.

Antonio spoke to our mother, but he looked at me. "Mami, I heard from an old high school friend just now. Jack Callaghan. You remember him?"

The hair on my neck stood up. Had Jack called Antonio the second I left the bar?

"*Por supuesto. El guapo.* Of course I remember." She moved to the counter, picked up a ball of tortilla dough, and slapped it between her hands, flattening it into a puffy disk.

Antonio drew out his next sentence. "I invited him here for dinner Sunday."

"What?" I wiggled my finger in my ear. Surely I hadn't heard right. "He's a *mujeriego*, remember, Mami? Always looking for a new woman." And after seeing him again tonight after so many years, I was pretty sure I'd welcome the opportunity to be one of those women, given enough time.

"I am certain that he has grown up, just like Antonio."

I held back my laugh. My brother hadn't grown up. He was still looking for a good time and not much else. There was no reason to think Jack wasn't still exactly the same. "No way," I said. "He can't come here."

My mother threw down her tortilla dough and gaped at me. "No way? *Dolores Falcón Cruz.* What manners are these?"

Ah shit. Pissing my mother off was not the way to keep my tummy full.

"We will not turn away a friend at our door," Mami said.

49

She picked up her dough again. I grimaced at her strength—I suspected that she wished it was my head she was slapping between her palms. "I raised you better than that."

I reconsidered. If we had dinner with Jack, maybe I'd come up with some more questions to ask him about Emily Diggs. Okay, that was an excuse. I *wanted* to see him again. I couldn't deny it. "You're right. You raised me better than that."

She slapped another ball of tortilla dough. "He is your brother's frie—" she stopped. "What did you say?"

I smiled to myself. God, it was good to throw her off every now and then. "I said you were right."

Antonio grinned. "Great. He said he misses your cooking, Mami."

If it hadn't already been a done deal, that statement would have carved it in stone. Appealing to Mami's culinary pride—checkmate.

"He will come to Sunday dinner." My mother squared her shoulders and waved her hand out toward Antonio. *"Punto."*

I heaved a sigh. She was being so melodramatic, even though I'd already given in. Hospitality was the cornerstone of her existence. Magdalena Cruz lived for visitors, and her kitchen had a revolving door.

I had a sudden thought. "It *is* too bad that Antonio can't find a good woman, what with the goatee and all. . . ." I trailed off, mirroring Antonio's Cheshire cat grin.

"Whatever it is, Lola," he said, peering at me, "the answer's no."

Mami looked from him to me. Years of experience had taught her how this worked. "The answer to what is no?"

"I have a friend who has a crush on Tonio." I spoke pointedly. "A really *nice* girl, Mami. A *secretary.*"

Her face softened as she pondered this. "A secretary. Ah,

much better I think than the—how do you say?—Hooter girl you bring home last month."

Antonio scowled at me. "I *liked* the Hooter girl."

"I know!" I exclaimed, smiling at my brother. Sweet revenge. My mother had my back now, so I went for the jugular. "Me, you—and Reilly. We should go out."

Antonio backed away. "No way, Lola. Not that girl from Camacho's. She's—" He looked at Mami. "—short."

I cocked an eyebrow at him and smirked. *You can't talk your way out of this one*, hermano. "If she wears high heels"—really, really high heels—"she'll be my height."

"But you're—" He flailed his arms around and looked me up and down. "—and she's—"

"All set to go dancing Tuesday night," I finished.

Mami went back to the tortillas. "How do you know this girl?"

I tore off a piece of hot tortilla and folded it into my mouth. "She works for Manny."

Her face softened. She might hate my job, and Manny might be my boss and divorced, but he was wickedly handsome, presumably Catholic, and *Mexicano*. And that was just too much of a good thing. "Now, there is a man you could marry."

"Mami, he's my boss. And we're not talking about me. We're talking about Tonio going out with Reilly."

She gave a curt nod, a smile tickling the corner of her mouth. "I will make *mole* for Jack," she said, "and Dolores will help me."

Her voice was terse and a little threatening as she turned to Antonio. "And you will see this friend—¿*cómo se llama?*—Reilly." She waved her spoon again like a magic wand. "*Punto.*"

And as if the word of God had been spoken, that was that.

Chapter 4

The pounding on my bedroom door jolted me awake. I jumped out of my bed, my muscles tightening as I cocked my arms and curled my fingers. For a second I thought I'd dreamed it, but the banging started again.

"Lola! Wake up!"

"What?" I demanded, shaking away the sleep. "Who's there?"

"It's Chely."

I slapped my forehead and fell back onto my bed, ignoring Salsa's garbled protest at her interrupted sleep. The day before flooded back into my mind: Manny, *Tomb Raider* girl, the ex-wife, Emily Diggs, Jack at the Forty-niner, Sunday dinner, Tonio's going out with Reilly. . . . What would today bring?

I closed my eyes and drifted off again. . . .

More pounding. "Lola!"

I shoved the covers off, stumbled across the room, and flung open the door. "It's too early for this," I said, frowning at her.

"You have to stop her." Chely was frantic, panic in her voice. "She's ruining my life with this *quinceañera*." She darted a glance at my pajamas. "Cute boxers, but the shirt's kinda thin."

I ignored her fourteen-year-old assessment of my pj's. "Don't you think you're being a little dramatic? A *quinceañera* can't ruin your life." But as I rubbed my eyes, I reconsidered. Knowing my aunt, it probably could be destructive. I'd barely made it through the whole rite-of-passage thing, and my mom had been relatively sane.

The delectable smell of dark roast percolating from the kitchen caught my attention. I followed the scent like a zombie. Chely padded behind me, Salsa trotting behind her. If we had Gloria Estefan playing in the background, we could have started our own conga line.

I talked to Chely over my shoulder. "You wanted this, remember? For what it's costing, you could have gone for braces."

She shrieked in my ear. "You think I need braces?"

I smacked my forehead and spun around to face her. "Your teeth are fine, Chely. It was a joke." Obviously not a good one, but still . . .

She bared her teeth at me. "Are you sure?"

"Yes, I'm sure. They're perfect. Now, what's today's drama with the party?"

"My mom wants it powder blue and baby pink!" she wailed. "And your mom, like, isn't helping. She actually *suggested* butterflies and clouds. Or worse, hearts. Can you believe it? *Butterflies, clouds, and hearts.* I'll never be able to show my face at school again." She buried her face in her hands and wailed louder. "My life is over."

Butterflies, clouds, and hearts sounded exactly like what my traditional mother and her even more traditional sister would suggest. My shoulders slumped slightly. My heart went out to my cousin. I started toward the kitchen again, desperate for coffee. "I'll talk to them, but I can't promise—"

I stopped short at the living room. Men's laughter and guitar strains? At this hour? In *my* apartment? Chely plowed right into my back, lurching me forward.

Antonio reclined on the couch, his black acoustic guitar

propped on his legs, his feet resting on the coffee table. As usual, he looked like he was up to no good.

"Hey, sleepyhead." Then he looked at my flimsy pj's, and his eyes darkened. Did his teeth just clench? "You remember Jack, don't you?"

I rubbed my eyes, sneaking a look at the man sitting across from my dopey brother. Oh my God, he looked good. All whiskers and tousled hair.

"Morning, Lola."

I choked on air. "Morning, Jack."

Chely's breath hit my shoulder, and her hand lightly touched my lower back. I couldn't tell if she was helping me keep my balance or helping herself stay upright.

Jack's gaze slipped down my body, and I froze. My nipples felt suspiciously perky. Shit. Double shit. Why was I wearing white?

Finally his gaze settled back on my face. *Yeah, that took a while, buddy.* His eyes were pools of blue, lighter and clearer than they'd been last night. I admit, I have a thing about eyes—mirrors into the soul. He gave me that cockeyed grin, and darn it if my body didn't actually quiver. What was wrong with me? I was an independent woman, a freethinker who was bucking culture and tradition. I could lust after this man, but I couldn't actually fall for him.

He was a womanizer, and I knew he'd never be my parents' or grandparents' first choice for me. He had too many Cruz strikes against him out of the gate. First, he wasn't Mexican. Not essential, but a definite plus to my parents. Second, his parents were divorced. Again, mine would freak over this. (Although my mother was able to accept that Manny was divorced, but then, he had the Mexican thing going for him.) Third, and most important, I couldn't remember if he was Catholic. And *that* was a deal-breaker for Mami and Papi. It

54

would be an uphill battle for me if I ever chose a Protestant as my one and only.

But it's my life, I reminded myself. I checked Jack out again. His arm was stretched along the back of the chair, all muscled and perfect. And then there was his chest and legs—and that face. He was like a movie star, back when movie stars had character, charm, and charisma. Even with three strikes, Jack Callaghan was beyond tempting.

I stood my ground, threw my shoulders back, and smiled sweetly. "Nice to see you again so soon, Jack." Then turning to my brother I said, "Antonio, could I see you in the kitchen?" I forced the smile to stay plastered to my face, but gritted my teeth. *"Now."*

As I did my best nonchalant walk through the living room and into the kitchen, I felt Jack's eyes on me the entire time. At least my boxers covered my ass.

I turned at the kitchen to see Chely lagging behind, craning her neck in a lingering gaze at Jack. She stopped at the archway, and I grabbed her wrist and yanked her in. Salsa yapped at the back door. I opened it and released her out into the yard.

"Who *is* that?" Chely whispered. "He's, like, so totally hot."

"He's too old for you." I patted my hair and grimaced at the tangles I felt.

"Um, you look fine," Chely said, staring at me with one brow arched. "But, like, the shirt . . ."

I peered down to see how bad it was, and my shoulders drooped. It was thin enough to see dark quarter-sized circles through the white. Oh. My. God. Had my mother put a curse on me because I'd been ungracious in not wanting to welcome Jack into her house? I coughed. Oh God. Did I have pneumonia?

I crouched down in front of the oven and shoved the dish

towel out of the way. My reflection appeared before me. *Mirror, mirror on the wall, who's the fairest—?*

Oh, forget it. I had a rat's nest on my head, and my soldiers were at full attention. It was hopeless.

Antonio finally strolled into the kitchen.

I sprang up and turned on him. "What the hell are you doing?"

He looked pissed as hell. "Me?"

"Yes, you. Why is he here at eight in the morning?"

He stared at me. "First of all, it's almost nine—"

I whipped my head around to look at the clock. Yep, 8:55.

"And second of all, what the hell are *you* doing walking around—" His face twisted. "—like that."

I leaned my back against the wall and banged my head on it, folding my arms over my chest. "This is *my* house. You need to tell me when someone's here."

"No, you need to wear some goddamned clothes when you walk around." He made the gagging face he used to make when he was ten. "At least until I move out."

"Don't tease me." I stared daggers at him. "You're not going anywhere."

"I will. Soon. Now, go put something on."

Easier said than done. If only I could beam myself back to my bedroom. Since I couldn't, I went postal, jerked my hand out, and grabbed the front of his shirt. He tried to knock my hand away, but I blocked him. "Why is he here?"

He stepped back, and I let my hand slip away. "Jesus Christ. Relax, Lola."

"Okay." I regrouped, folded my arms over my chest again, and arched a brow. "So, why is he here?"

"You're too wrapped up in this damn private eye thing—"

"This *private eye* thing is my career, and what does that have to do with him being here?"

56

"It's your career, but you have no life." He stroked his goatee. "I mean, be straight with me. When was the last time you went out?"

I cocked my head to the side. "Yesterday. With Reilly—you know, the girl you're going out with Tuesday."

He chose to ignore his upcoming date. "Let me clarify. When was the last time you went out with *a guy*? And going to the movies with me doesn't count."

I scratched my chin and frowned. It counted to me.

"Callaghan's a pretty good listener," he continued. "Cheaper than a shrink."

I punched his arm. "You think I need therapy?" And anyway, Jack was a reporter. Not the same thing.

He shrugged. "Couldn't hurt."

"Nice, Tonio. Thanks for the support."

He shrugged again. "He's always had the hots for you, so I figured, why not . . ."

My brain skidded to a stop. "What?"

He looked at me like I needed a straitjacket. People were doing that a lot lately. "I know. News to me, too. I thought he had better taste—"

I slugged him again.

"Hey!" He backed away before saying, "I would have beat the crap out of him in high school for even thinking about one of my sisters, but that was then. Let's face it. You're going to be past your prime pretty soon. Then where will you be?"

I was too shocked to speak. Past my prime? Who was this man, and what had he done with my brother?

"And he's, like, really *hot*," Chely said, sneaking a look into the living room. "Did you see that bod? You may not get another chance for someone, like, that good. Go for it, Lola."

I glared at Chely. If I had the same taste as my teenaged

57

cousin, well, that couldn't be a good thing, could it? But Jack did have a killer body.

"I am not anywhere near my prime, and you are not my fairy godmother, so butt out," I said to Antonio.

"So this is where the party is." Speak of the devil. Jack stopped in the archway of the kitchen.

He was taller than I remembered. I'd have to stretch up on my toes to kiss him—*Stop!* I shooed away the thought. Oh God, I was losing it. Where was the damn coffee? I needed caffeine.

Actually, I needed sex. The way my body was screaming, I needed it now. But coffee would have to do.

As if reading my mind, Antonio said, "It's cool, man. Lola just needs to feed her addiction." Then, bless his demented heart, he poured me a cup.

I took it gratefully and gulped, scalding my throat and not taking my eyes off Jack.

He smiled, and shivers shot up my spine. A good man could make my life so much more interesting. Even if it was short-term. But was Jack a good man?

"So," he said.

"So," Antonio said, pressing his fingertips together and frowning at me.

"So," I finally managed. Sparkling conversation. I set down my cup and suddenly remembered my shirt. I tried to cover myself, heat rising to my cheeks. Jack Callaghan reappears in my life, and suddenly my body was going haywire. What was wrong with me?

Jack forced a laugh. "I think you've ruined me for other women, Lola."

Join the club, buddy. Back at you.

Antonio looked at me as if he was sending me a message— *keep yourself covered*—then knocked Chely on the arm. "Hey, *prima*, let me play you the song I'm going to do at your party."

58

Chely was dreamy-eyed and goggling at Jack. "Later."

But he grabbed her sleeve and pulled her toward the front room. "Not later. Now."

She sputtered but let herself be dragged.

Subtle, Tonio. Real subtle. Yep, we were definitely back in high school.

When they were gone, Jack turned back to me. "You really have ruined me," he said.

"Do you say that to all the girls?"

His eyes smoldered. "I was thinking we should go out. Talk about old times. What do you say?"

I jammed my hands onto my hips and laughed. "What old times? We don't *have* any old times."

"Oh, come on," he said. "Sure we do."

I suddenly felt the effort of him trying to keep his attention on my face and quickly covered myself again. I had to get out of here. "Are you talking a date?"

"If that means we'd have a specific social engagement at a specific time—then, yes, sure, a date."

I tilted my head, suspicious, remembering my thin shirt. Why the sudden interest? But I chased away my doubt. Antonio had said Jack had liked me since high school. I found it hard to believe that I'd missed that little detail in all my early sleuthing, but I took it at face value. "Uh, okay."

Smooth. Lola Cruz—woman of words. "I can do lunch Monday," I said, thinking it'd be better to stick to broad daylight. The way my body was reacting to him, I was pretty sure I'd be putty in his hands the second the sun went down. I had to stay focused on my case and question him some more before I turned to goo.

The way he smiled, I wondered if he could read my mind. "Monday it is."

We made plans to meet at Szechwan House—if the date

was a disaster, at least I'd have a great meal and an inspiring fortune. He walked to the front door, nodding at Antonio. "Later."

"See you tomorrow, man," my brother said.

"Tomorrow?" I looked at them blankly.

Jack's smile got bigger. "Right, dinner tomorrow. Seeing you four days in a row. I'm a lucky guy."

How many dates before a good Catholic girl should succumb to carnal pleasures? Was two enough? Did the Forty-niner count? I frowned. The strikes against Jack ran like ticker tape in my mind: Not Hispanic. Divorced parents. "Are you Catholic?" I blurted, then immediately cringed.

He gave me a puzzled look. "Am I Catholic?"

Chely burrowed between us and gazed up at Jack. "We're Catholic. You have to, like, be Catholic to be in this family."

Oh my God, now he'd think I was trolling for a husband. I shot a look at Chely that said, *Shut up!* Then I smiled brightly at him. "Never mind. I was just curious."

"You can ask me anything, Lola," he said, and I felt a rush of flutters spread from my core. "We're an Irish Catholic family."

I did a mental cheer. Now there was a check in my "pro" column on Jack. I let my gaze drift over him and added another bold check for his body. *Muy caliente.* I tore my eyes away and split off from them at the living room. "I'll see you tomorrow," I said, and hurried back to my room.

"Why can't a guy like that ask *me* out?" Chely said, following at my heels. She closed the door and fell onto my bed, chattering at warp speed. "Who *was* that? He's, like, awesomely hot. I mean H-O-T. Think my mom would let me go out with an older guy? Could I borrow him for the *quinceañera*?" Then, apparently remembering the whole reason she was here, her face dropped. "What about the *quinceañera*? I really need your help,

Lola. You can talk to your mom and then, like, she can talk to my mom."

I gestured my hands in the air, unable to take any more drama for the morning. "All right."

She sat up, perky again. "Cool. Thanks."

I pulled her up by the wrist and shoved her out of my room. "Great. I'll call you later. Tomorrow."

She stood in the hallway. "Promise?"

"Yes."

She grinned. "What time?"

"When I can. Good-bye." I breathed a sigh of relief and checked the clock. Nine-thirty. I had to get moving.

I jammed over to Camacho and Associates first. Had to look up Allison Diggs's address and do a little background investigation on her. Turning into the conference room, I stopped short when I saw the associates sitting around the conference table. It was Saturday, right? Why were they all here? Indignation hit me like a horde of women at a shoe sale. And why hadn't I been invited?

"Dolores," Manny said by way of greeting.

"Morning."

"We're just finishing up some business." He waved his hand toward the vacant chair. "Since you're here, take a seat."

"I didn't realize there was a meeting today."

"Check your messages," Sadie said. "I called your cell phone myself."

I yanked my phone out of my purse. Sure enough, I had a voice mail. Damn phone needed the volume button fixed. "Guess I didn't hear it."

Sadie's lips thinned, her chin looking more pointy than usual. "So, Miss Marple. What's next on your agenda? Do you

61

have a plan, or are you just praying that Emily Diggs will materialize in front of you in a gracious act of God?"

Oooh, low blow, I thought just as Manny shoved his chair back. "Sadie. My office." His voice was measured.

She sat up stick straight, her upper lip curling. "Excuse me?"

I had to stop myself from gawking at her. Had she seriously thought her boss wouldn't call her on her attitude? Her condescension was so blatant, it was pathetic.

"Now." Manny's cowboy boots thumped against the tightly woven Berber carpet as he walked to his private office. When Sadie reached the door, he guided her inside by the back of her arm and then kicked the door closed with his foot.

I spread my hands out on the table and studied my fingernails, straining to hear. Damn Manny and his soundproof glass. As surreptitiously as possible, I stared at them through the flattened slats of the blinds on his window. It was like an overly dramatic silent movie. Sadie yanked her arm away from Manny and stood with her back to us. Her hands were on her hips, and her posture looked pretty damned defiant. Unlike with most movies, this time I wasn't rooting for the woman.

Manny leaned back against his desk. His lips were drawn tight, like a thin string splayed across his square jaw. Sadie's head jerked back and forth, and her right arm waved in front of her face every few seconds. If she'd been talking to me, I'd have been tempted to catch her wagging finger between my teeth and chomp down. God, I think I needed anger-management classes.

Another awkward minute passed before the office door swung open and they returned to their chairs. Looking at their tense faces, I had no clue who'd won.

"Dolores." Sadie turned so her back was to Manny. "What's on your agenda in the Diggs case? Can you share those details with us?"

"Sadie," Manny warned.

She threw him an innocent look and flung her hands up. "What? I have a right to ask."

I couldn't imagine why she had any right to ask, but I answered anyway. "I'm on my way to visit the older Diggs kids. And I'm going to see the younger one a little later today." I channeled my optimism and showed my determined face to Sadie. "I'll find Emily Diggs."

"Sadie, you're on at Laughlin's tonight and tomorrow night," Manny said. "Check in as needed."

She nodded at him, uncharacteristically submissive, and walked away. Neat trick. Guess Manny had won the battle. What the heck had he done to turn her into a Stepford detective?

My creative brain concocted the absurd theory that they were sleeping together—or had. Yuck. It was too horrible to contemplate, and yet . . . It might explain why he tolerated her unprofessional behavior and why she fell back into line at the slightest reprimand. I suspected that once a woman had Manny Camacho, it'd be tough to give him up.

Unless, of course, she had someone like Jack Callaghan waiting in the wings.

Still, I had trouble imagining Manny and Sadie doing the zigzag. I'd have to pick Reilly's gossipmonger brain some more about the idea. Maybe put it on my list of things to investigate off the clock. Inquiring minds wanted to know!

After I found Emily.

Neil headed off to work on his own confidential cases. And that was that. Class dismissed.

I went through Emily Diggs's file and found that Walter Diggs, Emily's brother and Camacho's client, had supplied the last known address for his niece. With any luck, she'd still live there—and she'd be home.

Chapter 5

Allison Diggs's small house sat close to the sidewalk on a seedy-looking side street off Del Paso Boulevard. There were no spaces available at the curb—didn't anyone on this street work? I parked in the short driveway, tucked my CDs into the glove box, and made sure nothing valuable was in plain sight. Slipping my backpack purse on, I peered up and down the street, climbed out of my car, and locked the doors.

Cracks in the driveway splintered out from underneath my car. The postage stamp front yard was overgrown, weeds long ago choking out any trace of lawn. I headed up the short walkway, stepping over cracks, not wanting to break any backs, least of all my own.

Something scurried past my feet, and I shrieked. It was either a small cat or a large rat. *Ew!* I toe-sprinted through the rest of the growth, leaping up to the front stoop.

A young woman stared blankly at me from behind a shredded screen door, clutching a smoldering cigarette between two fingers. Even through the aged mesh of the screen, I could see a tattoo creeping down her arm. Leopard print, in full color. Very high-class. "Hi," I said, darting a glance behind me, still on the lookout for the furry creature. The low buzz of a fan came from inside the house.

"Yeah?" Smoke crept out of the girl's mouth as she spoke.

"I'm looking for Allison Diggs."

Nothing. No response. More smoke.

I rifled through my purse and held out a business card, hoping to detect some sign of acknowledgment.

She pushed the screen door open and took the card from my hand. Her dwindling cigarette was in a death grip between her lips, and the smoke filtered up into her face. Very attractive. She must spend a fortune on Altoids.

The steady purr of the fan filled the dead air while she studied the card. It seemed to take an eternity. I couldn't tell if she was a slow reader or just high. Really, I didn't care. I was too concerned about the mutant rat that lurked somewhere behind me.

Finally, she cracked open the door and, just as the fan circulated in my direction, flicked the gray ash that hung from her cigarette onto the porch. I jumped back and turned my head to avoid a faceful of cigarette dust. Lovely.

She leaned against the screen door, holding it open. "So, are you Allison?" I asked again.

"Yeah." She smashed her cigarette butt into a rusted sandfilled coffee can that sat next to the door, and then she moved aside, making room for me to pass. No "nice to meet you" or "come on in." Whatever.

I pasted a smile on my face as I peered into the depths of her house, wishing I'd worn my crucifix or that I had a hunk of garlic in my purse—or a gas mask. The fan was clearly useless in the smoke dungeon.

The screen door slapped closed behind me, and I automatically tensed, holding my arms close to my sides. Another tattoo peeked out from the waist of her hip-hugger shorts.

More leopard spots. Judging by the utter blackness inside the cavernous house and her body decorations, I wondered if she thought she was part cat. Did her eyes glow yellow in the dark?

Allison perched on the edge of a saggy black velour couch. A leopard-skin throw lay haphazardly over the back. Big surprise. She gripped a fresh cigarette between her teeth. I searched for the resemblance between this young woman and Emily. It was difficult to find under the angst, but I detected similar cheekbones and the same deep-socketed eyes.

"So?" she said as she flared up a blue mini Bic lighter. The cigarette sizzled fiery red at the tip as she puffed it to life.

Right. Cut to the chase. "Thanks for talking with me," I said. "I'm looking into the disappearance of your mother."

"So they haven't found her yet."

Dios mío, where was the concern? "No, they haven't."

"So?" she said again.

I watched Allison, looking for the smallest sign of interest. *Nada*. "Emily *is* your mother?"

She gave a snide laugh. "If your definition of *mother* includes purposefully keeping a child from their father, then yeah, I guess she's my mother."

Okay, so Allison had been kept from her father, but Emily had fed her, wiped her bum, had the purse where Allison had probably stolen the money for her first pack of cigarettes. "Great, glad that's established," I said, trying to keep the annoyance out of my voice.

"She gave birth to me. That's about it." She took another drag, and her eyes rolled upward. She readjusted herself on her broken-down sofa. "What makes you think she wants to be found, anyway?"

Not another skeptic. "You think she walked out on Sean?"

She jabbed her finger in the air at me. "Who the hell *are*

you, anyway? And who gave you permission to talk about my brother?"

My gaze dropped to the card on the floor. Hadn't she spent a couple minutes reading it? She reached to pick it up, and I filled in the blanks, speaking slowly. "My name is Dolores Cruz. I'm investigating the disappearance of your—of Emily."

"Yeah, right. I got that part. Who hired you?"

"Your uncle—Walter."

She stopped middrag and leveled a stare at me. "Well, that figures. So, where is he?"

"Walter's going to meet me—"

"Not my uncle," she snapped. "The kid. Sean."

A second ago, he was her brother. Now he was "the kid"? I was hesitant to give away information for free, but Allison didn't look like the bartering type. I figured I'd have to ante up first and maybe she'd soften. "Sean's *with* your uncle. I'm going to see him"—I checked my watch—"in about half an hour."

Her eyes looked glassy, but she seemed to focus. The vein that had started to pop on her forehead subsided, and her face relaxed. "They're together?"

"That's right."

In a series of quick, jerky movements, Allison stubbed out her cigarette, snatched a black purse from the floor beside the couch—finally, something without spots—and headed toward the front door. I stared after her. What the hell, was the interview over?

She whipped her head around and stared at me. "Are you coming, or what?"

Okay, had I missed a vital part of the conversation? "Uh, coming, where?"

"I'm going to see my brother," she said, her voice incredulous as if we'd just spent the past ten minutes discussing just that.

67

"Right now?" I gaped. Allison had gone from the most disinterested person I'd ever met to being—what? A caring sister?

"Yeah, right now." And she actually smiled. And her teeth weren't too terribly yellow—at least not from this distance. "I'm coming with you. The kid needs to see a friendly face."

By whose stretch of the imagination was Allison's face friendly? I blinked and wondered how Manny would handle this. "Uh, Allison, I don't know—"

"I want to see Sean," she said again. She adjusted her weight to one hip and peered at me. "If you want to keep talking, you'll take me with you."

As my mother would say, Allison had me by the *huevos*. I didn't have a clue how she'd managed that when she probably couldn't even remember my name.

She smiled again, a full-on twisted grin. "I have some things I could tell you. About Emily."

Okay, she had me by the *huevos*, and now she was squeezing. I pushed past her and, with a quick look around for the mutant rat, speed-walked down the walkway. If I couldn't take the lead in conversation, at least I could take the lead to my car.

Allison locked the dead bolt, let the screen door slam behind her, and followed me, climbing into the passenger seat. I started the engine, and she immediately dug in her bag, pulling out a mashed box of cigarettes and knocking one out.

I leaned away from her, jutting my chin forward. "You can't smoke in here." No way. I was not disinfecting my car and my hair from her death sticks.

She hissed through her teeth, but jammed the cigarette back into the box.

"Thank you," I said.

She snorted.

Accommodating girl.

I'd arranged to meet Walter Diggs at the zoo in William Land

Park. It was a relatively short drive from Del Paso Heights, and we had time to kill, so I drove slowly. "You're twenty-one, right?" I asked, figuring that was, what, like 147 in cat years.

I caught her nod from the corner of my eye as we got on the freeway. She better not have gone back to her nonverbal mode.

"And your brother's eighteen?"

"Sean's six."

"I meant Garrett."

Her voice went flat. "Garrett's dead."

I stared at her for a beat, and my gut twisted. A layer of creepy, unsettling brightness settled on her face. I had a feeling this case was about to get more complicated. "What happened?" I asked, not surprised that my voice had gotten softer.

"Your investigation didn't turn up anything about him?"

"It just did." Her sarcasm didn't do anything to endear her to me, and I had to bite my lip to stop myself from lashing out. She had information I needed. And maybe I could head her off before we actually got to Sean at the zoo. I definitely wasn't convinced that her friendly face was one he needed to see. "How'd he die?"

Her voice lost tone again. "Heart infection."

Heartache, I knew about. And a broken heart, I'd experienced. But a heart infection? "How'd he get it?"

She glared at me. "None of your business."

Hello? Earth to Allison. "Like my card said, I'm a private investigator. Your mother is missing. Everything's my business." I jerked the car to the shoulder of the freeway. A horn blared behind me. "If you don't want to talk, you can get out any time you want. I'll say hi to Sean for you."

She knocked a cigarette out of the box again, twisting it between her fingers, popping it between her lips, taking it out again. "Oh, all right. Just keep driving." She huffed. "Nobody knows why Garrett got the infection."

"No idea?"

"We found out about it, and he was dead two weeks later."

Hitting my blinker on with my pinkie, I slammed my foot down on the accelerator and charged back into traffic.

I sneaked a look at her. She leaned back in her seat, one arm across her chest. Her unlit cigarette was gripped between two fingers, her other fist wrapped around a lighter. Was she going through withdrawals already? What had it been? Fifteen minutes? "Was Emily close to Garrett?" I asked.

She flicked her lighter to life a few times then finally shoved it back in her purse. "I guess." She started to slide the cigarette back into the pack, but it bent and broke. "Shit." She unrolled the window, crumpled the apparently empty box, and tossed it all into the wind.

My body stiffened. She was a litterer. Citizen's arrest crossed my mind. A bright orange city vest and a day on the side of the road picking up trash might smack some common sense and humility into the girl.

Of course, I knew turning her in would be self-defeating. I dragged my gaze from the rearview mirror and her trash. "How about you? Were you close to Garrett?"

She shrugged. "I guess."

"What about Sean? Are you two tight?" They couldn't be that close if she didn't know where he was and how to get in touch with him, but she was sure anxious to see him. Had she lost sister visitation rights somehow?

"Look . . ." She paused like she was searching her memory for my name.

"Dolores," I reminded her.

"Look, *Dolores*. I haven't seen Emily since the funeral. I don't know where she is, and I don't care. But Sean's my brother, and he needs all the family he can get. We can't pick our parents. It's not his fault he got stuck with Emily."

O-*kay*. I'd heard this melody yesterday—from Mary Bona-tee. Sucky parents seemed to be a running theme in this investigation—at least on days one and two. I changed tactics. "Cool tats," I said. "I've thought about getting one. Either that or a belly button piercing." The tattoo thing was a lie, but the belly button piercing was a fantasy. Nothing I'd ever *really* do, but maybe my interest would soften her up. "Know a good place?"

She clamped her mouth shut.

Guess not. We were silent the rest of the ride. The woman was like freaking Fort Knox. I just couldn't break in, and I had to know if there was gold inside.

In no time, the Sacramento Zoo was in sight. I sneaked a peek at Allison. Her fingers twisted around themselves, but her expression was like stone. Maybe Sean would be able to melt his sister's icy little heart. I slipped my car into a parking spot across from the zoo, put it in PARK, and opened the door to the heat.

From behind me, the passenger door slammed shut. I whirled around, and my jaw dropped. Allison had hurled herself out of the car and was sprinting across the parking lot toward traffic and the zoo entrance.

Chapter 6

"Wait!" I yelled, but Allison Diggs was already dodging cars in the parking lot as she barreled toward the street. "Oh no, you don't!" I grabbed my purse and Sean's stuffed dinosaur, but she had a good hundred yards on me by the time I made it across to the sidewalk.

Who'd have thought she'd have the lung capacity to run so fast? Of course, it didn't help that I was wearing two-and-a-half-inch heels. They may have looked fabulous with my jeans, but they were definitely not ideal for giving chase.

Allison's breakneck smoker's pace waned by the time she was halfway across the street—charcoal lungs will do that to a girl—but I was thwarted when the crosswalk light turned red on me and the backed-up traffic started inching forward. Horns blasted, and she picked up her pace again.

"Wait for me!" I yelled, edging into the street only to leap back as a car horn blared at me. She was almost to the ticket kiosk. Damn. She really wanted to see her brother. Bad.

And then a wayward thought struck me. Maybe Allison had insisted on coming with me so that she could *take* Sean. But if that was her plan, she had a few obstacles—namely that she had no car.

I gritted my teeth, afraid I'd lose her completely if I didn't catch her before she made it inside the grounds. Enough! I slung my purse across my back, shoved the stuffed toy under my arm, and darted into the street, kamikaze-style. Car brakes squealed, and I jumped. A red-faced man screamed at me through his windshield, honked, and jerked the wheel. His tires screeched and his car spun sideways on the road, the truck behind him skidding to avoid a collision.

I scurried out of the way, feeling guilty for causing such havoc, grateful there hadn't actually been a crash. But I was on a mission. I kept going. More horns bellowed at me.

"¡Basta!" I screamed at the cars, channeling my mother. Weren't pedestrians supposed to have the right of way? Couldn't these people see I was in a hurry? "Stop already!"

I dodged a car going in the opposite direction only to run smack into a shimmering red SUV. My palms slammed against the hood, and the driver glared at me. "You trying to get killed?" she yelled.

It may have seemed like it. I gave her that. Still, I grimaced at her. I was on a case, for crying out loud.

Finally, I flung myself onto the sidewalk and saw the line at the kiosk. Good God, was this place the only entertainment Sacramento had?

Groups of families with wide-eyed kids stared at me as I sprinted toward the ticket booth. I slowed down enough to dig for some money in my purse. Honesty was costing me precious time. I finally found a twenty-dollar bill, wadded it up, and as I cut though the line, I threw it at the lady behind the glass.

"Hey!" she called.

"Keep the change!" Honest *and* generous—that was me.

"Stop!" she yelled again, but I ignored her. I'd paid. What more did she want?

I crossed the courtyard and slowed down to catch my breath,

peering over my shoulder in case the zoo police were on my tail. I needed to find Allison, talk to Sean and Uncle Walter, and never come back to this place again. They might well have a WANTED sign with my harried picture on it hung up in the ticket booth next time I tried.

I beelined for the flamingo habitat—the scheduled meeting place—and leaned my back against the railing, panting. I searched the area, thinking Allison ought to be easy to spot with her leopard-print skin. She was nowhere in sight. My clean lungs were still recovering from that sprint. Allison was probably keeled over dead somewhere.

When, a little while later, she still hadn't materialized, I thought that maybe she hadn't come here to see her half brother at all. Maybe she'd come to visit her cat kin.

Ten minutes later, when I saw a tall man shepherding a boy through the front entrance, I immediately knew he was Walter Diggs. With his deep-set eyes, chiseled cheeks, and tuft of silver hair springing from his left temple, he was a dead ringer for his sister, Emily.

I walked toward them. "Mr. Diggs?"

He nodded and gave me a once-over. "Ms. Cruz?"

"Thank you for meeting with me."

"What have you found out?"

Looking at Walter Diggs, I felt like I was looking into the soul of Emily. He looked tired, just as his sister did in the photo I had of her—but he also looked serene and slightly exotic. My image of Emily expanded to include a peaceful aura.

"I'm working some leads. I'll let you know the minute I find anything helpful," I said. "This must be Sean." I focused on him for the first time, kneeling down. And drew in a sharp breath. He had amber eyes and slick black hair that hung around a light ebony face. It was the second time in two days

I'd seen those amber-colored eyes. Little Sean Diggs, I thought, was a fairer version of Mary Bonatee.

"Sean!" The high-pitched, borderline hysterical voice screamed from behind me.

I whipped my head around in time to see Allison careening toward us. "Sean!" she yelled again. "It's okay now. I'm here. Sissy's here!"

Sissy? I started to straighten up from my crouched position just as Allison's black-booted feet tangled under her. She plunged forward, tumbling, grabbing for me.

I tried to pull away from her, but her momentum was too great. She took me down with her, and we fell in a heap onto the pavement. The back of my head knocked against the ground, and the sky spiraled. I blinked hard, and then again, to clear away the kaleidoscope behind my eyes.

My fall had broken Allison's, and now she straddled me, gasping for air. I turned my head to the side. Ugh. Stale, cigarette breath. This girl needed to quit smoking, *rápido*.

I managed to whip my body sideways and knock her off me. She flipped herself over and started crawling toward her half brother. "Sean, are you okay?"

"Ally." Walter bent to help her up, but she ratcheted herself free and swept Sean up into a smothering hug.

"Why did she go, Ally?" Sean's voice was small and cracking. My heart lurched.

"I don't know, baby," she said. They clutched at each other, and I felt the love. I really did.

Walter watched them with rapt attention as they started walking down the fence line at the flamingo habitat. "What's she doing here?" he said to me.

I couldn't really answer that specifically. I still had my doubts about her motives. "She insisted on coming to see him."

My feet ached from the mad chase earlier. Too late, I realized

I shouldn't have bothered to run after her. I could have ruined my shoes—or twisted an ankle. And for what? To end up exactly where I was.

"Late's better than never, I guess," he said.

So it seemed Uncle Walter agreed that Allison wasn't sister of the year. There was a mind-blowing surprise.

Allison and Sean led us all the way to the tiger habitat and pressed their noses up against the thick Plexiglas. Walter and I sat on the bench across from the window, watching them. I asked him the question that was now first and foremost in my mind: "Do you know who Sean's father is?"

I had a very distinct suspicion about the answer, but thought how nice and tidy it would be if he could confirm it.

He shook his head. "Emily would never say."

Yeah, I knew it wouldn't be that easy. I'd know if my theory was correct soon enough. "You haven't seen your sister in a while, is that right?" I kept one eye on Sean, wanting to protect him. The tiger couldn't escape and hurt him, but I couldn't say the same about unpredictable Allison.

"Right." He stared straight ahead, sitting tall and rigid. "She kept her distance."

"You don't know why?"

"No idea. She started stepping back five or six years ago. Moved around a lot, like she couldn't settle down, would call out of the blue and visit occasionally, then she'd disappear again."

Huh, odd behavior. "You're keeping Sean for now?"

As if on cue, Sean turned to look at his uncle. His eyes glassed over, and he clutched at Ally. "We're going to try to make the best of all this, right, buddy?" Walter winked at Sean. He gave a heavy sigh. "You should come to the house, Ally. Play with Sean for a while."

Leopard girl smiled slightly and then drew Sean back to the tiger.

"Find out where Emily is," Walter commanded me.

Exactly what I intended to do.

I hated to leave Emily's son, but I couldn't see questioning him. He was a child. They needed some family bonding—and major therapy—and I needed time to think, and some Band-Aids for my blistered feet.

I knelt down in front of Sean again and handed him his dinosaur. "I brought this for you. Would you like me to get some of your other toys?"

He hugged the stegosaurus and nodded. I added *Get some more of his things from Mary Bonatee* to my mental list of things to do. At the top of that list was giving him back his mother.

I said good-bye and limped out of the zoo. Driving by Saint Francis, I decided on the fly to attend afternoon Mass. Sean could use an extra prayer. Plus, if I went now, I could sleep in tomorrow. Two birds . . .

I circled the block, found parking, and hobbled up to the front entrance of the church. Just climbing the stairs to the vestibule calmed me. Tension melted away with every step.

I zoned out during most of the service—thinking about Emily's children instead of the liturgy—standing, kneeling, and sitting at the appropriate times more out of habit than out of devotion. Obviously devotion wasn't a crucial element, because I already felt much better.

After Mass ended, I headed to the rectory. You really had to want to light a candle to pray for someone, because it required walking—or in my case, limping—across the street, buying a candle for a buck, and walking back to church to light it. I guess we Catholics weren't honest enough to be on the honor system.

If I was going to light one candle, I figured I might as well light a few. Three was a good number. I knew right off the bat that one would be for Emily and one would be for Sean.

I tapped my cheek with my finger. Who should I light the

third candle for? Mary Bonatee was pretty stressed. And then there was my mother. I could pray that she chill out and stop stressing over my career so much. Although Sadie could benefit from a candle in her honor, I immediately decided against *that*. I didn't feel inclined to waste a good prayer on her—especially since I was pretty sure it wouldn't do any good.

In the end, I decided on Allison. Her mother was missing; her brother was dead. She had real angst and could probably use a good thought tossed her way. I lit the third candle and prayed for Allison to get her life together and find some peace.

And then I headed home to scour Emily's notebook and try to figure out where she might have gone on the day she went missing.

After a midmorning kung fu class followed by an hour and a half of yoga, I was in the kitchen under the pretense of getting ready for the Sunday feast.

By midafternoon my mother already had the *mole* sauce cooking, the chocolaty scent of it filling the room. She stood at the counter, rolling out a fresh batch of flour tortillas. To her, no Sunday meal was complete without homemade tortillas. I usually agreed, but I didn't have much of an appetite at the moment. Jack was coming to dinner, and I couldn't help but count the thousand ways I could be humiliated in front of him.

"Are you going to change?" my mother asked.

I looked down at my outfit. "What's wrong with this?" How I managed to keep a straight face was a testament to my acting ability. I knew I looked flirty, if a little underdressed, in a low-waisted, flared white skirt and a stretchy lavender top with tiny decorative buttons up the front (which was, just possibly, a little too low-cut and a tad too tight). At least my shirt wasn't see-through. I had boundaries, after all.

My mother yanked at the hem of my top, trying to pull it over my naked belly button. "This is too small." When the fabric snapped back into place, she gave up. "We are having a dinner guest, Dolores. It is Sunday. You could dress nice, ¿no?"

"This *is* nice." For a rendezvous in the nearest bedroom.

She gave an exasperated sigh and went back to the *comal* on the stove, flipping over a bubbling tortilla. My stomach grumbled, but the thought of food was nauseating. I sat down at the table across from my father. He was flipping through the newspaper, grunting as he read bits of it here and there. I studied him, thinking that I resembled him more than I did my mother, though most of my family disagreed. Maybe it was wishful thinking. Papi had a strong jaw and warm olive skin. I wanted the depth that his soulful hazel eyes seemed to hold and the strength that emanated from him.

He caught me watching him and gave me a puzzled look. "*¿Qué?*"

"*Nada,*" I said. If I found myself a man who was half as thoughtful and committed as my dad, I'd be lucky.

I turned to Emily's journal and began flipping the pages again, still processing all the different information she'd scribbled. Apparently she and Sean shared the notebook, because his crayon drawings and careful large letters marked almost every page. He'd written, "I love you Mommy" next to a drawing of a woman. There was a portrait of a family on the lined paper, and on the next page there was a colorful drawing of a boat rocking on the ocean.

She'd written names and dates. I ran through them, hoping something would spark inspiration. Muriel. R. Case. Todd. They meant *nada* to me. Less than *nada*.

A knock on the front door interrupted my musings. I glanced at the clock—3:37. Sunday dinner was always in the afternoon, which gave us plenty of time to burn off the high-calorie meal. My imagination suddenly raced with thoughts about how Jack could help me burn calories.

My mother immediately slipped her apron off and tucked it into a drawer. Then she patted her hair and smacked her lips. Was Jack *her* date—or mine?

Actually, neither. He was here for Antonio today. My turn was tomorrow.

My father folded up the newspaper and joined her on the way to the door, welcoming Jack like a soldier returning home from the war. It was as if he wasn't the player who my mother had caught feeling up some cheerleader in our backyard when he was sixteen, Antonio in the opposite corner of the yard with another pom-pom girl.

If my parents knew he'd seen me in my underwear, knew I was going to lunch with him tomorrow, knew I wanted him to take *me* to some corner of our yard and make me cry out in ecstasy—I had the feeling the welcome would be different. Like maybe Mami would be chasing him down the street, wielding her biggest kitchen knife, instead of primping for him.

I stood up from the table just as Antonio walked in from the utility room. He looked me over, and his mouth quirked. "Subtle."

I rolled my eyes but grew a touch concerned. If Antonio thought my efforts to be alluring were obvious, I'd probably gone too far. Too late to change now. I leaned back against the counter and continued to flip through Emily's notebook while I waited for Jack's grand entrance. Nonchalant. Very cool. *Good job, Lola,* I thought. I was playing it smooth.

"Jack," I heard my mother say. I could just see her kissing both his cheeks in her old-fashioned way. "It has been too long."

"*Señor,*" my father's quiet voice greeted. "*¿Cómo estás?*"

"I'm good, sir," Jack said. "How about you?"

My father responded, but I was stuck on Jack's voice. It was a let-me-take-you-to-bed-*now* voice, and I bit my lip, feeling twinges in places I'd forgotten existed.

They walked into the kitchen, my mother's hand tucked in the crook of Jack's arm. "*¿Y tu familia?*"

Jack nodded. "They're fine, thanks. Keeping busy."

My mother nodded sagely, leaving out any mention of Jack's father. We all remembered Jack's junior year in high school when his dad had left his mom for another woman.

"*¿Y tu hermana Brooke?* We see her around. A police officer. Hmph. Y *mi* Dolores a detective," she added, shaking her head. *What is it with these girls and their dangerous career choices?* her words seemed to say.

He gave me a little smile. "They're strong. They can handle themselves."

Good answer, Jack. And he still had rudimentary Spanish-comprehension abilities. Two more checks in his "pro" column.

Mami's expression shifted and seemed to say, *What do you know?* Thank God she kept her thoughts to herself.

Antonio held out his hand to Jack, pulling him into a bear hug when he took it. "*Bienvenido,* Callaghan." Then he turned to Mami. "*No más.* Let the man alone."

Looking Jack straight in the eyes made my vision go blurry. They had the same soulful depth I saw in my father's. I couldn't form a single word.

My mother marched up to me and whispered, "*Saluda,* Dolores." If only she knew how I really wanted to greet him.

She went back to the stove as my father gathered up the sections of the newspaper from the table.

Jack's grin quirked up in one corner. "Lola." I think he tried not to check me out, but his gaze drifted up and down my body. Thank God my parents were otherwise engaged, or the scenario of Mami chasing him down the street with the knife might have become reality.

I arched an eyebrow at him and put my hand on my hip. He'd already had a preview of me. If he wanted the whole show, he'd have to buy the wine-and-dine ticket. Not that it mattered what I wore. I suspected Jack Callaghan might always make me feel naked.

I peeked guiltily at my mother, glad she couldn't read my mind. I needed some alcohol to calm my wild impulses.

"Margaritas, anyone?" I said, proud of myself that I'd managed to put a jaunty lilt in my voice.

Jack piped up right away. "Yep. I'll take one." Every word he spoke was smooth and sultry and reminded me of silk sheets and a cozy morning. No man had ever given me thoughts like this, least of all Sergio, the longest relationship I'd had. I'd spent two years of my life with a cookie-crumbs-in-bed and cold-feet guy. Even after ten years, Sergio was the kind of mistake a woman wishes she could erase.

I shook the silk sheets from my brain and focused on Jack. The pictures I had of him didn't do him justice. He'd been a boy back then. Now he was all man, from his dark brown hair to his loafers, and every millimeter of taut muscle in between.

His eyes seemed to sparkle at me. Could he read my mind? The moment splintered as Antonio slapped him on the back. "Good choice, *hombre*. Lola makes a mean margarita. Her own special recipe."

I pulled out my official margarita equipment: blender, premium bottle of *Tres Mujeres* tequila, triple sec, a bottle of beer, lime juice, and the ice bucket from the freezer. I rubbed the glass rims with a wedge of lime and dipped them in sea salt, coating the edges. Turning my back, I downed a shot of tequila. Who needed salt and lime when you were fighting nerves and lust?

Sufficiently warm inside, I blended the ingredients together, glad for the grating noise and distraction. When I couldn't stall any longer, I poured, turning and passing around the frosty glasses.

"Good to see you, Jack." My dad's voice rang thick with his Spanish accent. We raised our glasses. "*Salud*," he said.

"*Salud*," we all echoed.

"Good to see you all, too, sir."

Twice with the *sir*. Jack had gotten respectful since he'd been gone.

He caught me staring. "Excellent margarita, Lola."

"Thanks." I took a long drink then slammed the heel of my palm against my forehead. Brain freeze! But a voice managed to ring out from the depths of my body like a contestant for Miss America. "Margaritas are one of my specialties."

The corner of his mouth curved up temptingly. "Just one of the many."

I smiled back. Were we flirting? In front of my parents? I needed to pace myself. "I've liked your articles so far."

"So you've read them."

Should I have admitted that? "Oh, you know. Here and there."

He gave me a skeptical look, like he knew I scoured the paper every day for something written by him. "I'm always searching for new things to write about. Investigating, talking to people. That's where the ideas come from."

I narrowed my eyes. "Right, like Emily Diggs."

"I've been thinking about that." He shook his head. "Do you have a picture of her? I don't remember the name, but—"

I held up my index finger, told him to wait, and raced upstairs. Three minutes later, I returned, out of breath, my file of Emily in my hand. "Right here," I said, opening it up and passing it over so he could have a look.

He started. "Her?"

That looked like recognition to me. "Have you talked to her?"

He nodded slowly. "I have. She showed up at the newspaper kind of belligerent. Security took her out, but I gave her my card before they got her out the door. I'd forgotten."

My ears perked up. "When was this?"

He thought as he took another drink. "Two weeks ago?"

"She never called you?"

My mother piped up. "It is Sunday, Dolores. Stop this."

Jack held his palm out. "It's fine, Mrs. Cruz." He turned back to me. "No. She never called."

Antonio leaned against the counter, sipping his drink. Papi rifled through the refrigerator and Mami glared.

"Do you know what she wanted?" I asked. "Any idea?"

"Not really. I asked security. Something about her son. That's all I got."

I finished my drink and refilled my glass. Something about her son. Which son? And why go to the paper?

"Can we have dinner now?" Mami asked, staring me down. "*Por favor.*"

I took the file back from Jack and put it with Emily's notebook on the counter. "Sure, Mami."

She handed me an industrial pair of shiny silver tongs to pick chicken out of the stockpot. Standing over the stove, steam billowing around my face, I imagined I looked a little like an amber-skinned Cinderella, but deep down I knew I was Xena. What kind of girl did Jack want? I suspected that it was the dainty princess—and I didn't want it to be.

The smile he flashed at me as he refilled his glass melted my insides a little. Well, shoot. I could be Cinderella or Snow White if that's what he wanted—at least for a day.

Get a grip, Lola. I turned and downed another shot of tequila. Hell no, I couldn't be Snow White. Maybe Mulan.

That Disney character had it going on. And so did I. I couldn't pretend otherwise.

"You enjoy the *mole*, Jack, yes?" my mother asked from the stove.

"Oh yeah, Mrs. Cruz." He kept his eyes glued to me. "Sweet and savory. Love every last bit of it."

A shiver shimmied up my spine. I swallowed, flipped a tortilla, and then stirred the contents of the blender with blinding focus. I jumped a mile when the phone rang. We all turned to stare at the wireless unit. Saved by Ma Bell.

Mami cleared her throat. "Excuse me, *por favor.* I am expecting a call."

I cocked a brow at her back. She was *expecting* a *call*? From who? The pope?

She picked up the handset. "*Bueno.*" She listened for a moment then slipped into Spanish, her tone formal. "*Bien, gracias. ¿Y usted, señor?*"

Okay, so she really *was* expecting a call. I tuned her out, concentrating instead on finishing my margarita. If Jack's words and vague innuendos could make me shiver, what would touching him, and having him touch me, make me feel?

My mother thrust the phone at me with a glare. "*Para ti.*"

I took the phone. "Hello?" My lips felt heavy, and gravity pulled my eyelids into slow blinks. Man, good tequila worked fast.

"Dolores? It's Manny."

My eyelids flew open. "Manny." Why was he calling here? I bent at the knees and carefully set my glass on the wavy counter. Throwing my shoulders back, I stood up as straight as I could. I was professional and alert. "Is shomething wrong?" I slurred, my mouth working a step behind my brain. Okay, not so alert. I waited for Manny's explanation, my fingertips tapping my forehead. Damn, I shouldn't have had that last shot.

85

"I have a situation. Are you available tonight?"

What kind of situation? "Available? Tonight?"

I looked over my shoulder and caught Jack's expression. It was a combination of heady lust and disappointment.

Exactly what I was feeling.

"I need your help with a case," Manny said.

My heart did a double somersault. I didn't want to leave now. I *really* did not want to leave now, but this was my job. No man would get in the way of that. Flapping my hand at them, I made a serious face, pointed to the phone, and slurred loudly, "It's my bossh. *Mi jefe*," I said to Mami, although she'd answered the phone and already knew it was Manny. I sidestepped past them and into the living room.

"Dolores?" Manny barked.

I nodded.

"Dolores?" he said again.

Ah, revelation. He couldn't hear my nod. "Mmm-hmm. I'm here." I slapped my cheek, trying to knock the alcoholic blur out of my brain.

"Sadie can't make her shift at Laughlin's." His voice was tense. "I need you to fill in."

My stomach gurgled in panic. *Shit!* I forced my eyelids wide again and looked around. At least I could focus. I just had to ignore the haziness and soft edges around everything. "Right." I articulated so I wouldn't slur. "I can be there in fifteen minutes." Laughlin's was close by. Down the street. I could walk—since there was no way in hell I was getting behind the wheel of my car right now. I might be tipsy, but I wasn't stupid.

"Why are you shouting? Are you all right?"

Was I yelling? I lowered my voice into a conspiratorial whisper. "I'm fine, Manny. I'm on the job. I'll be right there."

"I'll pick you up. Five minutes." The line went dead, and that was that. Manny was on his way, and I was holding a dead phone.

Eight eyes were staring at me when I rushed back into the kitchen. I forged through the gawking crowd. "Something's come up. I have to go." I looked longingly at Jack. I really didn't want to leave him, but work was work. "See you later," I said.

The faint indentation of Jack's dimple taunted me, and I imagined squeezing his cheeks together as my mother had done to Antonio. There was a magnetic draw to it—to him—that I'd never understood. Even after fourteen years, it hadn't ebbed.

"¿Ahora?" My mother looked horrified. "You are leaving now?"

I spoke slowly, working hard to enunciate my words. "I have to. Manny's picking me up. I'm going to do some—" I dropped my voice again, whispering seriously, "undercover work."

"What kind of covers are you and your boss going to be un-der?" Antonio murmured.

Apparently Jack heard; his smile faded.

"Today is Sunday," my mother objected. "Your sister, *the teacher*, does not work on Sundays."

"Actually, she's probably doing lesson plans or grading pa-pers, Mami. That's why she's not here."

Mami scowled and went back to sipping her margarita.

"What is this undercover work?" my father asked, his jaw set.

"A case. It's no big deal."

Jack set his drink down and leaned against the counter. His folded arms pulled at the palm trees that decorated the bot-tom of his shirt. He looked as disappointed as I felt, but I'd chosen my career. And I was a team player. Manny needed me; I was there.

"I'll be fine, Papi." I gave him a peck on the cheek. "It's just Laughlin's, and Manny'll be there." Then with a wave good-bye to the group, I flew out the door and zipped upstairs to change.

Chapter 7

pulled on low-rise black jeans and Sketchers, then tucked my hair up under a wig from my growing collection—a shoulder-length redheaded bob. With a pair of black-framed prescription-free glasses, the disguise was complete. I looked in the mirror. Not half bad.

Manny's white Dodge Ram pulled to the curb just as I headed back outside. It was a lifted four-by-four, complete with sunroof and matching camper shell—an extension of his machismo but not exactly an inconspicuous undercover car.

I looked around as I raced down the stairs, wondering what kind of car Jack drove. Too many parked on the street to venture even a guess.

Inside the truck, I avoided looking at my parents' window. Guilt was second nature to me, what with my Mexican Catholic upbringing and all. A good daughter would have stayed and had dinner and helped clean up afterwards. A good daughter would not have become a detective. A good daughter would have put her mother first.

Apparently I was not such a good daughter.

Manny gave me a slow once-over as I tucked a stray strand of my hair under the wig. He raised a quizzical brow.

"People might recognize me at Laughlin's," I said.

He revved the engine and took off, the midtown houses flying by in a blur. Ten seconds later, he looked at me again. "Been drinking?"

My head skirted around a nod and a shake. "A few margaritas." And a couple shots of tequila. "I'm fine." I considered segueing the conversation to Isabel—just for the hell of it—but didn't have the mental deftness to tackle a subtle change of topic. "Where's Sadie?" I asked instead. "She's not going to like me taking her gig." Not that I cared.

Okay, I cared a little. Even if Sadie had wanted the Diggs case but was stuck at Laughlin's, our cases were our cases, and I knew she'd be pissed if the perps showed up tonight while I was working her turf.

"She's stuck out of town. She'll relieve you at seven."

Oh, well, that sucked. I was giving up dinner with Jack for just a few hours? My shoulders slumped for a second, but then I bolstered my attitude. Manny'd called me in to do a job, and I was going to do it well. "I didn't do—" A hiccup slipped out. "—the training," I finished, darting a glance at him to see if he'd noticed.

He stared straight ahead, his face impassive. "You're just bagging groceries. I'm sure you can handle it."

"Do—I—get—a—Laughlin's—shirt?" I enunciated each word, overcompensating for any alcohol-induced slur I might be harboring. I could feel him evaluating my behavior. Damn. PIs didn't work under a tenure system. Would he fire me if he found out I hadn't been straight with him about being tipsy? How long did a tequila buzz last, anyway? I wished I'd thought to down some water before I left. Or a quadruple espresso.

I popped a mint and muttered a nearly silent prayer that I'd be back to normal in no time. Meanwhile, I'd be extra cautious.

"Yes to the shirt. You can wear it on top of—" He paused, looking me over with a slow gaze. "—that."

Manny's silent appraisal of me was more than a little disconcerting. I tugged at the top I'd worn for Jack. Damn again. I should have changed it. Served me right for dressing all alluring for a man.

He dangled one arm out the window and turned his concentration back to the road.

"Are you going to fill me in on the job?" I had a rough idea from the last staff meeting, but details would be a little helpful. "What am I supposed to be looking for?"

He pulled the brown file from under his seat and handed it to me. "It's all in there."

I opened the folder. The information sheet contained the standard data—minus a photograph. We were on the lookout for a man-and-a-woman team, both purportedly in their thirties. They'd robbed four grocery stores in the immediate area, always between the hours of five in the afternoon and nine at night, taunting the police with notes, daring anybody to catch them.

Keenan D'Angelo, owner of Laughlin's, hadn't been hit—yet. He was taking no chances. He didn't want to risk his employees' safety for the money in the tills. The police would offer only nominal patrols.

So far, there had been no injuries during the robberies, no evidence of a weapon. I thought D'Angelo was probably more concerned about losing his hard-earned dough than losing his employees. Oh, man! The tequila had zapped my optimistic attitude and made me a cynic like the Camacho Associates. *Not good, Lola, not good.*

Trying to get my optimism back—and get focused—I went back to the file. The method was the same each time. The couple does a little shopping and waits in the line of a male checker. After the groceries are bagged, the woman flashes the checker. While he gawks—as they all do, I mean they're guys—the partner in crime jumps over the checkout counter, shoves the checker aside, snatches the money from the till, grabs the grocery bags, and then they both bolt. The checker is left speechless and his drawer penniless.

It was some high-class thievery.

Enter Camacho and Associates.

The one thing that all the robbery victims, and the surveillance cameras, could give as a description were the sunburst nipple shields and a spiral tattoo that started under the sunburst on the right breast and worked its way outward. I cringed. My head spun at the mere idea of a tattoo on the boob.

Not surprisingly, no one seemed to remember any details about the Bonnie-and-Clyde duo—except Bonnie's boob jewelry.

"So our goal is to prevent the robbery if they come in to Laughlin's?" Nothing wrong with a little clarification.

"And subdue the perps, if possible."

Check. "You'll be in the store?"

He shook his head. "Surveillance from outside."

So how was I going to capture both Bonnie and Clyde on my own? Assuming they showed up tonight.

Manny seemed to read my thoughts. "How are you going to subdue them if they come tonight?" He looked at me with an annoying little smirk on his face. "Are you hiding a gun on your person?"

"You know I don't believe in guns. All I need is a pair of handcuffs." I'd given him my philosophy on guns more than once. "My body is my weapon." My lip curled after the words left my mouth. That had sounded so much better—and so much less suggestive—when I said it in my head.

91

"You're going to have to prove that to me, *sargenta*," he said, his voice low and rumbling.

I jabbed my finger at him then grabbed the doorjamb to stop swaying. "Hey, I can subdue and restrain. You sure you want to go there?"

The corner of his mouth twitched. "Oh, we'll go there." His face was way too serious. "You're going to show me *all* your moves one day."

I swallowed hard and pressed the window button. *¡Dios mío!* I was suddenly roasting. "What's with the *sargenta* bit?" I asked when I'd cooled down a degree. As nicknames went, being called sergeant was good. Strong and tough. But Dolores from him was just fine. Anything else sounded too personal.

"How do you expect to catch bad guys when you're always the underdog without a weapon, Dolores?" He'd ignored my question, but I left it alone. Ignorance is bliss, and all that.

When I didn't say anything, he shook his head. Neil carried. Even Sadie, who could decommission like Medusa with her porcelain gaze, had a pistol. Manny had made it clear that when I got licensed, he wanted me to carry. That was two years ago. He was still waiting.

"It's against my principles."

"Then you need to reconsider your principles."

I hated to admit that he had a point. I was at a *slight* disadvantage against bad guys without a weapon. But was I willing to risk my freedom for it? I'd thought long and hard on the subject. I'd done firearms training, but I still wasn't willing to risk shooting an innocent person—or have my own weapon used against me. I flexed my muscles, bolstering my confidence. "I'll take it under advisement."

"We're not done with this discussion," he said as he pulled into Laughlin's parking lot.

I chose to ignore him.

"You need to wear a wire. I'll be out here watching and listening." He eyed me. "With a gun."

"Well, don't accidentally shoot me."

Manny had one arm stretched across the bucket seats of the truck and the other slung across the steering wheel. He looked away as I worked the black wire up underneath my shirt and clipped the miniature microphone onto my bra. What a gentleman.

"How's that?" I asked when I had it in place.

His voice was low as he trained his gaze on me. "Too obvious."

I looked down. Yep, even from this angle I could see it. I turned my back to him, stuck my hand underneath my shirt, and worked the wire to my side. I fed it beneath the fabric of my bra, flattened my shirt against it again, and turned back. "Okay?"

"*Perfecto*," he said slowly, and I had an inkling he wasn't talking about the wire.

He dug under his seat, handing me a pair of scratched-up handcuffs a moment later.

I dangled them from my finger. "What are these for?"

"You said all you needed was handcuffs. Here they are. Put them to good use."

Yikes. He was thinking only about work, wasn't he? He had Isabel to play hostage with. "I will."

"Introduce yourself to D'Angelo," he continued. "He'll set you up. If you see anyone suspicious, give me a signal. *¿Entiendes?*"

I nodded again and got out of the truck, forcing the handcuffs into my back pocket. "Got it." I pushed the glasses up the bridge of my nose and straightened my wig, feeling Manny's eyes burning against my back as I walked into Laughlin's Grocers. My head swam and I felt nauseated. Alcohol

93

and an empty stomach did not make a good combination for investigative work. But I was on the job, and Lola, PI always gets her man . . . or in this case, her nipple-shielded woman.

It didn't take long to slip a green Laughlin's shirt over my top and situate myself at the front of the store to pack groceries. Within an hour, my tequila buzz had worn off and I was actively studying each customer. No sign of Bonnie and Clyde, but it was still early.

Chances were they wouldn't show anyway.

It was five fifteen, and two checkers were working the registers: an attractive blond-haired young man in his late teens or early twenties, probably a college student; and an older woman with tight iron-gray curls running up and down her head. Working back and forth between the two, I packed bags, tried not to crunch eggs or smash bread, and made polite conversation.

I kept my eyes peeled for a couple with no specific features, hair color, hairstyle, or height. Since this wasn't a nudist market, the description I had of Bonnie's breasts didn't do me any good.

It took a while, but before long I found my groove, packing bags like I'd been doing it for days. "Paper or plastic?" I asked after each sale, disappointed that no one came in with their own environmentally "green" bags. Didn't people know about global warming? Didn't people care?

I kept an eye out for Manny every time I helped a customer to the parking lot with their groceries, but I didn't see him. Where in the world had he hidden the macho machine? It wasn't like you could slip the big-ass truck behind a tree. I knew he was out there somewhere. A shiver zipped down my spine—he had my back.

It was good to know someone did.

By 7:20, Sadie was still a no-show, I had no less than eleven paper cuts on my fingers, and I'd spotted at least seven nonde-script couples who could have been Bonnie and Clyde. But each had shopped, paid, and left without incident. At 7:25, another couple wound their way up and down the aisles, adding this and that to their cart. The way the woman's eyes darted around put me on alert. Was she casing the place?

I peered at her chest. *Nada.* Her shirt was smooth. It didn't look like any medieval jewelry lurked underneath, but I couldn't rule out the possibility.

"Potential suspects," I hissed into my bra, putting Manny on alert, too. There was a lull at the checkout lines, so I swept the floor in front of the registers, keeping an eye on the couple as they shopped. Another couple, two men, and a gray-haired man entered the store. Laughlin's was steadily busy. Saturday nights in Sacramento weren't just for dates anymore.

The couple in question approached the checkout line. "Be ready," I whispered into my chest.

I leaned the broom up against the checkout counter, ad-justed my wig, poked at my glasses, and began bagging the cou-ple's groceries. I peered at her front again. Perfectly smooth.

When I looked back at her face, she caught my eye and— *¡ay, Dios!*—winked at me.

I broke into a coughing frenzy and quickly walked away. Oh God, did she think I was checking her out? No, no, no! I needed to work on my subtlety.

Once my coughing was under control, I went back to the groceries, looking at the couple through my eyelashes. The woman cracked a huge come-hither smile at me as I bagged a six-pack of beer, a container of strawberries, whipped cream, a T-bone steak, and oysters from the seafood counter.

It wasn't hard to deduce that they were going to have an aphrodisiac kind of night. Ew, had she wanted to make it a threesome?

The guy caught the look his girlfriend was giving me, grabbed the bags, and dragged her out of the store. Good. Thank God. But what, I wasn't his type?

I pressed my hand against my forehead for a second and then turned my back to the checkers. "False alarm," I whispered as I contemplated taking a break and having a Snickers bar.

"Hello, there, boys." The sausage-curled checker's giggly voice brought my attention back to the register. The next customers moved up in line.

Jack and Antonio. My jaw dropped. "What the hell are you doing here?" I snapped.

Antonio flashed a wicked grin. "Geeky. That's a good look for you, Lola."

"Nice. Get out of here. I'm working." I paused and dropped my voice. "And by the way, since when do you step foot in a grocery store?"

"Since tonight. I had a hankering to see what one looked like from the inside." He winked at me. "I need a battery for my *camera*," he said, "so I can take some *pictures* later."

I peered at him, my lips tight. What was he talking about? Oh! Oh, no! My pictures of Jack. I'd dug through my drawer searching for my fake glasses. Had I left the photos in *plain sight*? Had Antonio been in my room and *seen* them?

My stomach coiled. Oh shit. I couldn't believe I'd be so stupid as to leave them lying around. Grabbing Antonio by the front of his shirt, I pulled him aside. "Did you——?" But I couldn't even say it. What if I was just paranoid? What if he *hadn't* seen the photos and he was just fishing?

He smacked an ultra-innocent look on his face—quite an accomplishment, considering his fearsome goatee. "Something wrong, sis?"

My blood scorched my cheeks, and I was afraid steam

might start shooting out of my ears any second. "What are you taking pictures of?" I asked as innocently as I could muster.

His grin widened. "I was thinking I'd hide somewhere and see what looks interesting. Maybe I'll catch someone doing the nasty." His voice dropped a decibel. "Candid shots are the best, don't you think?"

Shit! He *had* seen them. I growled and felt my face get hotter. Dropping my voice to a harsh whisper, I demanded, "What were you doing in my room?"

He notched his head toward the check stand. "Borrowing some cash for the beer." He stepped back into line. "I'm saving all of mine, remember?" He shot me a victorious smile. "Oh, and I guess we need to talk about that date with Reilly," he said.

"Oh no." I grabbed the six-pack of Corona and stuck it in a bag. "You promised."

He turned to Jack, who'd been watching us with a look of amused curiosity. "Hey, dude, you remember that girl you dated in school. Greta—" He paused, resting a finger on his lips. "What was her last name?"

"Pritchard." Jack grinned. "Greta Pritchard."

"Right." Antonio darted a look my way. "Pritchard."

I seethed, partly at Antonio's audacity, and partly at the look of blissful remembrance on Jack's face. "Okay, we'll talk," I snapped. "Now, I'm working. Do you mind?"

Antonio paid the checker as Jack smirked. "Nice hair." He was close enough for me to breathe in his clean outdoorsy scent. "Where's Scooby and Shaggy?"

I knocked his arm with the back of my hand, heat from the contact sizzling up my arm. "You're hilarious." I gave the store another scan. All clear. Lowering my voice, I leaned closer again, hyperaware that Jack, a man I was totally hot and bothered over, was next to me, and Manny, a man who had just put me on edge with his scrutiny and nickname, was outside listening. My only consolation was that I had finally sobered up. "I'm undercover," I whispered. "Now go away."

"Anything to do with the missing woman?" Jack asked.

"No. Completely different." I scanned the store again. A gray-haired man flipped through magazines. A mom chastised one of her kids in the cereal aisle. A couple, so nondescript that I'd hardly registered them before, stood in line at the college boy's check out. They had half the liquor department and a roasted chicken on the counter. The checker started bagging.

"Oh no!"

"What?" Antonio jabbered at me. "*Hell-o*. Earth to Lola."

I ignored him and reached for the broom handle, edging toward college boy.

"What the—?" The young checker's jaw dropped as Bonnie yanked up her shirt.

"Argh!" I snarled and lunged forward, brandishing my broom as if it were a light saber. I was a Jedi ready to battle. Nipple-shield woman would not get away.

My guttural bark startled Clyde midvault. His foot caught on the edge of the counter, and he tumbled over. The bottles slipped off the edge and crashed to the ground, exploding in a spray of vodka and rum, beer and gin. The chicken came undone from its plastic container and slithered, belly down, across the floor.

Bonnie spun to face me, and I cranked my saber-broom around, bristles poking toward her. My eyes bugged when I saw the bull's-eye target that doubled as her right breast. Holy shit! I stopped and stared, hypnotized. It was working on me.

I blinked, breaking the trance. Lunging forward, I jabbed the prickly end of the broom at her. Antonio and Jack rushed past me toward Clyde, and the next second, the three of them slipped in the puddle of alcohol. They sprawled on the floor and spun on their backs like they were break dancing. Antonio and Jack rolled onto their stomachs and clamored to hold on to Clyde, all the while trying to avoid the glass shards that littered the floor.

I couldn't do a thing to help them.

I wheeled back around to see Bonnie pulling her shirt down and starting for the exit. Shit! Where was Manny?

Oh my God. I hadn't alerted him. "It's them. They're here. Nine-one-one!" I plucked my shirt out and rasped into my bra as I flung the broom down and ran after her. "Backup, Manny. *Bingo!*"

I chased after Bonnie into the parking lot and saw Manny racing across the asphalt toward us. Bonnie tried to sidestep around him, but we sandwiched her. I grabbed her by the arm just as she flashed again, her bazookas aimed right at Manny. My grip spun her, but she yanked free and went flying, tripping over her own feet and sliding across the pavement.

Manny dived after her and deftly maneuvered her arms behind her back. He yanked her up, and even as her shirt flew open, he ripped a pair of handcuffs from his belt and snapped them on her.

Damn. My handcuffs were still safely in my pocket. Maybe I wasn't completely sober.

Thin threads of blood surfaced on the abrasions that ran down her chest. I cringed when I saw her nipple shield dangling and made an X with my arms across my breasts. *¡Dios mío!* That had to hurt.

Bonnie kicked at Manny. "Let go!" she shrieked.

"Not a chance." He took her by the shoulder. "Nice mutilation." His expression never changed.

She spit at his face.

He spun her around just as Antonio and Jack stumbled

99

across the parking lot, each of them holding one of Clyde's wrists. They stopped dead in their tracks, eyes rooted to Bonnie's chest.

"Oh, come on." I waved my hand in front of their faces before yanking Bonnie's shirt back into place. "I know for a fact that you've both seen breasts before."

"Not like those," Antonio said, way too much appreciation in his voice.

Clyde kicked at them, cursing.

As Jack stepped sideways, stretching out to avoid his flailing prisoner, Bonnie looked at him, flicked her tongue out between her lips like a lizard, and shimmied. "Want some of this, big boy?"

Oh, the nerve. As if.

"Thanks, but you're not my type," Jack said.

Good answer. But it left me wondering what *was* his type.

"Try it, you might like it," Bonnie said with another wag of her tongue.

"Shut your mouth," Manny said, jerking Bonnie and then passing her over to me. I took hold of her by the handcuffs while Manny flipped his cell phone open and called the police. We waited in awkward silence until they came to take away the grocery store bandits. Case closed.

Sadie pulled up seconds after the cops left. She stared at the four of us, me in my Laughlin's shirt, Manny grimly staring after the patrol car, Antonio looking smug, and Jack, hair tousled and palm tree shirt stained, leaning against my brother's green Mustang.

"What's going on?" she demanded.

Manny pulled her aside and filled her in. When they came back, he said to me, "We'll need to file a report."

I nodded, silently cheering. I'd captured the bandits with a broom for a weapon—no gun required.

Sadie's pointy jaw worked. "Nice disguise."

It was sarcastic, but I took it at face value. "I shop here. Didn't want people recognizing me and chatting me up. . . ." I glared at Jack and Antonio. "You know, blowing my cover."

She turned from me and, teeth still clenched, hissed something I couldn't hear to Manny. Then she walked away from him, storming across the parking lot.

Manny's nostrils flared, but, unbelievably, he followed her.

Antonio stared after her. "She's hot."

I stared after her myself, trying to be objective. "Really? You think so?"

"Oh yeah. Definitely."

I was trying to see Sadie from a man's point of view when Jack came up next to me. "Are things always this exciting around you?"

I had an urge to let my fingertips wisp against his chest. To brush his wayward locks of hair back into place. To show him that my proclivity for excitement wasn't limited to my job. Instead I slipped my fake glasses off and pulled the wig from my head, ruffling my hair back up to volume. "Comes with the job."

"Your mom might have a point about the danger—"

I started to mentally erase one of the checkmarks I'd placed in his pro column. Unconditional support. That's what I wanted in a man. I should have known Jack couldn't offer that.

Antonio turned back to us. "You're talking to a wall, Callaghan. Lola's wanted to be a detective since she was—" He looked at me, that duplicitous smile sliding across his face again. "What fourteen? Fifteen? Been spying since then, anyway."

"Spying?" Jack looked from Antonio to me. "Okay, what am I missing here?"

I swatted Antonio on the arm. "Nothing." I was going to have to burn those pictures, damn it—and I didn't want to.

He took me by the arm and led me away from Antonio.

"How about dinner?"

The adrenaline rush from Bonnie and Clyde was fading, hunger pangs beat against the inside of my stomach, and the tequila from earlier had zapped the rest of my energy. Dinner sounded like heaven. I opened my mouth to answer—

"Dolores!"

—and closed it again.

Jack and I both turned to see Manny walking toward us, his face tense, his cell phone clutched to his ear. Sadie walked double time to keep up with him, but they were oddly in sync.

"Dolores," Manny said again when he reached me. He shot a searing look at Jack as he clipped his phone back onto his belt. "I just got a call from a buddy on the force. They found a body in the river off Garden Highway."

The air was suddenly heavy and thick in my lungs. I felt faint.

Manny's face grew stony. "They identified the body. It's Emily Diggs."

Chapter 8

Manny placed an immediate call to Walter Diggs, spoke to him briefly, and clipped his phone closed again.

"Well?" I asked.

He glanced at Antonio and Jack, who were leaning against the Mustang, then turned back to me. "It's not over. He wants us to find out what happened."

"Won't the police investigate?" I didn't get why Walter would want to pay for services the police would automatically provide. "I'm assuming they think this wasn't an accident."

"It looks suspicious."

I covered my face with my hands. Murder. That was a far cry from subduing the freaky flasher thieves. I hadn't made much headway in finding Emily when she was missing. Sean's little face fluttered into my brain. I'd have to do better at finding her killer.

"Let's go," Manny said.

I tried to ignore the numbness in my fingertips and the chill that snaked through my body. "Go where?"

"To the police station. We'll file our report on Laughlin's and see what we can find out about the Diggs woman."

"Right." I wasn't thinking clearly. News of Emily's death had shaken me to the core. It felt like a personal loss, the weight of it like the water that had pressed down on Emily's body. "I'll take a rain check," I said to Jack, my appetite, like a wave receding from the shore, gone again.

Jack had been studying Manny with a piercing look. His face softened as he ran his fingertips down my arm. "You okay?"

"Fine. But I have to go." Even his touch couldn't erase Emily's tragedy from the front of my mind.

He nodded. "Sure."

"Lunch tomorrow," I said as I pulled my Laughlin's shirt over my head, tugging my lavender top down to keep it in place.

Jack's mouth tightened. "Yep."

Manny took the shirt from me and tossed it to Sadie. "Take it back inside."

I didn't want to leave, but what else could I do? My missing person was dead.

Sadie clutched the shirt, glowering as I climbed into Manny's truck. Red blotches appeared on her skin, creeping up her neck, coloring her cheeks. If she were a geyser, she'd blow any second.

I ignored her, mentally reviewing the things I'd learned so far in my search for Emily. Nothing that warranted murder. Of course, what *did* warrant murder?

I thought about Beatrice, Emily's crazy roommate and Mary Bonatee's aunt. I'd told her I'd find Emily, and I'd let her down.

Manny and I drove in silence. Despite the temperature— ninety-five degrees at 9:10 in the evening—my skin pricked with goose bumps. I was chilled to the bone.

At the station, I perched on the edge of a hollow metal chair, the cloth-lined frame scratchy against my arms and of-

104

fering no warmth. Manny sat in an identical chair next to me, unfazed. Of course. He was the perfect PI.

Detective Seavers, Manny's buddy, sat across from us. He had a crusty voice and an even crustier demeanor. His suit was rumpled, his tie wrinkled, and he looked completely disheveled. A thin layer of hair grew around his head in a dome-wrap. After brief introductions, he said, "We've got next to nothing. Coroner's report will be a few days."

"What can you tell us?" Manny asked.

"A boater found her near Riverbank Marina. Initial report indicates she's been dead several days." Detective Seavers straightened his files and stifled a yawn. I glanced at my watch—9:30. Where was his stamina?

I yawned. Where was mine? A wave of dizziness flitted over me.

Manny shifted in his chair. "Anything else you can tell me, Randy?"

"Not right now. I'll keep you posted." He looked at me and raised his caterpillar eyebrows.

Manny hitched his thumb in my direction. "Dolores is working the case from our end. I'll let you know if she finds anything." Then he shook Seavers's hand. "Welcome back to Sacramento, Detective."

Seavers gave me a quick nod, then actually smiled at Manny. "Good to be back. Gotta love the valley."

Manny stood up. "I'll be in contact."

Detective Seavers walked us out. He dropped his voice as he spoke to Manny. I could barely hear him ask, "So, are you and—?"

"Over," Manny said.

"Right. Too bad." The detective ran his hand over his sparse hair. "She was a feisty one."

Manny shot him a look, and the detective shut his mouth.

Then he strode out of the police station, leaving Seavers staring after him.

I hurried to keep up. Seavers and Manny must go way back if the detective knew the ex. Feisty? I just didn't know what that meant in relation to Manny Camacho.

Fifteen silent minutes later, Manny pulled his truck up in front of my parents' house and turned in his seat. "Not a bad job tonight," he said.

"Thanks." I think. It wasn't quite a compliment, but it wasn't criticism either, so I took it graciously. "See you tomorrow." I started to climb out of the truck.

"*Peleadora,*" he murmured, and I nearly fell.

Now he was calling me a fighter? I leaned back in and did a double take at the glimmer in his dark eyes. "What's with the nicknames?"

"Looking for the one that fits."

I was speechless. "I don't need one."

He smiled slightly. "But you deserve one, Dolores."

Whatever *that* meant. I slammed the truck door and went upstairs. Better not to think about it.

He didn't leave until I'd gone inside. The apartment was empty, no sign of Antonio—or Jack. First things first. I raced to my bedroom and immediately searched my dresser for the photos of Jack and Greta Pritchard. I tossed all my lingerie out of the drawers, dropped to my knees and looked under the dresser, even pulled it out from the wall to look behind it.

They weren't there. Damn Antonio. After fifteen years of having them, the thought that they were gone made my stomach feel hollow. I couldn't remember when I'd eaten, but I didn't think I could choke down water at this point. I hooked a leash to Salsa's collar and went out for a late-night run around the neighborhood. The streets were lighted, the neighborhood quiet and comforting. A half hour turned into forty minutes. And that turned into an hour.

Who would want Emily Diggs dead? I filtered through what I knew so far. I couldn't come up with a motive for Mary Bonatee. Allison had a chip on her shoulder the size of Mt. Kilimanjaro, but did she dislike her mother enough to kill her?

How did Emily get into the river? Maybe it *was* accidental. Had she been on a boat and fallen overboard? But whose boat, and why would she be on it? Or had she been killed somewhere else and dumped in the river?

I came back to why she'd wanted to talk to a reporter at the paper. She'd had something big on her mind, but what?

By the time I got back home, it was painfully clear that I didn't have even a fraction of the information I needed to figure out what had happened to her, and Salsa and I were both exhausted. I fell into my bed, names and ideas circling in my mind—Emily, Sean, Bea, boats, bodies in the river. Finally, as the sun started to come up, I drifted off to sleep.

Sitting at my usual table at Szechwan House, I pressed my fist to my cheek. Even with the yoga class I'd taken that morning and the extra primp time, I was still early. I dug out my phone and George Bonatee's business card, and placed a call to Emily's landlord.

Out of town until tomorrow, his secretary said. Damn. Visiting him would have to wait.

I always looked for signs of good luck—it was part of that eternal-optimism superstition thing—so when Helen brought over a single fortune cookie, a goofy grin smacked across her face, who was I to question it? "You need good luck, eh, Lola? Open fortune."

I cracked the cookie, and two small papers fluttered to the table. Ooh, was I double lucky today? The first one said YOU WILL MAKE A LOT OF MONEY. Great, but would I find a killer? That's what I wanted to know.

I picked up the second one. Much better. YOUR DESTINY AWAITS. Vague—and slightly menacing if I thought about it too hard. I flipped the fortune over to see my lucky numbers. Just in case I decided to play the lottery later so I could make the money the first fortune predicted. There, scribbled on top of the numbers in green ink, was a handwritten message: *Am I it?*

Helen giggled. "I slip it in for him." She nodded toward the waiting area.

I spun my head around. Jack stood there, looking far better than lunch possibly could.

My destiny awaits. I felt encouraged.

"You're early," he said, his voice smooth and velvety. Like a layer of scented lotion, it seeped right into me, working its magic.

"I'm hungry. I like to eat. You should know that about me right from the start." Until I knew the man Jack had become, I thought I should keep my distance. That included prattling on about whatever inconsequential thoughts came to mind. "I'll probably end up round, just like my mother."

Jack slid into the chair across from me. "Your mom's not that round." He grinned wickedly. "And there's always exercise to help keep a person in shape."

It was perfectly clear that the exercise he was referring to included a bed and lots of heavy panting. I pretended to be naïve. "I run. Very fast. I like to run. And do yoga. I'm very active."

He leaned forward, resting his forearms on the table. His navy polo shirt matched the smoky blue of his eyes and hung on him perfectly, accentuating the hard body underneath. If he was trying to impress me, he was doing a fabulous job. "I had a different kind of exercise in mind," he said.

Ay, Dios, the man was bold. I felt myself blush and hurried to change the subject. *Keep your distance*, I reminded myself. "Exciting night last night, eh?"

His smile faded slightly, and he leaned back in his chair. "Yep."

"Sorry about missing dinner." My mother's voice in my head reminded me of my manners. "But thanks for your help."

"My pleasure," he said. "You needed backup."

"Manny was there for backup." I sat up taller and folded my hands in front of me. "And I can take care of myself. You and Antonio being there just made it a little easier." I wished I hadn't sounded so defensive, but something about Jack's scrutiny made my back go up.

"If you say so." He turned his attention to Helen, who was back to take our order. "We'll have Happy Family with prawns and—" He looked at me.

"Mapo tofu," I said.

He added hot and sour soup and an order of paper-wrapped chicken. He had a healthy appetite and good taste. Another check in the pro column—if I was keeping track. Which, of course, I was. He was still down one from that comment last night about my mother having a point about the danger in my job. And his attitude today seemed to corroborate that sentiment.

"What else is new with you, Lola?" he asked after Helen disappeared into the kitchen.

My lust-filled crush on him was completely renewed; that's what was new. "Nothing." I made myself blink. "You were in San Luis Obispo for a long time, right?"

He nodded. "I was."

"Do you miss it?"

He paused for a beat too long, and there was a vague change in his expression. "Not much."

My Spidey senses went on alert. There was something he'd left unsaid. "How long were you there?"

"A little more than ten years."

Ten years and he didn't miss much? He'd left behind his job, friends, and the life he'd established. That he was indifferent didn't seem right. "What about your friends?" I prompted. *Or girlfriends*, I thought, wishing I could just cut to the chase. "There must be *something* you miss."

He considered for a few seconds. "The ocean. The drive along the coast. And the mountains, I guess. There's definitely something about the beauty of that place." He looked out the window as he took a sip of his water, the sparkle gone from his eyes. "But sometimes home is the best medicine. Too many obligations . . ."

Medicine for what? "Obligations?"

He looked at me again, and I felt the intensity of his gaze as if the light inside him could somehow illuminate my soul. Was he talking about obligations he'd left behind, or ones he'd returned to? It was crazy to think that I was one of those obligations, but my mind went there anyway. Tonio had said Jack had wanted me back in high school when I was off-limits. In my wishful thinking, I wanted to believe he'd come back to find me after all these years.

"I had to leave," he said.

Oh. The way he said those four little words, and the unspoken heavy meaning underlying them, made my fantasy that he'd come back for me vanish. He'd left something behind; that seemed clear. But what it was, and his seeming conflict over it, was what I wanted to know.

He cocked his head and smiled, the wistfulness I thought

I'd seen in him gone. "I didn't realize there was so much here to miss."

"Right. Like Greta Pritchard. She's still here, isn't she?"

He laughed, choking on the water he'd just taken a sip of. "What is it with you and Antonio and Greta Pritchard? I haven't thought about her in years. God, how long ago did we even date?"

"Fourteen years," I blurted. *Six months, ten days* . . .

He laughed. "You have the memory of an elephant."

When it came to Jack, I sure did. "The beach and the mountains sound nice," I said to change the subject. "I'd even move if these hundred-and-five-degree days keep up."

He gave me a skeptical smile, the faint outline of his dimple in his cheek. "You'll never leave your family, Lola."

"You're probably right. I actually like fall in Sacramento—and it's coming." I shrugged. "I'd probably get tired of the beach anyway."

"There's more than weather and topography to consider about where you live." He propped his elbows on the table, and his face grew serious, his dimple flattening out until it disappeared, the line of his jaw creating a strength in his face that seemed to define him. He was a man to take seriously, despite the playful side I'd glimpsed. "Grass and sky aren't enough to keep a person happy."

Jack had been a staff writer for the *Bee* for the past six months or so. The first time I saw his byline, I knew something big had brought him back to Sacramento. "You're not going to tell me why you came back, are you?"

He slipped his chopsticks out of the paper wrapper and broke them apart. "Nothing to tell."

"I don't believe it."

He shrugged. "Everyone's entitled to a few secrets, right? Lola, PI?"

My heart skittered at the way he looked at me, as if he knew every last one of my deep, dark secrets. The fact that my biggest secret was that I had pictures of him—of which I was no longer in possession—was one I hoped he'd never learn. Once I wrung Antonio's neck and had those photographs back in my hands, I was going to dispose of them, pronto. Or at least I'd hide them better. The fact that I'd been a voyeur and had snapped those pictures was a secret I'd take to my grave.

"I guess," I said, grateful when Helen popped up out of nowhere and delivered a plate of paper-wrapped chicken and two bowls of steaming soup.

Jack ignored the food, watching me instead. "You've changed."

I didn't know if he meant that in a good way or not, so I chose not to respond.

He didn't seem to notice, instead digging into the food, unwrapping the foil triangles and effortlessly manipulating his chopsticks to pop the chicken into his mouth.

He pushed the plate toward me, and I couldn't resist taking a triangle. I was not one of those girls who ordered only salad for lunch. No way. I'd earned my size 8—sometimes bordering on 10—and I wore my curves with pride.

Helen returned with the rest of our lunch, and we ate in silence.

"What made you get into private investigation?" Jack asked after all our lunch had been decimated.

I sucked in air, trying to expand my bloated stomach over my suddenly too-tight jeans. Size 10 would definitely have been better to be wearing at the moment. I longed to stand up and stretch so gravity could help suck the food in my gut down to my toes. "I'm good at it. Ever since—" I swallowed, stopping myself from revealing the surveillance I'd done on him. "—I realized I like snooping and spying, it's been my dream."

"You were always reading mysteries in school."

I nodded, my eye twitching as a cramp gripped my gut. "You were a senior when I was a freshman. How do you remember that?"

He leaned back in his chair. "I used to see you go into Mr. Chow's classroom at lunch. You were always there with a book."

I shook my head, stunned to realize that maybe Antonio hadn't been pulling my leg, that Jack's apparent attraction to me wasn't new—and that mine wasn't one-sided. "Guess you have an elephant's memory, too."

"Why'd you and Sergio break up?"

"Jeez. That was so long ago. You know, we grew apart."

"I never thought you grew together in the first place."

"You weren't even here when we were together."

He rubbed the back of his neck, his bicep flexing. Mmm, he had great arms. "I heard things."

Muy interesante. Had he been keeping tabs on me? I shifted in my chair, trying to loosen my waistband. Fact was, I was the detective and had tried to keep tabs on him. And had failed. Jack's past after high school was a big fat blank. "I take it you're single?"

"Oh yeah."

That was a little too enthusiastic, but I let it alone.

"What's the deal with your boss?" he asked.

"No deal." Except for the sudden nicknames and his desire for me to show him my moves. "He's good at his job, is a total professional, and dates models." I threw in that last tidbit to drive home the point that Manny and I weren't dating. At all.

"He hired you, so he must be smart."

My pride swelled at that. It was a nice compliment, I

thought, but my smile faded as he continued with, "Dangerous line of work, though."

Here it came—the inevitable criticism and doubt about my
ability to be a private investigator. "Look, I've been doing this
for four years. I've done the required training, I've been licensed for a couple years now, and I'm pretty good."

His gaze was unnerving. "Uh-huh."

"I deduce and follow leads that unravel a muscle—um, I
mean puzzle. I find it stimulating." I pressed my fingertips to the
space between my eyebrows. Did I seriously just say *stimulating*?

He stifled a smile. "Is it really safe, though? What if those
two last night had had guns?"

Not this again. "I can handle myself." I felt a wall creep up,
and my voice tightened. I got enough of being doubted by my
family. I didn't want to hear it from my hot lunch date. "What
about investigative reporting? You're digging around where people don't want you. Can *you* take someone out in one move?"

"Can you?" When I nodded, he arched a brow in disbelief.
"Right."

I bristled. I could knock him flat on his back in mere sec-
onds. "Hey, I'll show you right now if you don't believe me."
Might as well get it over with. Find out if he wanted Buffy or
Susie Homemaker.

He looked skeptical. "What, you want me to attack you so
you can bust a move?"

"I wouldn't be busting a move." I wagged my finger at him.
"I'd be kicking your ass." Standing up, I ignored my bloated
stomach, grabbed his arm, and yanked him out of his seat.
"Come on."

He threw up his hands in protest. "I believe you, Lola."

"No, you don't. We're doing this." I spotted Helen. "We're
going into the banquet room for a sec."

She giggled and nodded, obviously misreading my inten-

114

tions. I didn't care. I pulled Jack with me, out of the dining room and into the huge deserted back room reserved for large parties . . . and sparring.

Jack let himself be dragged. "This should be interesting," he said.

I pushed a table out of the way and turned to face him.

He looked intimidating—all six muscled feet of him. He crossed his arms, a smile tugging his lips. "What do you want me to do?"

"Attack me. Come at me." I stood with my arms limp at my sides.

"Lola—"

"You're not going to hurt me." I bent my body at the waist, held my arms out, palms up, and wiggled my fingers. "Come on, Jack," I taunted. "Are you chicken?"

He lunged, darting toward me like a hungry wolf. He caught me around the waist, pinning my arms to my sides.

"Ooh, good move, Callaghan." He smelled like soap and musk and evergreen trees. I could get used to that scent. I was torn between the urge to burrow into him—my head fit perfectly into the crook under his neck—or drop him to the ground. But my instincts, and the challenge of taking him down, took over, and I twisted. I could have kneed him, immobilizing him in an instant—but if we did end up, uh, snuggling—I didn't want that part of him damaged.

I forced my arms up through his, breaking his lock on me. Then I shot my arm forward and up, stopping short just under his chin.

He took a step back, and I dropped my arm. "Impressive," he said.

"I could make you beg for mercy if I wanted to."

"I'm sure you could make me beg—" He gave me a scorching look. "—but not for mercy."

My legs started to turn to Jell-O. Fighting him felt like foreplay.

We went back to the table, and Jack plucked a twenty and a ten from his wallet. "I really hate to cut this short, but I have an appointment."

I checked my watch. It was one thirty. "I need to get back to work, too." I had a murderer to catch. "We can go dutch," I said, reaching for my purse.

"No, I got it." He laid the money on the table. "And for the record, I'd like to do this again."

My insides warmed. "So you like Xena."

"What?"

I shook my head. "Nothing. Never mind."

His voice took on that low, smooth timbre again. "What other secrets do you have, Dolores Cruz?"

I threw my arms open. "I'm an open book." Almost.

"I bet it's a good read."

We walked out to the sidewalk. I only had to go next door, so we stopped in front of his car. "Oh, by the way," he said, "I looked through my notes this morning. I got a message from a woman last week who wanted me to write an article about her son."

I leaned against his sedan—a sporty Volvo. It mirrored him. Solid, safe, and sexy. "Uh-huh."

"She gave me her son's name, but hung up before she left hers."

My curiosity was piqued. "And?"

He unlocked his car and pulled a narrow notebook from a dark leather satchel. "The son's name is Garrett Diggs."

I inhaled sharply, furious that he'd waited until now to tell me this tidbit. Luckily reason kicked in. The truth was, I'd been so wrapped up in our lunch and our sparring that I hadn't followed up with him about Emily Diggs. "Are you sure?"

"Oh yeah, I'm sure. I write down my messages—"

"All of them?"

He nodded. "That's where half my stories come from. I get a call with a lead or a tip. Someone wants to meet me and give me confidential information—"

"Sounds very Deep Throat."

He cracked a suggestive grin. "What do you know about Deep Throat?"

"Nothing." I felt my face heat from the innuendo. "Never mind. What did she say?"

"According to my notes, not much. Something about her son and wanting me to write an article about him."

"He died," I said.

"Ah, too bad." He flipped the notebook closed. "So she may have just been grieving."

It was possible, but I doubted it. My instincts were telling me that Emily had been looking for answers, not condolences.

He checked his watch again. "I really have to go."

I nodded. "It was good to see you, Jack. Thanks for the tip."

The corner of his mouth inched up. "You bet."

I ran my fingers through my hair, tucking it behind my ears, and smiled. "So, I guess I'll see you around."

"Definitely," he said, and he gave me that dangerous half smile.

A few seconds later, I was staring at Jack Callaghan's tail-lights as he drove away. *Ay, caramba.* I fanned myself with my open palm. There was no doubt in my mind: The idea of seeing more of Jack was going to give me sleepless nights.

Chapter 9

At the conference table at Camacho and Associates, I snapped open the *Sacramento Bee* and went straight to the obituaries. Emily Diggs's name was listed under the death notices. I looked for an expanded entry on her. *Nada*. No picture, no information, no memorial. Not a word written about her. I felt a tug of sorrow. Did nobody care?

I decided then and there to make it known that when my number came up, I wanted a full-on celebration, complete with mariachis and bottomless margaritas. As I watched life unfold from heaven, I wanted to know that I'd been loved.

I flipped back to the front page of the Metro. There was a too-big picture of local Assemblyman Ryan Case and his family. Of course, election year meant mondo coverage. I spent a few minutes perusing the rest of the paper—nothing by Jack Callaghan today. A nagging feeling pulled me back to the front page. I scanned the articles again, but couldn't put my finger on what was bothering me.

Neil lumbered by. "Yo."

I translated his greeting to mean "What's up?" but responded in Neil lingo.

"Yo," meaning "nothing." Unfortunately.

"The case—copacetic?"

Wow. I was impressed he knew how to use *copacetic* in an almost-complete sentence. I gave him a thumbs-up. "A-plus."

He gave me a single nod and continued on his way.

My cell phone broke into song, and I picked up before the second verse of "La Bamba" started. "This is Lola."

"Hey *chica,* can you play tomorrow?" my cousin's wife, Lucy, bubbled.

If you considered following leads playing—which I did—then yes, I could. But I was afraid Lucy wouldn't like my kind of play. "Not really . . ."

"You sure?" Her voice fell flat. "Zac's taking the day off to spend with the kids."

"Oh, wow. The whole day without kids?" How could I turn her down? "I guess—"

"Is that a yes?" She perked right up again. "What should we do?"

"You don't have anybody to wax or massage?" Lucy was a killer aesthetician.

"I canceled everyone. I *never* get to have any fun. I need a day off!"

"Shopping?"

"The mall," she agreed. "I want some new Birks."

That was one thing about Lucy and me. Our styles were completely—and I mean 100 percent, 360-degrees, flower child–to–Sarah Jessica Parker—opposite.

But we both had a passion for shoes. Maybe I'd go for some pink heels with a frilly bow. Ooo-la-la. In case Jack asked me out on a *real* date that included dressing up.

Lucy and I agreed to meet the next morning, and we hung up.

I relegated shopping to a back compartment of my brain and returned to my case. With a blue dry-erase marker, I penned key phrases and words from Emily's notebook onto a large rectangular whiteboard on the wall. The woman didn't appear to have had a rhyme or reason to her journaling. But I persevered. She had to have left me a clue—something that would lead me to her killer. Or at least help me understand why she was killed.

The words ran like ticker tape in my mind: INFECTION, FUNERAL, JUST BECAUSE, MY PLACE, SEAN'S FATHER . . . Practically everything was printed in caps and written very neatly.

My mind screeched to a halt, and I backtracked. Just because, just because what?

Something knocked around my brain. I closed my eyes, and a minute later, the drive out to Sloughouse, the farm where my father had always bought his produce for the restaurant, popped into my mind. Highway 50 to Bradshaw to Jackson Road. Weren't there bars along Bradshaw with unusual names? My mind went blank.

I flipped open my cell phone and called my brother.

It rang twice before his voice came over the line. "Yep?"

I rolled my eyes. "Mom lets you answer the phone like that, Tonio?"

"Yep," he said again. "What's up, Lola? Need some old film developed?"

"You're hilarious. And I want those pictures back," I said, jabbing my finger in the air as if he were right in front of me.

"Not going to happen."

That's what he thought, but I dropped it and got to the point of my call. "What's the name of some of those bars on the way to Sloughouse?"

I heard a bang, the phone dropped, and Antonio cursed. "I don't know," he said after he recovered the phone. "Why, feel like getting sloshed with the alcohol enthusiasts?"

"No, it's for a case. There are a couple of bars out there in the country. They have weird names. . . ."

He sighed. "Yeah, I know what you're talking about. There's The Office, the Why Not, Just Because." His voice took on a Southern drawl. "Hey, baby, I'm stayin' late at the office." He chuckled, and I heard metal bang against metal as he worked in the restaurant kitchen. "Whoever named those places was a genius."

"Thanks, Tonio." It seemed like a long shot, but sometimes long shots paid off. It was possible that when Emily wrote JUST BECAUSE, she'd been referring to the bar. "I have to go out tonight," I said. "Want to come?"

He was silent for a moment. "See, this is what I was talking about. You gotta go out with *other* people."

"Yeah, but I love your company *so* much." I rolled my eyes again. Why'd he make everything so hard? "Come on. Papi's working Abuelita's tonight, right?"

He sighed. "Maybe I have a date."

"You do. With me."

"What, to one of those bars?" he asked slowly; I heard the suspicion in his voice.

"Yeah."

"Sounds like a blast. Now tell me why."

"I'm checking a lead on my case." He didn't need to know more than that. Besides, my logic was a stretch, at best. If I told him I was basing the whole trip on connecting JUST BE- CAUSE in Emily's journal to a bar on the way to Sloughhouse, he'd hang up on me.

As it was, he hemmed and hawed.

I sweetened the deal. "I'll buy the drinks. . . ."

Antonio was easy, so I knew the next pause was just to torture me. Finally he said, "What time?"

I heaved a sigh of relief for his benefit and looked at my watch. It was 3:05 now. "Six?"

He agreed to meet me at Abuelita's. For all his faults, I

knew I could depend on him when it counted. Family was family, after all.

I went back to my scrutiny of Emily's notebook and was on the verge of having a revelation—a thought tickling at the edge of my brain, just out of reach—when Manny called me into his office. He leaned back in his chair, propped his boots up on his desk, and looked at me. "What's your hypothesis?" His MO was to form a hypothesis and then prove or disprove it. Easier said than done.

"I'm still working on it." I frowned and tucked my hair behind my ears. Something about this case was just off my radar. . . .

Manny folded up the newspaper that he'd been reading and tapped it against his knee. Distorted newsprint faces stared back at me. *¡Dios mío!* My spine stiffened. Case. "Assemblyman Case," I murmured.

"What about him?"

My foot shook under the chair as excitement surged through me. "Emily wrote 'R. Case' in her journal. She could have been referring to the assemblyman."

Manny nodded, looking satisfied. "Get on it and report to me when you have something."

I practically skipped out of his office. Justice for Emily. I was on my way. I looked up the address of Assemblyman Case's office and headed out.

It took me all of ten minutes to locate the reelection headquarters for the assemblyman, a storefront office three blocks from the capitol. Just a hop, skip, and a jump from George Bonatee, I noticed, recalling the address from the lawyer's business card. At least the guy's office would be easy to find tomorrow.

It took me another fifteen minutes to find parking, my adrenaline pumping with anticipation. One big break. That's all I needed. Maybe this would be it.

I pushed open the door of the office, expecting to see a bustle of activity like election central in any movie or TV show. This was not *Taxi Driver,* and a fresh-faced Cybill Shepherd was not poised primly behind a desk.

The closest thing to a fresh face was a sporty girl pushing desks and boxes around. Light-brown hair pulled into a ponytail, running shorts, tank top, shiny watch, diamond earrings. And a dour face. Poor thing. I wouldn't want her job either.

"Excuse me?" I said, walking with my arm outstretched.

She wheeled on me, startled, holding a box like she might hurl it at me and bolt. A split second later, she relaxed. "Yes?"

I dropped my arm. "Sorry—"

"Joan." A woman's sharp, tinny voice echoed in the space. "This bottle is empty. You have to keep the prescription filled—" She stopped when she saw me, dropping a small plastic container into her jacket pocket. Her voice turned harsh. "Who's this? You know I don't want your friends here."

The girl, probably in her early twenties, curled her lip up. "I don't know her."

Guess I didn't look like a big money campaign donor. Still, I was a voter. Didn't I warrant some respect?

I turned my attention to the older woman, a Nancy Reagan clone, right down to the powder blue suit. "My name's Dolores Cruz. I'm looking for the assemblyman."

"What about, may I ask?"

Well, she just did ask, so now I was forced to answer. I went for shock value, holding my gaze steady to gauge her response. "Emily Diggs."

She didn't flinch, didn't bat an eye. Damn, she was good. "Is that name supposed to mean something to me?" she said in full bitch mode.

Since I didn't know who she was, I didn't know if the name was supposed to mean anything to her. "I'm sorry, you are—?" I prompted.

She narrowed her already beady eyes at me. "Beverly Case," she finally said. "The assemblyman's wife. And I'm afraid we can't help you." She started toward the door. "Now, if you'll excuse us."

I stood my ground. "Is the assemblyman expected anytime soon? Can I make an appointment?"

"No," Beverly Case said. "He doesn't take appointments here." She went back to her paperwork, a silent dismissal.

Joan came up behind me, propelling me forward until I was out on the sidewalk. Next thing I knew, she'd shut the door on me. Wow. That was a record. In four years, even tailing Sadie, Neil, or Manny, I'd never been so effectively handled. Beverly Case was *good*. Damn good.

What now? I put my hand back on the door handle, ready to try again, when the door suddenly pushed open. The girl, Joan, poked her head out. "Sorry about that."

Oh, an ally. "Joan, right?" I stretched my hand out to her, thrilled when she actually shook it.

"Joanie. Only my mom and—" She broke off. "Joanie's fine."

"Your mom's not into chitchat?"

Joanie rolled her dull brown eyes. "She doesn't like people." She darted a glance over her shoulder and then turned back to me. Mommy dearest had her on a short leash. "You want to see my dad?" she asked.

I suspected that I had only a second before her mother ordered her back inside. "I do. Can you help me?"

She made a face, scrunching up her lips. "He's probably at the capitol. Are you a reporter?"

"No, just a voter."

"Who's the woman you mentioned? Emily something?"

"She was a mutual friend. She passed on, and I thought Mr. Case would want to know."

Joanie nodded, darting another look over her shoulder. "I'll

124

tell him—" A muffled voice came from inside, and she jerked and looked behind her. She pulled back and started to close the door. "Gotta go," she said.

"Wait!" I jammed my foot into the opening to block her, my brain scrambling to come up with a way to get her outside. "Your mom's prescription!"

"What?" Joanie stared at me like I'd lost my mind.

I nodded enthusiastically. "I could go with you while you fill it, and we could talk some more."

"There's nothing to talk about." She glanced over her shoulder before turning back to me. "I'll let my dad know about Emily," she said, and then before I could stop her, she slammed the door closed. My toes barely escaped amputation.

The lock turned, and that was that.

I waited, silently hoping she'd change her mind and reopen the door, but after two minutes, I realized I was dreaming. Damn.

I headed back to my car, passing business folks, moms and dads with strollers, a police officer or two, and assorted home-less people with their shopping carts of treasures piled high. Most of them had more goods than I'd seen in Emily's room at the Bonatee rental—a sad fact, I thought. Poor Emily had died without much to her name. What had brought her to Bonatee's, and what was it about her son that had her worked up enough to call a reporter?

I mulled this over on the drive home. I'd succeeded in gain-ing lots of questions, but had very few answers. For the time being, I shifted my thinking to the evening ahead of me. The fact that I had discovered a potentially vital clue from Emily's journal bolstered my spirits. Maybe my big break was waiting for me at Just Because.

●　　●　　●

It was still light outside—way too early to be heading to a bar, in my opinion—when Antonio and I left Abuelita's.

Antonio pulled his vintage Mustang into the gravel parking lot of the bar off Jackson Road. "Remind me to watch out for drunks on the way home."

"Just Because," I said, reading the red neon sign. The *B* was blackened, and the *c* flickered erratically.

Inside, my eyes adjusted to the dimly lit bar. Round tables ran around the circumference of the room. A small stage sat in one corner, and a long shellacked counter ran the length of one wall.

A tall, lanky man leaned his back against the mirrored backdrop behind the bar. Glass shelves held the top shelf liquor, the standard labels hidden in the well. The bartender's cheeks were hollow, and his pumpkin-colored hair and mustache were straight out of the disco era, long and feathered.

"Like I said," Antonio whispered, "an alcohol enthusiast."

I looked at the guy more closely. Pasty skin. Bloodshot eyes. He took a long swallow from a lowball glass. "Seven and seven," I muttered to my brother. "Maybe some speed to top it off."

Antonio nodded his agreement.

I ordered a couple of Dos Equis and debated whether to try to engage the guy in conversation or play it straight. Direct, I decided. The guy didn't look like he messed around. Drinks in hand, I slid a copy of Emily's photograph across the tacky counter and held my breath.

The bartender stuck his drink back in the well and reached for the picture. "What's this?"

"Do you recognize this woman?" I watched his face with Clint Eastwood scrutiny as he picked up the photograph.

He squinted and held the picture up to a dusty fixture that hung from the ceiling. The light from outside couldn't penetrate the tinted windows and the dimly lit bar.

"I've seen her around here a few times." He sounded hoarse, as if he'd just woken up and hadn't found his voice yet. He slid the photo back to me.

"Really?" I asked, probably sounding a little too excited. My hunch had totally paid off. God, I loved these moments.

"Are you cops?"

"No, no." I shook my head emphatically to convince him. "This woman turned up dead. I'm trying to find out what happened to her."

He took a long drink and then leaned forward, both hands resting on the bar. "She met with Muriel once or twice."

I slid onto a barstool and sipped my beer as casually as I could muster. A minor in Acting should be a required degree for private investigators. Luckily I'd had several years to perfect my innocently curious expression. Muriel. The name rang a bell. Another entry in Emily's journal, I thought. "Muriel?" I prompted.

"She runs the place." I pulled out my notepad and scribbled.

"Does Muriel have a last name?"

He squinted at me but said, "O'Brien."

"And, I'm sorry, I didn't catch your name."

"'Cause I didn't give it, missy."

I looked him square in the eyes. "Could you give it to me now? For my notes."

"Notes for what?"

"Like I said, Ms. Diggs is dead. I'm looking into it."

The bartender's suspicious gaze settled on Antonio.

My brother leaned in beside me, one elbow resting on the bar. If only he had a cowboy hat, he'd fit in perfectly. As it was, with his clenched and goateed jaw, his Raiders cap pulled low over his eyes, and his pumped-up biceps, he looked like a damn menacing bodyguard.

"You sure you're not cops?"

Antonio laughed. "Not even close."

He lifted an eyebrow, but he looked back at me and shrugged. "Tom Phillips."

I scribbled the name in my notebook and then glanced around at the nearly deserted bar. Just a few lonely California cowboys sipped their drinks. "Is Muriel here tonight?" I asked, turning back to Tom.

"Nah, she runs a couple places in Sac Town."

So Muriel was busy. "And they are . . ."

Grumpy attitude notwithstanding, Tom Phillips was more than willing to talk. "Tattoo Haven over off Del Paso and My Place."

"My Place. Isn't that bar out on Bradshaw, too?"

He nodded, and I scribbled the names of Muriel's businesses down.

"Do you know why Emily and Muriel met?"

Tom's bony shoulders moved up and down. "Nope. Muriel don't tell me shit." Poor guy, he was kept out of the loop. I hated that. He tilted his head back as he took a long drink. "Don't pay me shit, neither."

"She doesn't care that you do all the work, huh?" I shook my head, trying to win him over. "Bosses."

His bloodshot eyes brightened. "Damn straight."

I smiled. He was putty in my hands. "Do you remember when Emily was here last?"

He thought for a few seconds, nodding his head at me like we were part of the same union, fighting against the man. "'Bout a week ago, I reckon."

"Do you remember the day?"

He dumped the remains from his glass in the sink, refilling it halfway with ice. Then he took a bottle of Seagram's from under the counter and poured the glass three-quarters full. He topped it off with Sprite, gave it a quick stir with his finger, and gulped, draining half the liquid with one mouthful. I wondered if he'd be able to stand at the end of his shift. I was getting tipsy just watching him.

"Muriel splits her time between the places. She's here Tuesday, Wednesday, Friday, the Tattoo gig Thursday and Sunday, and My Place Monday and Saturday."

"Busy woman," I said, writing her schedule down.

Tom shrugged. "That lady, the one in your picture, she was here last week."

"What day, do you remember?"

He thought for a second. Nodding, clearly satisfied that he'd figured it out, he said, "Must have been Wednesday."

A jolt of energy shot through me. Now I was getting somewhere. The day Emily had disappeared. "You remember what time?"

"Round lunch, I think."

"Did she talk with Muriel?"

"Yeah, they talked." He finished his drink and dumped the ice. It seemed to be his routine. "Argued, you might say."

"Did you hear what about?"

"Didn't want to." He shrugged again. "I tuned 'em out most times."

"But you know they were arguing," Antonio said.

My thought exactly.

"Look," Tom said, "I mind my own business. Life's easier that way."

"But you did hear what they were saying," I prompted.

Reluctantly, he nodded. "A little bit. Something about her kids and some of their friends. Don't know what Muriel had to do with it, and I don't care neither."

129

"Have you seen Muriel today?" I asked.

He shook his head, giving me an *I just told you her schedule a second ago* look. "It's Monday."

I smiled brightly and checked my notes. Sure enough, Muriel spent her Mondays at My Place.

Tom Phillips didn't seem to have any other information for me, but who knew when I might need him again. "You've been very helpful. I hope Muriel smartens up and gives you a big fat raise." I passed him a business card.

He stuck it in his back pocket. "I hear anything, I'll be sure to give you a call."

Wow, wasn't he accommodating. Looks and drug use could be deceiving. I smiled and thanked him. "Are you up for another stop?" I asked Antonio when we were back in the car.

"You buying another round?"

I nodded. "Of course."

He revved the engine, and we were off to My Place.

It was clear the second we walked in that Just Because could have been lifted and dropped whole on top of its sister bar and no one would have noticed the difference. They were nearly identical inside, from the dim light and tinted windows to the shellacked bar and pasty-skinned bartender. The only difference here was that the bartender was a woman.

"I do believe we've found our Muriel O'Brien, Holmes," Antonio whispered, the *H* in *Holmes* sounding like he was hawking a loogie in an East L.A. way.

I grinned. "Right, Watson." Memories of childhood detective antics flashed through my mind—Jack playing the villain—God, I'd forgotten about that. I'd tied him to a tree once after I captured him. If only I'd known what to do with a restrained Jack Callaghan back then, but the opportunity had been lost on my innocent twelve-year-old self.

I looked around at the mix of people—an older couple at

the jukebox, a leather-vested man with a navy bandanna snugly wrapped around his head, a black-and-white couple that looked from the back like a May-December affair. It was an eclectic bunch.

"What can I get you two?" the bartender rasped at us. Looking at her, I found it hard to believe she had the ability and skill to actually run three businesses. Her brittle hair was pulled back and clipped at the base of her neck, steel gray strands poking out like bits of spiraled wire. Her teeth had an awful tint to them, like the slimy coating on a peeled hard-boiled egg. I swallowed a gag.

I opted for bottled water this time, and Antonio ordered a Corona. I ponied up the cash and perched on a stool while Antonio leaned in beside me, elbow on the bar, his cap tugged low over his eyes.

"Are you Muriel O'Brien?" I asked.

Her eyes immediately became wary, and she took a half step backwards, pulling her flannel overshirt closed. "What do you want? You come in here to drink or what?"

Wow, this lady was on edge. What happened to chatting up the customers? I handed her a business card. "I came across your name in relation to Emily Diggs."

She mulled that over for a second, then let out a throaty cackle. "That lunatic? I ain't no relation to her."

Oh, this one was bright. "But you know her."

She darted her eyes around the bar as she huffed, shrugging her shoulders. "We've had the unfortunate pleasure."

"Well, unfortunately for *her*, she's dead."

Muriel blinked, and blinked again, her gaze skittering around again, finally settling blankly on the May-December couple. They seemed blissfully unaware of anyone else. Oh, to be so in love.

Apparently, Muriel hadn't read the obits in the *Bee* this

morning. She threw her hands up and retreated even more. Her voice lowered to a raspy hiss. "You two just get on outta here. I don't want nothin' to do with this."

I threw my own hands up in an effort to calm her down. "Emily's brother just wants to know what happened to her. Can you help me out?"

"I'll tell you this," she muttered sharply. "If she's dead, she probably asked for it." She doubled over in a hacking cough. "She was looking for trouble, gettin' mixed up where she don't belong."

Antonio notched up the bill of his cap. "Can you be more specific?"

Muriel bared her yellowed, crooked teeth. Her eyes jerked around the room, and her eyebrows lifted when she focused on us again. "She done screwed the wrong people, and she didn't even know it. Made all kinds of trouble." She dropped her voice to a whisper. "I tried to warn her."

Muriel seemed to have forgotten she'd wanted us to leave, so I seized the moment. "Who'd she screw over?"

She hacked, her head thrusting forward like a cat coughing up a fur ball—only Muriel's fur ball was a glob of brown phlegmy goop that she spit onto a napkin, crumpled in her hand, and tossed into the garbage can.

"*Qué asco*," Antonio muttered under his breath.

It was *totally* gross, but I flashed him a look that said, *Shut up.* Who knew if this woman spoke Spanish?

Apparently she didn't. She ignored Antonio and knocked a cigarette out of a battered pack. With the cigarette gripped between her thin lips, she managed to light it with a yellow Bic held in her shaky hand.

After a deep inhale, she hacked again. I tried to keep my face impassive. Guess I didn't do a very good job. "You got a problem?" she rasped.

Shaking my head, I flattened the wrinkles that lined my forehead. "I was just thinking smoking might aggravate that cough you have." Or make her cough up a whole blackened lung.

"Shee-it," she drawled. "Smokin' and drinkin' are my only pleasures." She pulled a glass out from the well of the bar and held it up in a toast before swigging a mouthful of her poison and swallowing hard. She leaned in toward me and hissed like she was divulging a world-class secret. "Only Myers's, Coke, and Marlboros. Nothing else passes these lips." She took another healthy swig before replacing the glass under the bar and out of sight. "I'm dead serious. Nothing."

Good to know. "So, um, Muriel, who was Emily screwing over?"

"You ain't the cops, right? You have to tell me if I ask, right?" Her eyebrows puckered, and she snaked her gaze at Antonio. "Hate to think a good-lookin' man like you was a cop."

Antonio nodded. He even managed a small smile, bless his heart. Maybe he deserved a kickback.

"No, we ain't police." I cringed, but if poor grammar was what it took to relate to her . . . I was willing to go the distance.

"So you ain't shittin' me. Someone really knocked off the old bat?"

The photo I had of Emily put her in her mid-forties. If she was an old bat, that made Muriel a walking corpse. Probably she thought she was hot stuff for a crotchety old broad. Rose-colored glasses. Was my perception of myself that warped? Twenty-eight and single to me meant wise and independent. What did it mean to an outsider?

"I ain't shittin' you." My high school English teacher would take back every one of my A's if she heard me talking now.

"Now what were you saying? About Emily screwing someone over?"

She surveyed the room, her expression turning hard when it returned to us. She was certainly conscientious of her other customers—I had to give her that. She shrugged. "When you go messing around in other people's business, people get mad at you." She doubled over again, coughing. After she stubbed out her cigarette, she moved the ashtray to the back counter. "How'd she die, anyway?"

"Her body washed up in the river."

She grunted. "Drowned, huh?"

"Yes, drowned." She was like a train-of-thought child. I had to redirect the conversation. "When did you see her last?"

Her gray eyes peered at me through the coils of her hair. "Last week sometime, I think."

"Do you remember what you talked about?"

"Shee-it. How could I forget? She was trying to shut down my tattoo parlor, that's what."

Tattoos. A flash of Bonnie, the tattooed bandit from Laughlin's market, shot into my brain. The tramp stamp on her breast was like a bull's-eye right over her heart.

A knock sounded from the end of the bar, and Muriel ambled away to serve a customer. She pulled out two bottles of beer and flipped off the caps before sliding them over. She made acerbic small talk for a minute, collected a fistful of dollar bills, and knocked her fifty-cent tip against the bar with two quick flicks of her wrist. She'd been doing this a long time, and it showed.

"Relax, Lo," Antonio said, rubbing my shoulder as if I were a heavyweight champ ready to go another round. "Don't let her rattle you." He adjusted his hat. "You're doing great."

I didn't know why Bonnie's tattoo was stuck in my mind, but I took a couple of deep breaths and had refocused by the time Muriel returned to us. "Why did Emily want to shut down your business?" I asked again.

"Get this," she said, smacking her thin lips together. "That woman, Emily, said that a tattoo killed her son. She was nuts."

"Crazy," I echoed. But my heart was pounding in my chest, and my attitude toward Muriel improved dramatically with this new little tidbit of information. My adrenaline surged. Allison had said Garrett had had a heart infection. Bull's-eye to the heart . . . Could a tattoo cause a heart infection? Is that really what Emily thought? "Was Emily's son's death ever investigated?"

She harrumphed again and shrugged.

"No?"

"Like I'm supposed to know?" She hesitated, and then continued. "Seemed to me like she was a one-woman show trying to shut our place down. It was bullshit, I tell you. She made the whole thing up."

"When you saw her at Just Because, did she say something about her kids?" I asked.

Muriel rolled her eyes. "Just how she and her daughter don't talk no more. Something about not doing right by her son, and she wasn't going to let it happen again. I didn't understand it at all."

I couldn't get any more information out of her, but I filed the conversation away for future consideration. How had she let Garrett down the first time? "Did she have proof about the tattoo and the heart infection?"

Muriel scoffed, her raspy voice filled with disdain. "Said she talked to a doctor and that she'd met with another family whose son died from a tattoo."

Something to follow up on. "Interesting."

Muriel slammed her palm down on the tacky counter. "No, it isn't! That lady thought that if someone else died from a

135

tattoo, it meant that's what killed her son, too. She didn't know what she was talking about."

The telephone rang, and Muriel snatched the handset from its cradle and held it to her ear. "Pffft. I didn't mean to. Sorry 'bout that. For a hundred?" She made another sound, pinched her eyebrows together, and said, "Two hundred."

Not three seconds later, she said, "Two hundred and fifty"; then she lowered her voice and turned around to finish her call more privately. Her attitude had shifted dramatically for the caller, and she'd lost her prickly edge.

She returned a minute later. Her lips were pursed tight, and her irritableness had returned, times a thousand. She scowled at us. "You two gotta leave now. I got work to do." And just like that, our conversation with Muriel O'Brien was over.

I tossed a couple of quarters on the bar to feed Muriel's habit, and we reluctantly left. The gravel crunched under our feet as we crossed the parking lot toward the car.

The sun had finally set. A group of straggling stars clung in the blanket sky.

Antonio walked around to the driver's side of the Mustang, and I put my hands on my hips. "That was weird," I said.

He cocked an eyebrow at me and straightened his Raiders cap. "Understatement."

"Yeah." A shiver crept up my spine as a shadow passed over the moon. Lucky I wasn't superstitious. At least not very superstitious. As a general rule, I tried not to step on cracks in the sidewalk, I didn't walk under ladders, and I held up my end of the bargain when I made a prayer offering. No sense in pissing off God.

Antonio laid his palms on the roof of his car. "Who do you think was on the phone?"

"Good question. It's like someone told her to shut her mouth and get rid of us."

The sound of a car starting interrupted my train of thought. Tires spun against the gravel, the screeching sound like a jet plane taking off.

I whipped my head around, startled by the booming rev of the engine. The shadow of a car jolted forward and into the light. Gravel ricocheted off the steel undercarriage. The headlights flashed on, blinding me. "Holy crap!" I gasped as I heard the car's tires finally take hold.

"Lola!" Antonio yelled. "Get out of the way!"

I blinked, registering what was happening. The car barreled toward me at full speed.

Chapter 10

Shit, shit, shit! My heart pounded furiously. I sprinted to the left.

Antonio's urgent voice rang in my ears. "Get out of the way!"

"I'm trying!" I yelled, but the car was like a heat-seeking missile, and I was the target. I stopped, faked left, then dodged to the right. Was the driver blind? My throbbing heart had climbed to my throat. Didn't he see me? I dodged again, but slipped on the loose gravel, sliding like I was making the winning run at home plate.

I caught a glimpse of Antonio waving me down. "Get in the car!"

The headlights bore down on me. I scrambled up and sped toward the Mustang, trying to see through the spirals spinning in front of my eyes. I pulled frantically at the locked passenger door, my hands white-knuckling the old chrome handle. It wouldn't budge.

At the last second, I managed to hike my foot up onto the door handle and heave myself onto the roof. Antonio reached for my arms to help pull me higher. The menacing car sideswiped the Mustang, the hair-raising screech of steel against steel worse than ten thousand metal claws scratching down a chalkboard.

The car pitched, and I catapulted off, knocking my head on the ground before skidding belly-down across the gravel.

Somewhere in the recesses of my mind, I heard tires squeal and grip the asphalt as the attack car skidded onto Bradshaw and sped away.

Antonio's voice drifted in and out of my brain like a light-house beam circling around in the fog. "Lola! Lola, can you hear me?"

I lifted my head as I felt his hand on my shoulder. I felt three sheets to the wind, even though I'd had only half a beer and a bottled water. Finally the fog lifted. *Holy shit!* That had not been an accident. Someone had just tried to kill me, and I did not like it.

I murmured a slurred prayer of thanks that it had not been my day to die—not with plain gray Jockey underwear on—and rolled onto my side.

"Lola?" The concern in Antonio's voice was almost as disconcerting as my nearly being roadkill.

"Argh." I struggled to push myself onto my forearms.

He reached behind me and pulled up, holding me at arm's length to examine my wounds. "Are you okay? Need to go to the hospital?"

My tongue licked the corner of my mouth. Blood-laced gravel dust had replaced my lipstick. "I'm okay."

"You're pretty scraped up."

"I'm fine. Superficial injuries." I took a tentative step, cringing at the pain that shot up my leg.

Antonio caught me. "No, you're not." Holding on to me with one hand, he pulled open the driver's-side door of the Mustang and eased me onto the seat.

"Just give me a minute, okay?" I said.

139

He gripped my elbow. "We can clean this up."

I looked at the missing layers of skin on my arm, tiny bits of gravel and dirt embedded in the abrasions. *Ay, Dios.* My first PI injury ever, and it was a doozy. So I wasn't invincible. Kung fu wouldn't do squat against a kamikaze car. Neither would a gun, for that matter. Good to know, and I'd make sure to drive that point home with Manny, but it didn't make me feel any better. Did someone actually want me dead, or had this been a warning?

Either way, first thing in the morning, I was going to demand a raise.

"Is this the worst?" Antonio said, examining my arm. "What about your leg?"

"It's okay." I'd banged my knee, but it didn't feel more than bruised. I looked at the Mustang and frowned. "Is the car going to make it?"

He looked morose. "It'll drive."

"Tonio," I said. "Go see if Muriel's still inside."

He gaped at me. "You think it was her?"

"I don't know. Go check. Please."

He nodded, just once, then jogged toward the entrance. He was back thirty seconds later. "She's behind the bar."

Damn. There was no way that lady could be in two places at once. If it wasn't her, then who had tried to run me over?

"Let me get you home," Antonio said. He walked around the Mustang and tried to pry open the passenger door for me. "Jammed."

"I'll climb over the seats." I winced as I struggled to crawl through the inside of his vintage car to the passenger side.

Once I was settled, Antonio started her up and headed for home.

Talk about guilt. Tonio loved his Mustang more than any

woman he'd ever dated. It was operational, but it looked like hell. "Sorry about your car."

He grumbled. "Insurance'll cover it."

We were silent the rest of the drive. Inside our flat, he looked me over. "You going to be okay? Need help?"

"I'm fine."

"That car came out of nowhere, Lola. *Hijo de la chingada*," he muttered. "You were a sitting duck, you know that?"

What could I say? He was right. Either I was lucky beyond belief, or I'd just been sternly warned. I left him on the couch and went off to lick my wounds. I showered, and twenty minutes later, I was tossing and turning in my bed, trying to figure out who the hell I'd spooked. And why.

After a fitful sleep, I awoke to the sun. I piled my hair on top of my head in a loose bun, pulled on shorts and a T-shirt, and scrubbed the kitchen like a woman possessed. The silver lining of pent-up anxiety was a germ-free house.

I squeezed the excess water from my sponge and was giving the sink a final rinse when Antonio walked into the kitchen. Jack was right behind him.

They stopped short when they saw me. Somehow Jack seemed taller than his six feet this morning. He wore jeans and sneakers, and an olive green T-shirt with an El Toro Brewery logo. Okay, I was totally superstitious. His shirt had to be a sign. Taking the bull by the horns was exactly what I intended to do. Whoever had tried to run me down would be sorry.

"You're awake." Antonio checked my bandaged arm then took my chin in his hand and turned my head. "It's not too bad. How're you feeling?"

My eyes darted to Jack. Hadn't I just told him that I could take care of myself? "I'm fine."

Jack's face was tight. "You look like you had a run-in with a gravel parking lot."

Clearly Antonio had given Jack every last detail. I stared him down. If he said one word about my dangerous job, I'd drop him—right here, right now. *Terminado. Finito.* All before it ever officially started.

He stood stone still, his jaw pulsing.

Finally I turned to Antonio. "Did you take the car in?"

"We just dropped it off. Needs a new door and side panel."

I sighed and nodded. "Will insurance give you a rental?"

"I have to call." Antonio shrugged away his anger. "So. You're really okay?" I'd barely started to nod when he said, "Good. Are you still hell-bent on your detective career? The folks are going to have a fit when they hear someone tried to kill you."

He'd taken a page straight from the Magdalena Falcón Cruz book of guilt. "They don't need to know." Wink, wink. "Can't it be our little secret?"

"Oh, yeah, you have lots of those," he said, his gaze shifting to Jack for a split second.

I wanted to slug him. I did *not* have a ton of secrets. Only a few choice ones.

Jack leaned back against the refrigerator. "Do you have any idea who it was?"

Finally, a rational question. "No."

"Any leads?"

I wanted someone to bounce my ideas off. Jack seemed like a good prospect at the moment. "Ever hear of a heart infection?"

He shook his head, but his interest looked piqued.

I wagged my finger as my thoughts spilled out. "I think that's what Emily was calling you about. Her older son died of

142

a heart infection. I think she was pissed about it and wanted to blame someone. I think she wanted you to investigate, I don't know, the tattoo industry—"

"The body art industry."

"Whatever." I didn't have all the details worked out, and I wondered if I sounded completely insane.

Antonio nudged Jack over so he could peer into the refrigerator. "How about breakfast? Chorizo?" he asked me.

"You cooking?"

"If Mom has any."

"Sounds good," Jack said, his eyes never leaving my face.

"I'll be back." The refrigerator door swung shut, and Antonio headed out the back door and down to our parents' kitchen.

After a beat, Jack's eyebrows pinched together. "You *are* pretty scraped up."

My hand brushed the abrasion on my arm. "Yeah."

He strode across the kitchen and stood in front of me. "This isn't a game, Lola. It seems pretty likely that this woman was murdered and you're getting in the way."

Here it came. I took a deep breath and tried to control my frustration. "Why, Jack Callaghan," I said in my best Southern belle voice, "I need a man who'll have confidence in me. Are you questioning my ability to solve my case?"

He smiled wryly. "Your drawl could use some work, Scarlett." But then his face tensed. "Be serious. You were almost killed last night. Have you considered that dropping this case might be a smart idea? Let the cops handle it."

I counted to ten so I wouldn't blow up at him. "When I want your opinion, Callaghan, I'll ask for it."

He smirked. "I'm going to give you my opinion, *Cruz*, whether you ask for it or not. You were fighting crooks with a goddamned broom on Sunday."

143

Anger inched up my spine. I struggled to beat it back down. "The broom worked. And it's really none of your business anyway. No one asked you to be there."

"The hell it isn't my business." He ran his fingertips over my arm. "I'm worried about you."

My tension started to evaporate. He was worried about me. "There's no need. I can handle it."

Antonio kicked the door open, holding an armload of treasure. "Fresh tortillas," he announced. And eggs, chorizo, tomato sauce, onion, garlic. Why did he need to grocery-shop when he had a direct supplier right downstairs?

I checked my watch, grateful for Antonio's horrible timing. Jack had managed to get under my skin in a split second, and that wasn't a real good idea, considering his love 'em and leave 'em philosophy. It was 8:34. "I need to get ready for work."

I left them to cook breakfast, went to my bedroom, and immediately phoned the office. Manny's voice rumbled across the line. "Toxicology's back."

"What'd they find?"

"Codeine and cough medicine in her system."

"Okay. So what does *that* mean?"

"Nothing specifically. Seavers mentioned suicide."

"He thinks Emily downed some cough syrup and codeine and threw herself into the river?" I didn't buy that theory for a second. Especially in light of my near-death experience last night.

"I don't think he believes it. Just mentioned it as a possibility."

"There's no way it was suicide," I said. I leaned back against the pillows on my bed. "You asked me about my hypothesis—"

"Let's hear it."

"Emily believed a tattoo caused her son's infection. She

went to Assemblyman Case and the newspaper about it. She was making waves everywhere. She hit a nerve, and someone wanted her stopped."

There was a brief pause. I bit my lip, worried that he was going to burst out laughing any second. "Go with it," he said quietly. "And keep in touch."

The line went dead.

Only after I hung up did I realize that I hadn't told him about the car accident. I picked up the phone to call back, but immediately changed my mind. I could fill him in later.

Paying a visit to Tattoo Haven, Muriel the bartender's third business, was on my list of things to do. I also had a date with Lucy for a day of shopping. Would she mind tagging along?

Hopefully not. My cousin's wife had no kids for the entire day. Even a tattoo parlor would look good to her.

I took a shower, gave my hair a quick blow-dry, and let it fall around my face to mask the scrapes as much as possible. All my good underwear was in the laundry, and I couldn't bring myself to wear the one ratty, only-in-emergency pair I had left. What if another car tried to run me over? I couldn't take the chance of having raggedy panties if I ended up in the morgue. Ridiculous as that sounded, I had standards.

I turned to my thongs. They were okay, in the right situation—like with a slinky silk dress. But when I was on the job, I preferred full butt coverage. Call it a quirk.

But with no other choice, I selected a sheer pink strip of lace and string and slipped it on. I pulled on a pair of capris and a ruffled long-sleeve blouse to cover the scrapes on my arms.

Grabbing my purse, I headed to the kitchen. Jack was finishing up the last of his *chorizo con salsa*. My dog sat next to his chair, looking up at him with her droopy face. He scratched her head and gave her a bit of tortilla.

145

I breezed by Jack, stopping at the counter to spoon some *chorizo con salsa* into a tortilla. I felt his gaze on me, and my body tingled with awareness. Could he tell what I had on under my clothes?

"Lola—"

But he hadn't asked me out again yet (even if we had only gone out to lunch yesterday), no matter how worried he was about me. "I have to go work," I said, rolling my tortilla into a burrito. I tried not to worry that I was leaving him in my flat with Antonio and the incriminating photos. "See you later."

"But your—"

Sanity had kicked back in; I'd made too much of his concern earlier. He was a family friend. No more. I couldn't stick around hoping he'd come through with an invitation for a date, and I certainly wasn't going to ask *him*. Not after years of being invisible to him. The door slammed behind me as I trotted downstairs and pushed through the gate to the driveway.

I stopped short. My car was gone! I slung my purse over my shoulder and ran to the sidewalk, peering down the street. Jackie's Volvo was parked alongside the house, but otherwise the street was empty.

I ran back upstairs, grimacing against the pain in my legs and torso as I took the stairs two by two. I burst into the house. "Jack!" I panted. "Someone stole my car."

He was leaning against the counter, arms folded, looking like he'd been waiting for me. "I tried to tell you—"

"Tried to tell me what?"

"That Antonio borrowed it."

I threw my hands up in the air. "But I need it."

He looked amused, the corner of his mouth creeping up and his dimple carving into his cheek. "Can I help?"

I gritted my teeth. "When's he coming back? I have things to do."

146

He shrugged. "Don't know, but you can use my car."

Well, why hadn't he extended that offer to Antonio? "Don't you have people to meet, words to write, your own places to go? . . ."

His dimple deepened in his cheek. "Not right now. And if it'll help you out . . ."

I peered at him. "Twenty minutes ago you were telling me to get a new job. Now you're helping out?"

"I never told you to get a new job, Lola. I said I'm going to worry about you as long as you have *this* job."

He had a knack for phrasing things in a way that defied argument. "Okay," I said. "Thanks." I followed him down the cement stairs and out to the street. He looked as good from behind as he did from the front. A broad back that tapered to a narrow waist. Jeans that hugged his lower half perfectly. A body that I longed to touch and explore.

He seemed to move extra slow, as if he knew the torrid thoughts that raced through my mind. Evil.

Finally, the torture ended. We made it to the street, and he unlocked the door for me. I fell into the driver's seat of the Volvo. The car was so low to the ground and the deep bucket seats so enveloping that I wondered if my bruised body would be able to maneuver me back out of it.

He crouched down next to me, his smile all but gone and his eyes smoldering. "Go out with me tonight."

I sputtered on the outside as I jumped for joy on the inside. "Tonight?" Then I remembered Reilly and frowned. "I can't. I'm going out with—"

His face fell, and I stopped. To hell with my old-fashioned upbringing. Independent, single, and in lust. I was going for it. "I'm setting a friend up with Antonio, and I'm kind of the chaperone." I hesitated. If Jack came, there was no way Tonio would back out. "I guess you could come along. . . ."

A slow grin slid onto his face. "Then it's a date."

Oh yeah. Date number two. What were the rules for a good girl? Could I kiss him on date number two? Go to second base? Did we have to wait until tonight? "I can drop you at the paper," I said.

He opened the passenger door and slid in. "I'd rather tag along for a while. See Lola, PI, in action."

I shot a suspicious look at him. "Not like a bodyguard, right?"

"No. Not like a bodyguard. I'll do a little investigating of my own. I might just write that article for Emily Diggs if there's anything to it."

The idea of spending part of the day—and then the night—with Jack was thrilling, but did I want on-the-job scrutiny? Especially with my plans for the day. Then again, how could I refuse? He was lending me his car. "I'm working. You can't distract me."

He smiled wickedly as his gaze slid down my body. "I'd say I'll be the one distracted."

I clutched the wheel as I zoomed off. *Thong.* Thank God Lucy was coming with us, or I'd be tempted to chuck my plans and be distracted with Jack all day. So far, I was liking the man he'd grown up to be, his feelings about my job notwithstanding.

The car veered. Jack grabbed for the wheel. "Lola!"

I snapped out of my fantasy and straightened the car. "Sorry."

"Maybe I should drive."

Never show weakness. I focused on the road. "Nope. Little lapse. I'm fine."

He paused for a beat, watching me. "Where are we going?" he finally asked.

I went for distraction. I didn't know if he'd approve of our destination. "Someone tried to kill me. You sure you want to hang around with me? It's not too late to change your mind. I can drop you—"

He rolled down the window and propped his elbow on the frame. "Where are we going?" he asked again.

"You know, I'm supposed to meet Lucy at the restaurant. We can probably take her car and you'll be off the hook." He didn't need me to investigate Emily Diggs. Let him follow his own leads.

His look told me he was probably cursing me inside like I'd been cursing Muriel about just answering a simple question. "Lola. Where the hell are we going?"

I was saved by the short drive to the restaurant. "Oh, look—we're here." Lucy stood on the sidewalk by the front entrance. "There she is."

I pulled up in front of her and rolled down the window. "Hey."

Lucy's blond hair was pulled back into two low ponytails, her long flowing skirt nearly dusting the ground. She was whole earth personified, right down to her beaded choker and anklet. She looked at the car, then at Jack in the passenger seat. "Hey."

"Lucy, this is Jack. Jack, Lucy."

She studied him, and her forehead wrinkled. "Weren't you at my wedding?"

Jack nodded. "You're Zac's wife."

She beamed at him with her California girl smile. "That's me." She looked back at me. "Where's your car?"

"Antonio has it."

"Where's his car?"

I made a face. "Long story. It's in the shop."

She leaned closer, peering at me. "What happened to your face?"

"Part of the long story." I didn't want to go into it again. "Can you drive today?"

"No can do. Zac dropped me off. He needed the van for the kids."

I caught Jack's grin. "No problem. We'll take my car," he said.

A zing shot through me. His smile was beginning to make me crazy.

Lucy climbed into the backseat. "Are you going shopping with us, too, Jack?"

No way. I was ditching him before we hit the mall. The shoes I was going to buy were for tonight—and, of course, I'd need a new outfit to go with them. No sneak preview. I was going to make him give little Lola Cruz the attention she deserved. "He's going to drop us downtown later. First I have to check into something for my case. Is that okay with you, Lucy?"

She nodded. "I'm going to be your sidekick? Cool!"

"No," I said. "No sidekick." I looked at each of them. "Can you both stay in the car while I do my, you know, *stuff?*"

"Stay in the car? No way!" Lucy squealed. "I'm on a vacation day." She looked at me in the rearview mirror. "I'm not leaving your side."

Jack didn't even bother to respond. I knew there was no way he'd sit in the Volvo while I was in a dive tattoo parlor. I'd given it a shot. What else could I do? They were both adults, and I couldn't very well handcuff them to the steering wheel. "Oh, all right. But let me do the talking, okay?"

Lucy closed her lips with an imaginary zipper but couldn't hide her smile. Jack didn't look nearly so enthusiastic. In fact, he looked suspicious—and like he'd suddenly gone into full bodyguard mode despite his early protestations.

Considering my plan, I thought his suspicions were probably well founded.

Chapter 11

I did a double take as a rickety old red truck bounced down the street in front of Tattoo Haven. It looked an awful lot like Muriel O'Brien behind the wheel. But it wasn't her day to be at the tattoo shop, so I figured I was hallucinating. Still, I waited until the truck disappeared around a corner before I let out the breath I'd been holding. After last night, I couldn't be too careful.

I glanced at Jack and Lucy. "Ready?" They nodded. We trooped across the street, and I gave them a final reminder. "Remember. Pretend I'm not a detective."

Jack considered me. Had he figured out what I had up my sleeve? "You can pretend I'm not a reporter," he said, "and maybe later, we can both pretend—"

"Hey." I stopped and whirled to face him, my index finger pointed sternly at his chest. His slow smile had me withering inside, but I held my ground. "Stop right there."

"It was just a suggestion—"

I continued across the street. "I'm on the job right now. Are you with me?"

Shooting a sideways glance at Lucy, I caught her raised eyebrows, but she nodded. She looked like she was beginning to wonder what the hell she'd gotten herself into—both with me and Jack *and* with the run-down looking Tattoo Haven.

A bell dinged as the door swung open. A velvety curtain separated the front room from the back and hung on a single suspension rod between the doorjambs. Muriel obviously wasn't socking money into interior decorating.

A tall, lanky young man sauntered out from the depths. He ran his fingers over a thick chain that hung from a front belt loop to his back pocket. My heart raced as I studied him. He looked familiar. Had I seen him last night at the bar? Could he have been behind the wheel of the kamikaze car?

No. That wasn't it, but my brain was ticking.

I did a quick survey of the room. Jack stood on sentry duty behind me, his arms folded over his chest and his jaw clenched. He was an obvious attendee of the same school of protection as Antonio. Not exactly blending in, Callaghan.

"Help you?" the tattoo guy mumbled.

I looked at him with his shaggy hair, nose ring, and multiple ear piercings. Mr. Clean-cut he was not.

He knocked a cigarette out of a mashed pack and backed it into his mouth. "What's your poison?"

Interesting choice of words. I looked around for a stray bottle of cough syrup or codeine. *Nada.* Of course not. That would have been too easy. I turned back. "You do piercings?"

He gestured at the list of services on a display board behind the counter. I read the sign. Yep. He'd pierce any body part I chose. *Nothing* was off-limits. "What'd ya want done?" he asked.

In a flash, Lucy was next to me, her eyes wide with curiosity. "Yeah, Lola. What do you want pierced?" The second she said my name, I realized I should have thought of using an alias. Too late. Damn. Hindsight and all that. Manny wouldn't have made that rookie mistake. Sadie or Neil either. Being around Jack was throwing me off.

Reading the body parts listed, I grimaced. Even when I was pretending, like now, my self-imposed piercing options held me back. I already had triple earrings in both lobes. A nose ring was completely out of the question. The tongue? No way!

I'd considered a tattoo—for about a nanosecond. A hypothetical piercing I could remove. A tattoo I was stuck with for all eternity, assuming I didn't die of a heart infection as Garrett Diggs had. I could just see myself, at eighty years old, hobbling to Mass, a colorful crucifix emblazoned on my wrinkled back.

Tattoo? Don't think so.

I looked at the tattoo guy again and shuddered. There was no way he was touching any part of me below the hips. That left only one place that I was willing to let a stranger poke a needle through. Not that I would actually let it get that far. I'd use my super detective skills to finagle information from Shaggy here and get out before he actually came near me with a needle. "My belly button."

Now Jack was beside me, his hand on my elbow. "You're not serious," he said with a hiss.

I yanked free and feigned a loving tone. "Aw, baby, I'm doing it for you. You said you'd like it." I snuggled up next to him, smiling sweetly at Shaggy.

"*Right.*" Jack slipped his arm around me and settled his hand on my hip. A jolt of electricity shot through me. He muttered in my ear, "Do you know what the hell you're doing?" Then aloud he said in his I-wanna-take-you-to-bed voice, "I *know* I'll like it, lover."

Lover? ¡Ay, Dios! Right here, right now, Callaghan.

"Hey," the tattoo guy said.

Jack and I looked up at him, but his focus was intent on me. He jerked his head to the side. "Lemme talk to you a sec."

My curiosity piqued, I wriggled out of Jack's arm and leaned over the counter.

The tattoo guy glared over my shoulder, then trained his beady gaze first on my lip, then my arm. "He do that to you?" he asked, his lips barely moving.

My fingertips fluttered over my swollen lip. "No, of course not!" Jack wouldn't lay a hand on a woman. I wanted to throttle the tattoo guy for suspecting such a thing, but then again, he'd been looking out for me. He had to be a good guy underneath the badass façade. "Thanks for asking, though," I added.

I moved away from the counter and backed right into Jack. His arm snaked around me, his fingers splayed protectively across my stomach. I held my breath for a split second, reveling in our proximity.

Lucy piped up, breaking the spell. "I'm getting a piercing, too. Or should I get a tattoo?" She stuck her lips out and looked up at the ceiling. "Yeah, a tattoo. That'll add spark, don't you think?" she said to me. But before I could answer, she turned to Shaggy. "I'm married and I need spark. I'm ready."

Oh, no! She thought I was serious. "Um, maybe you should look at some samples—"

"Oooh, good idea!"

The tattoo guy nudged her out of the way and pulled out two thick black binders filled with designs.

"If you're doing a piercing on me and a tattoo on her, I guess we should know your name," I said, pulling away from Jack before I melted into a puddle at his feet.

"Zod."

Zod? What had his mother been thinking?

"So, uh, *Zod*, I'm a little nervous about this." Complete truth. If there was any way Garrett's heart infection could be traced back to this place, there was no way I was going behind that velvet curtain.

I needed information, now. "Do you have to train to do

this?" I channeled my cousin Chely. "Like, at tattoo school or something?"

He leaned against the glass counter, watching Lucy flip through the binders, the chain dangling from his hip clanking against the case. "Yeah, it's my friggin' life's dream. When the rocket science thing didn't pan out, I thought, *Hey, I'll draw tattoos.* Went right out and got my master's."

Funny man. "Right. Well, I bet rocket science isn't all it's cracked up to be." He smiled at me, and I went on. "You must meet some, like, interesting people."

"Yep." He jerked his eyebrows up and looked at me like he thought *I* was interesting. Jack took a proprietary step toward me.

I pressed on. "So, how'd you get started? You know, when the rocket science thing fell through."

His fist jutted out toward my face. I stifled a yelp, and my hand shot up to block.

"Jesus, you're skittish," Zod said. He stuck his fist out again and rotated it. "Chill. I'm just showing you my tats. A year ago, I didn't have a single one. I was the sorriest-looking preppy dude you ever saw. Not even a piercing." He shook his head. "Pathetic."

I squinted and leaned forward, making out crude upside-down letters on each of his fingers just above the knuckle. The ink was blue and dull. There were two *L*'s. Maybe an *A*.

He pulled his hand back and studied his own knuckles before I could decipher the other letter. "I did these a little over a year ago."

"You tattooed yourself?" They were on his right hand. "So you're left-handed?"

He nodded, crossing one skinny leg over the other, cigarette hanging loosely from between his lips.

My deductive powers were astounding. Sometimes I impressed even myself. Not that Zod being a southpaw meant a damn thing. "They're blue." I gave myself an imaginary pat on the back. *Good job stating the obvious, Lola.* "I mean, why aren't they, you know, like, colorful? I like colorful."

Zod's cigarette bobbed as he took a drag. "I was experimenting." He blew a smoke ring and gave me a knowing look. "Little tidbit for you, sweetheart. Anybody who has tats like these was in the joint." He stopped, sucked on his cigarette again, and did a freaky French inhale thing through his nose. "Well, let me amend that. I did teach a friend how to do it a while back." His expression changed almost imperceptibly. "He died. Had a bad heart, poor SOB."

Pay dirt! That statement was proof enough for me that Zod had known Garrett. "Wow, that's too bad," I said. This case was going to be way too easy if Shaggy fessed up about being involved in Garrett's death.

"*Almost* anybody who has plain tats like this was in the joint," he said, changing the subject.

"The joint as in prison?"

He nodded, squinting his eye as smoke wafted over his face.

"Were you?"

He rattled his chain and looked down. Almost remorseful. "Nah. Have a buddy who was. You could say I have convict envy." He cracked up at his own joke, slapping his long thigh with his hand.

Did Zod seriously regret having a clean rap sheet? "How does self-tattooing work?"

"E string from a guitar, a cassette tape—" His cigarette hung from his lips, and he gestured wide with his arms. "—piece of cake."

"Eww, sounds scary," Lucy said.

And it *did not* sound sanitary. "Isn't that, like, dangerous?"

Ooh, Chely would be so proud of all my *likes*. "Hepatitis and stuff like that?"

He shrugged.

Okay, so did he have a death wish? "How'd you get from self-tattooing to this, uh, joint?" I asked, trying to use his lingo. The effort was giving me a headache.

I sputtered when he actually answered. "My sister and one of our father's friends showed me an ad. Muriel—she's like the manager—hired me on the spot."

So Muriel didn't own the place. No big surprise, but good to know.

Zod looked at me and Lucy. "You stalling, or what? Let's rock and roll. Who's first?"

I jumped. "That would be me." I had to get more out of him, so behind the velvet curtain it was. Plus, there wasn't a chance in hell I was letting this guy touch Lucy. My cousin, Zac, would never forgive me.

Zod pulled on his cigarette, and his eyes wandered to my chest. "Where'd ya say you wanted it? Through the nipple?"

I froze. "Uh, no, I did not say that."

His gaze lingered. "You sure?"

"Yeah, I'm sure."

"Too bad." He grinned—a little demonically. "I bet you have killer nips. And if they were pierced?" He blew out a mouthful of smoke. "Outstanding."

Jack tightened his grip on my hip. What it meant, I didn't know. Either he also thought pierced nipples on me would be outstanding, or he thought beating the crap out of Zod would be.

"Thanks, but the belly button's fine," I said.

Zod looked disappointed, but he pressed on with the details. "You want the fourteen-gauge or the post?"

I picked out a stainless steel post—what did it matter, since

I wasn't going through with it?—then passed behind the velvet curtain. Jack was at my heels. "You shouldn't do this," he said through clenched teeth.

I whispered as softly as I could. "I'm not." Then I winked, hoping he'd catch my drift. With my voice back at full volume, I said, "I think they're sexy." And I did, but hello? Heart infection. I'd see what other information I could get from Zod, then back out at the last minute. "Of course, I don't think my parents will think so—"

Zod showed me where to lie down. "What the hell do parents know?" he said. "Their plans backfire half the time."

Zod's pierced tongue was wagging, and I went with it. "What do you mean?"

"It's all about control. My dad thinks he can get me to live the way he wants, but he can't. He can't bribe me with Prozac like he can my sister."

I looked at his tattooed body and the gigantic hole in his earlobe. Looked to me like Zodman had won the control battle. "Don't I know it," I said in full pretend mode. "Parents."

"Lay down," he commanded.

¡Dios mío! My head started swirling, nerves encroaching on my clearheadedness. But I reclined in the chair, and Jack settled in the seat next to me. I had to expedite this or I'd end up with a needle through my belly.

Zod kept talking. "Yeah, hmm. Imagine my surprise when I found out my frickin' father owns this dump. B.C. Enterprises my ass."

"Wow, that's pretty deceptive," I said. "Why didn't you quit?"

"And let him win? No way."

I didn't see how Zod quitting let his father win, but it didn't really matter. He stuck his tongue out, Gene Simmons style. His demonic grin was back in place, and my thoughts derailed. "You gonna watch me stick your old lady?" he said to Jack.

Jack's jaw tightened, bless his heart. "I'm not moving."

His protective nature was really very sweet, albeit unnecessary, since I wasn't going all the way with Zodman. Still, when the tattoo guy snapped on a pair of latex gloves, I tensed. My words sped out of my mouth. "Everything's sterilized, right?" Just in case something sharp acccidentally pricked my skin somehow.

"We follow normal protocol here. I keep it clean. Never had a problem. Relax and enjoy the ride."

This is not Disneyland, Zod, I thought. More info. *Muy pronto.* "No problems with tattoos? Aren't they dangerous?" Zod gave me an odd look, and I hurried on. "My friend, uh, Glenda over there—" I nodded to the front, where Lucy was still looking at tattoo designs. "—she's going to get a tattoo. I don't want anything weird to happen to her. She can't, like, die or anything, can she? Your friend with the heart problem, he didn't die from a tattoo, did he?"

"Shit, why do people think that?" he muttered. Louder, he said, "Lady, I gave my buddy three tats over the years, and he was as healthy as a frickin' horse. I got a great little sterilizing machine off the Internet. No worries." Zod looked me over. "Now, pull up your shirt and open your pants."

I gulped. Jack's eyes were glued to me. "Uh, right. Will it b-bleed?" I stammered, sure my exaggerated acting would give me away.

Zod just shook his mangy head. "Nah."

I pulled up my shirt a fraction of an inch and undid the button on my capris. Would they be able to tell I was wearing a thong? Shoot. I should have gone for the safe Jockeys. "So if you self-tattoo, do you sterilize the equipment, er, the guitar string?" I asked.

159

Zod smirked. "Now pull 'em *down*, sweetheart." He held up a bottle. "See this? Orange antiseptic. Good for guitar strings and bellies. I'm going to smear it on you then clamp your skin. You don't want to ruin your pretty little outfit, now, do you?" He stood over me with his gloved hands and his cotton swabs. The thought of orange antiseptic staining my clothes was too much. I steeled my nerves, pulled my top up to my rib cage, and unzipped my pants, folding the sides in. I loved these pants.

Zod and Jack suddenly grew still. Their eyes were riveted to my midsection. What could they see? I propped up on my elbows and peered down at my navel. A triangle of sheer lace— and everything dark and curly underneath—stared back at me. My eyelids fluttered. *Ay, Dios.*

Jack scooted his chair behind my head and slowly slid his arms down my sides until his palms lay flat against my hips. He whispered in my ear, his voice like silk. "Is driving me crazy on your list of things to do?"

I managed what I hoped was a coy smile. "It's at the very top."

He made a low, breathy sound in my ear that shot straight through my body, awakening nerves in hidden places. Well, in partially hidden places. *Think about the case*, I told myself, not about the feel of Jack's hands against my skin. Or the startlingly masculine scent of him. Or the feel of his lips so close to my cheek.

Finally, Zod stopped leering enough to swab my stomach. I still had plenty of time, and I grinned up at Jack. A smack of cold metal pinched my skin together, and I jumped, back to reality.

I could fight off crooks with a broom, survive getting run over, beat the shit out of anyone who got in my way, but Zod was getting way too close to piercing my skin. I gave myself thirty seconds before I bolted out of the chair.

I bit my lip and braced myself. "Zod!"

"Hmm?"

He ran a finger over the needle and I felt faint. I squeezed my eyes shut. "Do you ever get any people in here bugging you?" I blurted. I had to get more information before I stopped him.

Jack's hands pressed hard against my sides. "Lola, he's—"

More information! "Ever been blamed—?"

I stopped cold. A harsh prick followed by a raging sting zeroed in at my belly. "No!" Zod was plunging the needle into my flesh. Oh my God, I'd waited too long! He was piercing me!

Jack held tight to my arms and put his head next to mine. His lips brushed my cheek as the needled stopped. Zod pulled it back and, like he was getting a running start, plunged again. I screamed as he forced it out the other side.

"Holy shit!" I screeched. "Are you trying to kill me?"

Zod looked at Jack. "She'd never make it through a tattoo, dude."

I gritted my teeth. "Your bedside manner needs work, Zod. Give a girl a warning, would you!"

My whole body trembled as he wiped my stomach with alcohol swabs—not exactly the trembling I would have liked to experience, considering Jack's arms were still around me.

A dull ache radiated from my belly.

"Clean it twice a day," Zod said. He handed me an instruction sheet and stood back while Jack slipped one arm under my body and propelled me up. My shirt fell over my stomach, but my pants were still undone. I didn't even care. The pain precluded any possible pleasure I might experience being in the vicinity of Jack. It looked like the piercing was going to be my chastity belt tonight.

I slung my purse over my shoulder and gingerly stepped through to the front room, laying my cash on the counter. To think I was actually paying for this pain. And the information I'd gotten for it was negligible at best.

Lucy was *still* searching the binders. God, I hoped she'd managed to snoop while I was getting tortured. I should have communicated that to her somehow. "I can't decide," she said.

"You shouldn't get one today, *Glenda*." I was not putting Lucy's life in danger. Wait and see if I died first. Anyway, I seriously doubted that Zac wanted the mother of his children sporting a tattoo.

"Glenda?" she mouthed, but she seemed to get the point and slammed the binder closed. Truth be told, she looked a touch relieved. She didn't really want the tattoo; she just wanted to do something wild. "Let me see you!" Before I could stop her, she pulled up my shirt. I looked at Jack and saw him swallow hard as his gaze drifted over my navel and my still-unbuttoned pants.

The pain was already dissipating, and I was feeling pretty good with the piercing. Or at least with the effect it was having on Jack. The ends sometimes justified the means.

The bell on the front door of the shop dinged. Lucy dropped my shirt, and we all turned our heads to look at who'd come to be tortured.

Allison Diggs skulked into the dim shop.

Her jaw dropped, and she pointed two fingers at me, a burning cigarette clutched between them. "What are *you* doing here?"

"What are *you* doing here?" Good comeback, especially considering her proclivity for tattoos.

Zod, Lucy, and Jack just stood there, looking puzzled. "I work here," she said.

Even better. Another dot to try to connect. "Small world," I said. My brain whirled. Emily's daughter, Allison, knew *Zod*, who may have had something to do with *Garrett's* allegedly fatal tattoo. Muriel had said Emily had messed in other people's business. Had she pissed Zod off with accusations of murder? God, my head hurt. This case was like a bad *telenovela*.

She frowned. "Like I said, what're you doing here?"

I flashed a bright smile. Go with the truth, or at least a modified version of it. . . . "I just got my belly button pierced. Remember? I told you I wanted to."

She rolled her eyes. "Right."

"Really." I lifted my shirt, just a little bit excited about my new body jewelry. "See?"

Zod knocked a cigarette out of his pack and offered it to Allison. "You know her, Ally?"

Total mental head thump. A L L Y. Those were the upside-down kindergarten letters on Zod's knuckles. Were they love tattoos? Were these two a couple?

She took the fresh cigarette and lit it with the dwindling old one before crushing the stub out under her shoe. She sucked in a deep drag of the new one. "She's the private investigator I told you about. She came to see me about Emily." She gave him an irritated look. "I went with her to see Sean. Tell me you didn't talk to her."

"Why shouldn't he? Does he have something to hide, Allison?" Obviously the candle I'd lit for her hadn't given her any peace yet.

Zod pushed his stringy hair back behind his ears and suddenly looked menacing rather than just mangy.

"Emily's dead, by the way." It was callous, I know, but I wanted to see her reaction.

She started, and her face seemed to crumple slightly. But then she recovered, deadening her eyes until she looked indifferent.

When she didn't respond, I blew. "Damn it, Allison, she was your mother. Don't you care, even a little bit? I know you have a heart. I saw you with Sean."

163

She lifted her leopard arm and pointed to the door. "Get out."

I crossed my arms and looked from one to the other. "Where were you last night?"

"Why?"

"Someone tried to run me over." Lucy gasped, but I ignored her. "Where were you?" I repeated.

"I didn't try to run you over," she said, but her voice cracked, just slightly, and I wondered if it stemmed from anger or sadness.

Of course she hadn't run me down, hence my need to drive her to the zoo the other day. "Where were you?" I repeated.

"She was here," Zod said. "Getting a new tat."

It was my turn to be skeptical. Was he covering for her, or making up an alibi for himself? I peered at her. "You don't have a square inch of bare skin left."

She whipped down her stretch pants, turned around, and mooned us. I slapped my hand over my mouth. Oh. My. God. One cheek was—big surprise—covered in leopard print. On the other side of her flat behind was a rectangular white bandage.

Jack coughed. "Classy," he muttered from behind his hand.

"Holy guacamole, Batman," Lucy said.

Allison pulled her pants back up. "Satisfied?"

Not even close. Jack had me hot and bothered, and Little Miss Sunshine and Zod, the Tattoo Man, were each other's alibis. I was extremely unsatisfied—in every way—but I smiled sweetly at Emily's daughter. "Was anyone else here with you?"

Allison shot a nervous look at Zod. Her hard-ass exterior seemed to be cracking just a little. She shook her head. "We were alone."

"Convenient," I muttered. "One more question."

She huffed, but crossed her arms and waited.

"How many tattoos did Garrett have?"

Her beady eyes studied me, probably trying to discern if it was a trick question. I wish it was and that the answer would reveal the killer. In truth, it was just curiosity. I wanted to know if he had been as rebellious as his sister. She shrugged, then looked to Zod for the answer. "How many?" she asked him.

The chain at Zod's hip jangled as he moved. "I already told you. Four," he said.

"Where were they?"

Allison smirked. "That's another question."

God, she was annoying. "Indulge me."

Her smirk deepened, but she looked at Zod again. "One on each gun—"

"His biceps," Jack translated when I raised my eyebrows.

"—one on his forearm, and the last one he did was above his knuckle."

I thanked God I hadn't been insane enough to have gotten a tattoo in place of my new piercing. Boundaries, I reminded myself. The line blurred sometimes, but I had them, and Allison and Zod had become my temporary moral compasses.

"Thanks," I said to them, adding, "I'll be in touch." As soon as I figured out what had happened to Emily, and assuming Zod, or whoever the killer was, didn't get in touch with me first.

Chapter 12

Jack dropped Lucy and me off at the downtown mall. He rolled down the driver's window. "I might need to check your belly button later, make sure it's healing properly."

He seemed to have a voice set aside that he pulled out for seduction. It dropped to a low come-hither tone and drew me in until my insides were melting. I was going to have to use super strength to keep myself lucid tonight and not fall into his arms. As much as I wanted to lose myself with him, never allowing myself to be a one-night stand was one of my hard-and-fast rules.

I raised my eyebrows at him, and he added, his voice like black satin, "Research. I need to get every detail and fact correct for my article."

"Of course you do." Despite my reservations about Jack's motives—and my own willpower—I added some flirt to my smile. "If it's in the name of research, then I'm sure I can't deny you a belly button inspection."

The second he drove off, Lucy grabbed my arm and whirled me around. Her California tanned face blotched red with pent-up curiosity. "Oh. My. God. Spill it! What's going on, Lola?"

"Nothing's going on. He turned up as part of my

investigation—that's all." I started walking toward Macy's. "We're going out tonight, which I'm afraid," I added, "might be a mistake."

"A mistake?" She squealed and yanked me back. "Are you serious?"

"Dead serious. He's not a settle-down kind of guy. I don't know what I'm doing."

She sputtered, clearly holding in her laughter. "You're going to have fun! You deserve it. And who cares if he doesn't want marriage and children? He's gorgeous."

I stared at Lucy. "Who cares? I've seen him love and leave plenty of girls. I have no intention of joining their company. I want marriage and children someday. Why waste my time with someone who doesn't?"

"People change, Lola."

"Not all people. Look at Antonio. He's the same as he's always been. Noncommittal."

We started walking again, but Lucy kept on. "You know Jack well enough to know that's how he feels?"

It was a fair question, and the truth was that I didn't know . . . Jack. Maybe I was just trying to protect myself.

"Look," Lucy hurried on. "You're going out with him. Just have a good time. Now, what are you shopping for? Where are you going? Do your folks like him?"

It was hard to get a word in edgewise, but I managed to answer her questions in order, ticking them off on my fingers. "I'm looking for a whole new outfit, we're going to Club Ambrosía, and my parents like him, although they don't know that we've been—" I dropped my voice to a heavy whisper. "—somewhat *intimate*."

She dug her fingernails into my flesh. "What! You just said he's noncommittal and you don't want to waste your time. And you've been intimate?"

God, I was a mess. I pulled away and jabbed my finger at her. "I know, Lucy! That's what I'm talking about. I lose all control around him."

She wasn't laughing. "What's the scoop, Lola? I need details."

I managed to laugh. "Well, *intimate* may be a stretch. He's seen me in my pajamas."

"Oh." Her face fell. "Is that all?"

What had she been expecting? "It was a thin white top. He got an eyeful."

"So he's hot for you. Lola, just let loose, for goodness' sake."

Maybe she was right. What would it hurt to really do myself up and let my boundary lines blur? With new intent, I pulled open the door. Cool department store air washed over us. We made a beeline for the shoe department, and I immediately zeroed in on a four-inch stiletto. After examining it this way and that, I put the shoe back and moved on. I didn't want to break an ankle on my first night out with Jack.

"Look! Mulberry!" Lucy practically ran through the racks to pick up a displayed Birkenstock. "I don't have one like this," she said.

I laughed. Lucy and her Birks. I flagged down the saleswoman for her and looked around. Not a minute later, a ray of light seemed to shine from the ceiling and onto the perfect red, flirty heel. It had straps that wound around the ankle, and most important, a three-inch heel that would put my lips in perfect proximity to Jack's. "This is it," I announced, holding it up as if it were the Holy Grail.

Lucy cocked an eyebrow at them. "Those look like strip shoes."

"What?"

"Strip shoes. You know, like you'd use for your strip list." I stared blankly at her, and she looked at me like I was straight out of the loony bin. "Don't you have a strip list?" she asked, sounding horrified.

"What is *that*?"

"A list of guys you'd strip for?"

An image of me dancing around a pole in the red shoes and sexy lingerie, with Jack's smoldering eyes taking in every slow, deliberate move, slid into my mind. "Uh, no." I swallowed. "Do you?"

Her face flushed. "Never mind. Forget I mentioned it."

Gladly. I didn't want to know who Lucy would strip for. I went back to the shoes, but she'd got me thinking. I could go the distance getting a piercing for my job, but strip for Jack on the second date? What *were* my limits?

I bought the shoes. I had no plans to strip for him tonight, but shoes were a state of mind, and I was gearing up for salsa dancing. "Come on," I said to Lucy. Now I need an outfit to go with them."

"I need to make one more stop," I said to Lucy. It had taken less than an hour for me to find the perfect red-and-black flamenco-like outfit. Now I was ready to get back to business.

"Where to?"

I pulled George Bonatee's business card from my purse. "It's three blocks from here."

"I'm digging this detective stuff. So cool."

I put my finger to my lips. "It's confidential, though."

She closed her mouth and turned an imaginary key. "Mum's the word."

We started down the sidewalk, hauling our shopping bags with us. By the time we reached the law offices of Bonatee and Craig, I'd reviewed the nuts and bolts of the case with Lucy. "I'll do the talking," I said.

She frowned. "Again? But I want to participate."

She looked so dejected that I gave in—a little. "Let's play it by ear."

The lawyer was in, and even though it was an unscheduled visit, Mary Bonatee's father, Emily's landlord, agreed to see us. We stashed our bags behind the mousy receptionist's desk, and she escorted us into the man's office. Bonatee was finishing a phone call. Law books lined the dark wood shelves, and photographs of the family on vacation—on a boat, in Old Sacramento, with the current governor—were strategically scattered here and there.

"That doesn't matter. It's over. You want me to say it'll be all right? Fine. It'll be all right." He paused, flashing a practiced smile, and held up a finger to us. I was immediately taken by his charisma. It seemed to fill the room, as if he exhaled pheromones. His skin was the color of milk chocolate, his tightly wound hair cut close to his head. And his eyes—as expected, were like amber just like his daughter, Mary's, and plain gorgeous. "Right. Me, too." He smiled at Lucy and me again, but spoke into the phone. "I'll see you then."

He hung up the phone and stretched his hand out to us. In three strides, I was face-to-face with him, grasping his hand firmly, trying to hide my satisfaction. This man was definitely Sean Diggs's father. Emily had good taste, assuming he wasn't a killer. "Thank you for seeing me," I said.

"Not a problem. Ms. Cruz, isn't it?" Then he looked at Lucy.

I gestured toward her. "My colleague—"

Lucy thrust her arm out and strode forward. "Clarice Clooney. A pleasure to meet you, sir."

I stared at her. Oh. My. God. Apparently George topped Lucy's strip list.

Bonatee gestured to a pair of black leather chairs facing his desk.

I started to sit, grimaced at the ache in my belly, and straightened back up. "I'll stand." This navel piercing was proving to be a big pain in the ass. It hurt like hell. I needed some Advil. Bad.

Bonatee pushed himself back under his desk and directed his full attention at me, his fingers steepled and perched under his chin. The man had a lethal mixture of suave sophistication and base animal magnetism. "That's a nasty abrasion on your arm." He peered at my face. "And your lip. Were you in an accident?"

"Yes, they are, and I was. Played chicken with a car last night."

He stared at me for a beat, but when I didn't offer any more information about my injuries, he went on. "What can I do for you ladies?"

"Emily Diggs." I paused, waiting for him to blurt out that she was the mother of his child. Or, at the very least, his tenant. He sat silent, his face like chiseled stone.

I kept waiting. A good screw, maybe? Anything?

No dice. Bonatee's poker face was stellar.

"Yes," he prompted.

"You are aware Ms. Diggs disappeared last Wednesday."

"Disappeared," he repeated. His eye twitched slightly, and the crack in his voice when he spoke revealed a tiny bit of . . . something.

"Your daughter told you your tenant was missing, didn't she? I assume the police have been to speak with you."

Bonatee shifted in his chair and sputtered a cough. "No, I haven't seen the police. Mary e-mailed me, but I haven't read it. I've been tied up on a case. Disappeared. That word has strong implications. You're sure Emily's not on vacation somewhere?"

"Do you read the newspaper?" I supposed it was possible he

hadn't heard Emily was dead. Was I the only person that read the obits?

"Of course, Ms. Cruz." His spine seemed to stiffen. "But as I said, I've been out of town."

Likely story, but a little too convenient. "You arranged the rental for Ms. Diggs, is that right?"

He nodded, the muscles in his face pulsing. "Correct. We were actually, er, old friends. She needed a favor."

The small repetitive movement of his jaw only added to his attractiveness. "Is that right? How far back do you go?"

He folded his thumb under the lip of his desk, sliding it over the edge. "Our daughters went to kindergarten together."

I stood up straighter and drew an imaginary line between Allison and Mary. I didn't know what it meant, but Allison was the common denominator.

"Really, Ms. Cruz," Bonatee said, interrupting my thoughts, "what's this about?" His voice had tensed, and a transformation seemed to take place. The cutthroat litigator materialized, replacing the congenial man he'd been a moment before. He didn't want us here.

"Emily's not on vacation."

There was a knock on the door and he pushed back from his desk. "Yes, Margaret. What is it?"

The mousy receptionist shuffled into the room a few feet. "Sorry to interrupt, Mr. Bonatee. You—you have a call. You can take it out here. . . ."

Bonatee smiled indulgently, if a little forced. "Of course." He looked back to Lucy and me. "Excuse me a minute, won't you?"

Lucy popped out of her chair the second the door closed. "He's hiding something. Did you see his shifty eyes? What do we do? What do we do?"

"Good question, *Clarice*." This guy was a lawyer, probably

172

trained in cross-examination. I snapped my fingers. "How about good cop, bad cop?"

Lucy smiled, big and diabolically. "So we need to get him to admit he was boinking the woman, right? I can do that. He's good looking." She winked at me. "Probably topped Emily's strip list."

That was an image I could have done without, but it did get me thinking about exactly what had transpired between Emily and Bonatee since she'd moved into his rental house. Had their old relationship been rekindled?

Lucy settled back into her leather chair. "Okay, I'm ready," she said a split second before Bonatee came back into the room.

Lucy would make the perfect "good cop." She was bubbly and exuded innocence. The question was, could I be a convincing "bad cop"? Manny, yes. Sadie, without a doubt. Neil could just charge. Me? I could take Bonatee down, but without resorting to kung fu, I was a little less confident. . . .

"I apologize for the interruption," Bonatee said, rounding his desk. He was back to Mr. Congeniality. "Where were we?"

"Emily and her son did not go on vacation—" I started.

"Do you know where they are?" He asked the question a little too quickly to be indifferent.

"Sean is with his uncle," I said, waiting for the right moment to unleash my bad cop.

Anxiety seemed to flow off him. He relaxed and slid back under the desk. "I'm relieved to hear that. I'm sure Em, er, Ms. Diggs will turn up."

Lucy rearranged herself in her chair, fanning her skirt out and shaking her Birkenstocked foot. "She did turn up, you son of a bitch, facedown in the river. Now cut the bullshit, and tell us what you know."

I gawked at Lucy. No! The sweet, bubbly, mother was not

taking on the role of bad cop. ¡Ay, *caramba!* I shifted gears. Good cop. Good cop. I fumbled for words. "*Clarice*, I'm sure Mr. Bonatee knows the seriousness of the matter. Let's give him a chance to cooperate—"

Bonatee's voice snapped as he looked from me to Lucy, his pleasant demeanor gone. "You just said she was missing—"

Lucy jumped up and slapped her palms on his desk. "She *was* missing. Now she's *dead.*"

"That can't be right—"

"It's exactly right. She was killed. Now, where exactly *were* you last Wednesday?"

His face froze, his amber eyes looking fossilized. "Wednesday?"

"That's right, sir," I said. A good cop should sit. I gripped the arm of the chair, grimaced, and lowered myself down. "The day she disappeared."

"I—I was out of town, working on a case. I told you that." Finally, he managed to quash his bubbling emotion and bring his face back to a normal expression. "How? How did she die?"

Good question if he was innocent. Diabolical if he was guilty. "We're waiting on the autopsy—"

"Autopsy?"

Lucy marched up and down the room, her Birks slapping, her skirt flowing. She wheeled around. "That's right. Au-top-sy. They do that with a wrongful death. As an attorney, I'm sure you know that. Now, stop playing dumb and tell us about your relationship with Ms. Diggs."

Damn, she was good. Even with my black belt, she had me on edge.

"You're sure it wasn't an accident?"

I watched Bonatee carefully. This guy was either Samuel L. Jackson good, or he was genuinely shocked. And maybe even upset. "She had drugs in her system—"

Lucy interrupted. "Yeah, like a Cuban boatload full."

"Drugs?" He coughed. "What kind of drugs?"

Lucy didn't know the specifics, but she was in full improvisational mode. "You tell us, *George*. What kind of drugs did your *lover* do?"

His face grew hard and calculated, like Lucy had said something that pissed him off. "My lover?"

I covered my eyes with my hand. Shit. She was beyond bad cop. She was out of control. I maneuvered myself out of my chair and took her arm, jumping in to smooth things over. "We know Sean's your son."

I could see him relax slightly. "Is that why you're here? To confirm your suspicion that Emily and I have a son together?" He threw his hands up, like he was giving up. "I confess. We had a relationship years ago. Sean was the result of that union."

"What happened with your relationship?" I asked.

His expression didn't change, but his eyes seemed to sadden. "Let's just say it didn't work out."

There were all kinds of reasons why relationships didn't work out. Who had been the one to call theirs off? "I'm trying to understand Emily," I said. "Can you tell me what happened?"

He lowered his head for a beat, and I felt his sadness. "It was my fault," he finally said. "I—I met someone else and—" He broke off.

"And she found out?" I finished.

He nodded. "But it was a mistake. I tried to apologize, but she wouldn't forgive me. I didn't see her for years. When she called me a few months ago and needed my help, I didn't hesitate."

"What about Sean? Did you see him much?"

"I didn't even know about him." His gaze dropped to the

175

desk. "When I saw him, I—I—" The glimpses of emotion he'd shown slowly faded. "I couldn't believe she never told me."

After having kept Sean a secret for so long, why would Emily have introduced him now? And if he'd cheated on her, why would she have come to him, of all people, for help? "What about your daughter?"

"What about her?"

"Why'd you set Emily up in the same house with her?"

"Emily came to see me, said she was having a hard time making ends meet. She'd lost her job, was struggling with some—" He cleared his throat. "—some personal issues."

"And Mary?" I asked, silently thanking God that Lucy wasn't unleashing her bad cop anger again.

"She's a student." He gave a proud smile. "Pre-law."

So Mary was following in her dad's footsteps. "Have you told Mary about you being Sean's father?"

He shook his head. "I only told—" His expression froze and then took on a touch of remorse. "No, I told no one. I wanted Mary to know, but I didn't want to hurt her, I thought if they got to know each other . . ."

Lucy was right. The man was attractive, and there was an underlying charm about him. The way he held himself. The line of his shoulders. There was almost a familiarity about him. I liked him and actually wanted to believe him, but Bad Cop Lucy was back. "You said she came back and asked you for help. Did she need money? Child support?"

He shook his head, but Lucy kept on. "She took a risk having you meet Sean. You could have fought her for custody. And you might have won." She sucked in a quick breath and glared at him, accusation in her eyes. "It's way more convenient for you that she's dead, don't you think? Once paternity's established, and if you want him, Sean will be yours."

He shook his head, looking indignant. "I would never take

176

a child from his mother. I set her up in the house. I offered to help her. She wanted—" He stopped abruptly. "As I said, she had some personal issues."

"Right," Lucy said. "Her other son and the tattoo." His mocha-colored face paled, and Lucy rattled on, spitting out the words. "Did she want your help as a lawyer? Did it piss you off that she wouldn't take you back after you betrayed her?" Her face lit up as if she'd had an epiphany. "Did you try to be with her again? Did she reject you? Is that why you killed her?"

"Clarice!" I jumped up and grabbed her arm, giving it a hard warning squeeze. "Back off," I murmured, and Lucy stepped back, letting me take the lead. "What she means," I said to Bonatee, "is that we have to look at all possible scenarios."

He rose slowly. "I did not kill Emily."

"Of course not," I said. "Clarice here always suspects the worst." I threw in a small laugh, hoping to lighten the moment, but it flopped. Emily was still dead, after all, and Bonatee hadn't forgotten that little fact.

"You said she was in the river?" he asked.

"Near the marina off Garden Highway," I confirmed. "I'm so sorry for your loss." And I was. The hum of emotion in his voice was real. Whatever Emily's motives for contacting him again had been, it seemed clear to me that Bonatee had seen it as another chapter in their story. Or a chance for a rewrite.

Or maybe it was just the rose-colored glasses I wore. I wanted to believe that Emily had known love at the end of her life, and that Sean's father was the one to offer it.

"What have the police concluded?" he asked.

Lucy jumped back into the conversation. "We're asking the questions, Mr. Lawyer Man—"

I stared at her. Mr. Lawyer Man? Where was she getting this stuff?

177

"I don't buy your story," she said, marching toward him, skirts flowing. "I know your type. All smooth jazz and shit. You could convince a girl that the sky is green with all that sweet talk and charm. You want us to believe you loved her, but she didn't want your love." She shook her head. "Tsk, tsk."

I could see anger pooling behind Bonatee's tiger eyes. "She was the mother of his child, *Clarice*," I said, trying to signal Lucy so she'd lighten up.

She bunched her fists. "But cheating is never, ever okay. Shoulda kept your pants zipped—that's what I say. A cheating man is enough to drive plenty of women postal. Poor Emily. She did the right thing by just walking away."

Bonatee's face turned stony.

"Clarice," I said as sweetly as I could, "we're trying to find out who killed Emily, not judge Mr. Bonatee's personal life."

"We're done here." Bonatee was at the door in three determined strides.

No! No! I channeled all the good cop I could. "Love doesn't always fit in a tidy little box, Clarice." I squeezed her arm again and smiled sweetly at the lawyer. His shoulders seemed to tremble under his suit. He looked like a volcano, bubbling and ready to erupt. I decided to quit while I was still ahead. "Thank you for your time."

He opened the door, standing stiffly alongside it.

I had one more question to ask. "Emily's personal issues . . . did they involve her older son and how he died?"

"From a tattoo," Lucy threw in.

He stared her down. "People don't die from tattoos."

"No, but they can die from infections."

"The kid had a bad heart," he said. "No one was responsible for that. I encouraged her to let it alone."

Lucy scooted back into the office and plopped down on the leather chair, her back to us. "He's dead. And now she's dead.

Is someone responsible for *that*, or should we just let that alone, too?"

He let the door close and came around to face her. "Emily wanted someone to take the blame for Garrett's death. She had circumstantial evidence, but nothing empirical. She wanted me to help her sue the tattoo artist, and I talked her out of it. End of story." He picked up his phone and dialed. "Now, we're done. Or if you prefer, I can have security escort you out."

"We're going," Lucy grumbled as we left the office. I grabbed our shopping bags and followed her to the elevator. Lucy's bad cop persona had come on with a vengeance. What the hell was behind it?

I heard the faint ring of my cell phone from the depths of my purse. Something in there must have been knocking against it to lower the volume. Damn, I had to find a way to set the ringtone so that didn't happen. I dug for the phone, adjusted the volume back to HIGH, then flipped it open.

"Lola!" An hysterical Chely was on the other end of the line. "We're running out of time! Help!"

Her voice sent a jolt of guilt through me. I'd been seriously slipping with cousin duty. Only four days till the *quinceañera*. I racked my brain. When was I going to have time to help? "It's okay, relax," I said, taking a deep breath myself. "What do we still need to do?"

"Flowers. The party's Saturday, and we don't have the flowers!"

Flowers. I could make the time to order flowers in between hunting down Emily's killer. "Don't worry. I'll pick you up in the morning, and we'll take care of it."

Chely breathed a trembling sigh of relief. "Thank you."

"Be ready at eight thirty. Don't be late."

"I will. I mean I won't. Eight thirty."

179

A hunched woman shuffled past us in the hall, her flannel-clad arm brushing mine. A tickling sensation shot up my spine. "Gotta go, Chely. See you in the morning."

I shoved my purse and phone into Lucy's arms and took off after the woman. She turned at the end of the corridor. "Muriel!" I yelled.

"Where are you going?" Lucy called after me, but I couldn't take the time to answer.

I rounded the corner and came to a hard stop. The corridor was empty. One by one, I threw open office doors. I received a slew of surprised stares from the people inside. "Sorry," I said before hurrying on to the next door. Each time, I came up empty. There wasn't an old woman wearing flannel anywhere.

I found the stairwell door at the end of the hall. I flung it open, half expecting a phlegm ball to come flying at me, a straight shot from Muriel's lungs. *Nada.*

Muriel had no big stake in Emily's life (that I'd found) and there had to be other women in Sacramento who wore flannel, right? Was I losing my edge?

I walked back to the elevator. Lucy's defiant stance—hand on her hip, one Birkenstocked foot flung out, and her head at an angle—didn't escape me. She hadn't liked being left behind. "Where'd you go?" she said, a bad cop snap still lacing her voice. "I'm supposed to be your assistant today."

"I thought I saw someone. . . ." I pushed away the paranoid nagging feeling that I was being followed by a flannel-clad prune, picked my purse up from the ground where she'd dropped it, and turned on her. "I was supposed to be the bad cop."

She raised an eyebrow at me. "Why would *you* be the bad cop? I'm a housewife with a truckload of suppressed frustration to draw from. *You're* going out with Jack tonight. You have stripper shoes in your bag that you're going to put to good use." She wagged her finger at me. "You're too happy to be a bad cop."

"You're delusional. I am always ready to do my job, stripper shoes or not." I looked at her Stevie Nicks outfit. "You seriously think you look tougher than I do?"

Her gaze flicked to my stomach. "You have a girly belly button ring." She flattened her palm against her chest. "*I* was going for the tattoo."

"You didn't *get* the tattoo," I reminded her.

"But I would have if your cover hadn't been blown."

I rolled my eyes, not believing it for a second. Frustrated housewife or not, Lucy was still a sweet California girl who wouldn't permanently ink her body on impulse. "If you say so. But next time, I'm the bad cop."

She bobbed her head, her sun-streaked blond ponytails dragging up and down over her shoulders. "Right. Like tonight with Jack." She grinned, a little wickedly. "Do you think he likes games? Oooh, I bet you'd have a good time being *bad* with him, Lola."

I bet she was right. I momentarily forgot about Bonatee, another Muriel sighting, and the ache in my navel. Only a few hours till the date. Did Jack have handcuffs, or should I bring mine?

Chapter 13

W ow!" I did a double take at Reilly when she met me at the entrance to Club Ambrosía. She'd put a bright red wash through her hair—bye-bye blue—and had on a gold shimmering dress with a deep plunging neckline. Even with four-inch heels, she still couldn't be more than five foot six, and she wobbled as she stepped up on the sidewalk.

"Do you like it?" she asked, all bright-eyed and bushy-tailed.

"It's flashy. I like the hair." She'd swept it up into a tight ponytail and stuck beaded combs here and there to add sparkle. As if she didn't stand out enough.

"I don't look as good as you—Lola!" She leaned forward and peered more closely at me. "What happened?"

Apparently lip gloss doesn't work miracles. Luckily my scraped-up arm and leg were covered by my outfit. "It's nothing," I said. "Just a run-in with some gravel. You look amazing. Ready?" She nodded, and I guided her by the elbow. "Come on, then. I'm ready to dance."

Inside the club, I looked around. Twinkling white lights crisscrossed the ceiling and framed each archway. Parquet flooring and sections of Mexican tile lent an old world rustic look to the setting, while strobe lights gave it flair and disco ambience. ¡Fantástico! My heart pounded in anticipation of a night of dancing as much as from the impending appearance of Jack Callaghan.

At eight o'clock, there was a salsa instructional hour. The band leader was a blond Colombian woman named Soledad who had a heavy Spanish accent and an hourglass figure. She went over the steps for salsa and merengue. Reilly and I staked out a table with my lacy black shawl and her gold lamé purse; then I shepherded her onto the dance floor to help her learn the basics.

I led—the best choice, since I knew my way around the dance floor and I had a good three inches on Reilly. Not to mention I needed to hold her up. Despite my best efforts, her feet buckled under her after the first series of steps, and she hobbled off to the table to await the arrival of her prince.

Who needed a partner? With my arms cocked at the elbows, I let the Latin music seep into me. My body began swaying, my hips rotating, my feet and the drum-heavy rhythm in sync.

"Lola!" I heard my name screamed from the bar and searched the dark club. Someone waved both hands overhead and called again. "Lola! ¡Ven! It's Coco!"

"Socorro?" It was! It had been months since I'd seen her. I gestured to Reilly that I'd be right back and headed to the bar.

"Coco." I kissed her on both cheeks, laughing and wiping away the brick red lipstick marks I'd left behind. She looked at my swollen and scraped lip, and her eyes widened. "It's nothing," I said quickly, stopping her before she could ask me what had happened. I changed the subject. "What are you doing here on a Tuesday?"

"It's my night off." She swayed to the music, her second-skin jeans and skintight white top not leaving much to the imagination. "Who are *you* here with?"

"Antonio, a girl I work with, and—" My eyelids spontaneously fluttered. "—an old friend."

She leaned her skinny butt back onto her stool and dropped her voice. "Uh-huh. What old friend? *Dime todo.*"

Coco and I went way back. All the way to elementary school. She knew Jack, knew about how I'd spied on him, and I wasn't sure she could separate the high school boy she'd remember from the man he'd become. Heck, I was having a hard time separating them, though it was getting easier. "You remember Jack Callaghan?"

She almost fell off her chair. "*¿Quién?* Jack Callaghan? The guy who went out with every single cheerleader in high school? The same big spender who took all the *chicas* to the levee?"

Well, when she put it that way . . . Still, I put my hands on my hips and defended him. "He's all grown up now, Coco. He's smart. And nice." And damn hot.

She looked over my shoulder, and I turned to see what had caught her attention. Antonio and Jack stood on the edge of the dance floor. My heart skidded to a halt and, I swear, an electrical charge passed between us because Jack turned and looked at me as if there wasn't another woman in the room.

I smiled then caught Antonio's eye and gestured toward our table. He saw Reilly, and the next second flashed me a *you're so going to pay for this* look—which, of course, I chose to ignore. At least her hair wasn't blue tonight. He had to be grateful for the small things.

"That's him," I said, turning back to Coco.

She fanned herself with her hand. "*El es buenísimo, pero* don't let him being gorgeous make you stupid, Lola. You did that already. Does the name Sergio ring a bell?"

"You can't even compare them, Coco. And I'm just here to dance." Or at least that's all she had to know about.

She stood up and caught me in a hug. "Okay, then—whatever you say. Go for it, *chica*. Have fun."

"*Gracias*," I said, smiling bigger. "Do you want to join us? Who are you here with?"

"My cousin, Lupe, and some of her friends." She cocked her thumb down the bar at a row of women dressed to the nines. "Maybe I'll hook up with you guys later."

"Good to see you," I said, and then I headed back to my table and the tall, gorgeous man who was waiting for me. Be still my heart.

They all greeted me at once.

"Lola," Antonio said through gritted teeth.

Reilly stood and grabbed my arm. "Thank God you're back! I'm so ready to dance."

Jack's gaze was glued to me and slid down my body. My pulse kicked up. "You look amazing."

I just said the same thing to Reilly, but the way Jack said it to me filled me with longing. I shook my arm loose from Reilly and handed her over to Antonio. "Tonio, Reilly. Reilly, Antonio. You remember each other, right? *Bailan*. Dance. Right now."

I turned away from them and gave my full attention to Jack. He looked damn handsome himself in a short-sleeve black pseudo-guayabera and gray pants. Thank God for Advil. It hadn't killed the pain of my navel completely, but had deadened it more than enough to be able to dance with abandon. And that's what I was going to do. All night long. With Jack Callaghan.

Soledad's lessons were over, and the band was in full salsa mode, the rhythm pulsating and hypnotic. I took Jack's hand and led him to the dance floor.

185

When he slipped his arm around my waist and pulled me against him, I knew I was in trouble. Dancing salsa wasn't the solution to lust. It was more like a catalyst.

My new shoes had done the trick; my lips were within kissing distance of his, and it took every ounce of self-restraint not to let them meet. *Get a grip, Lola. You're here to dance. Let him make the first move.* I wrapped one arm around his shoulder, he took my other hand in his, and we moved together in a slow rhythm like we'd been partners forever.

He led and I followed, and after a minute I pulled away—as much to get myself under control as to ask, "Where'd you learn to salsa?"

The corner of his mouth curved up, the faint indentation of his dimple skimming his cheek. "I went to just about every wedding, baptism, and first communion your family ever had when we were kids, remember? Some things you never forget."

Then he slipped his arm behind my back again and spun me around. A shiver shot up my spine as his hand skimmed my stomach then settled back on my hip. Facing him again, I laced my fingers behind his neck, looked into his smoky blue eyes, and rocked my hips under his touch. I wanted to close my eyes and throw my head back. To feel him drag his mouth along my neck. To slide my hands down his sides.

Dios mío, was it hot in here? To hell with dancing. To hell with lack of privacy. To hell with ensuring he had good intentions that included more than one night. I couldn't resist him another second. I moved my hands to the sides of his face and pressed up against him. A small groan slipped out as one of his hands slid from my hip downward, his fingers pressing against the outer side of my leg. He got with the program real quick and edged his knee between my legs, fitting our bodies together like puzzle pieces. His roving hand slid to my backside

186

and then to my lower back. He pulled me closer until the tantalizing ache in my inner thighs spread upward. I moved to brush my lips across his and—

The music stopped, and chills of disappointment circled through me. "It is time for a break, *bailadores*," Soledad said into her microphone.

Damn it! Didn't that woman know I was on fire here? I needed sultry music. Now. Jack and I stayed frozen, my lips against his, my insides melting, until the dance floor cleared. He finally let out a breath and released me. "Timing is everything."

Damn straight. My legs felt weak and my heart threatened to beat right out of my chest as he took my hand and led me back to our table. Antonio looked miserable. Reilly looked ecstatic. I didn't care at the moment. All I wanted to do was pull Jack into a dark corner somewhere and be ravished by him.

I curled my lip. What happened to the independent, kick-ass part of my personality? I tried to channel it, tried to imagine myself as the one doing the ravishing. Impossible. I wanted him in charge, exploring me, tasting me . . . I buried my head in my hands. Oh God, I had it bad.

When I raised my head, Jack looked like he'd completely recovered from our moment on the dance floor. Didn't he need a cold shower or something? Maybe he was just working his tail off to mask his frustration. I watched him, trying to glimpse the lust I'd felt from him. *Nada*. Unbelievable. I tried not to be offended by how quickly he'd gotten over our near-orgasmic moment by concentrating on the original reason I was here. I scooted my chair closer to Reilly. "How's it going? Everything okay?" I asked.

She beamed. "*Fabuloso.*"

I cringed at her accent.

"We're going to go out to Denny's after we're done here. Won't that be fun? I mean, I've always heard it's a blast to go out and order breakfast at two in the morning, but I've never actually done it—"

I could think of a hundred more exciting things to do at two in the morning, every one of them involving Jack and none of them involving Denny's. Waffles or sex? No contest. I wondered again about those handcuffs. Jack's laughter broke into my thoughts. He leaned back in his chair, grinning at something Antonio had said. Hmph. He didn't seem to have sex on the brain.

So maybe waffles would be the more rational choice.

"We've only been here an hour and a half," I said after glancing at my watch. "Let's dance some more before we start making after party plans."

When the band came back twenty minutes later, Jack had gone to the bar for more drinks, Reilly had dragged Antonio out to the dance floor (but not before he'd shot another payback look my way), and I joined Coco and her crew.

"How's it going with *el guapo*?" Coco asked when she caught me sneaking a look at Jack perched at the bar. "You looked pretty cozy. You need a bedroom?"

I flipped my hair behind my shoulder and smiled, determined not to let a little lust, and the fact that Jack seemed to be over his, get in the way of my good time. "*Fabuloso*," I said with way too much perk. Except that now I sounded like Reilly. I distracted myself with conversation, laughing and joking with Coco and company.

Eventually, I saw Jack head back to the table, fresh drinks in hand. Antonio and Reilly ended their dance session and joined him. Finally I went back, too. "Let's dance," I said to Jack just as Soledad announced another short recess for the band.

Double damn. Sinking into my chair, I propped my chin on my fist. "That band takes way too many breaks."

Reilly gazed adoringly at Antonio. "But they're fantastic." Then she looked at me and winked. "Just like penne." Her eyes grew wide. "Or macaroni. Oh, hell, they're both fabulous. Don't you love pasta?"

Antonio frowned and checked his wrist. No watch. "Is it two yet?"

"Oh, you're excited to go to Denny's, too? How sweet," Reilly gushed. "Are we *simpatico*, or what?"

"Or what," Antonio muttered.

I gave Reilly a *chill out* look. "It's ten after ten. You'll have to wait for your waffles," I murmured to her.

If she heard me, she didn't let on. She jumped up and grinned at Antonio. "I'll get you a fresh drink." And before he could tell her what he wanted, and before I could tell her to let *him* buy *her* a drink, she hobbled off to the bar, her ankles angling in directions that didn't look natural.

Antonio watched her for a second before snarling at me. "Does she think she's Jennifer Lopez, for Christ's sake? You owe me big, Lola."

Jack took a swallow of his Corona. "She's not exactly your type."

I bristled. Reilly was a sweet woman with killer boobs who only wanted to please Antonio. He'd never wanted much more than that before. "What's wrong with her?"

One of Jack's eyebrows arched. "Her hair's purple."

The red wash over the blue did give it a purple hue. "So?"

"She's too short for me," Antonio said.

Not with those stilettos on. Jeez. Did he have no appreciation for the trouble Reilly'd gone to so she'd look hot for him? "Have you even tried *talking* to her?"

He smirked. "I'll have plenty of time to talk to her over

189

waffles at Denny's." Then he wagged a finger at me. "Which you're paying for, by the way."

"Ooh. You're such a gentleman."

He looked at me a beat too long. "You have some pictures you wanted to share tonight, didn't you, Lola?" He slapped his leg. "Or are they still at home?" He looked at Jack. "Dude, did I show you—?"

"¡Cállate, Antonio!"

Jack looked from Antonio to me and back. "What am I missing here?"

"Nothing," I snapped.

Thank God he ignored my attitude. He looked back to Antonio. "Why'd you go out with Reilly?"

"Payback. And Lola owes me. Double."

"We're even." I crossed my legs and caught Jack's gaze following the movement. At least I still held his attention.

"Not even close. That dinner—"

I'd already told him to shut up once. Did he just want to humiliate me? "¡Cállate, Tonio!" I snapped again. Jack didn't need to hear that I'd agreed to Sunday dinner only if Antonio went out with Reilly. I shifted, letting my dress slide up my leg a bit more, wondering how I could distract Jack. Maybe a lap dance?

But damn it if Jack couldn't multitask. He checked my legs out again as he asked in a thick voice, "What's the payback for?"

I shot Antonio the sternest expression I could.

He ignored it. "You didn't even stay for the whole dinner, Lola, so it doesn't count. You left to go—" Antonio made air quotes with his fingers. "—'undercover.'"

Jack's face grew stony. "Dinner on Sunday?" He looked at me, his eyes like lasers that were intent on penetrating my guilty conscience. "You didn't want to be there, so you made a bargain—"

"I'm ba-ack." Reilly stumbled as she set a tall drink down in front of Antonio. She teetered, lost her balance, and fell into his lap.

Poor thing, but I had my own problems at the moment. I let Antonio deal with her and turned to Jack. All his good cheer had vanished. My humiliation over spying on him, and his playboy past, had made me hesitant to see him five days ago, but I was over it now.

"So what is this?" His usually playful dimple had an angry edge to it, and the planes of his face were shadowed. "I'm a bargaining tool?"

"That's just how it started—" Gloria Gaynor's "I Will Survive" queued up on the club's speakers, music piped in while the band was *still* on break. *Come on, Soledad.* I needed salsa to get Jack back in the mood, not disco. But nobody else was disappointed. Squeals came from all directions—this was the broken-hearted girl's therapy song.

Before I could elaborate on what exactly this thing that Jack and I were doing was, someone grabbed me from behind and yanked me out of my chair. I nearly pulled a Reilly, toppling onto Jack.

"Come on!" Coco shouted in my ear. She took hold of my hand and dragged me onto the dance floor. Apparently all the women in Club Ambrosía had had broken hearts. They were singing at the top of their lungs, arms swinging above their heads, and of course, I joined in. Why not? I'd been brokenhearted once upon a time. And who knows. If I fell hard enough for Jack, I might be again. Singing "I Will Survive" now might just give me a leg up on the recovery process.

I was laughing by the time the song was over. The disco

extravaganza continued with "Boogie Shoes" and then a Bee Gees revelry.

Jack came up beside me and put his hand on my elbow. His mouth moved, but I couldn't hear what he said. "What?"

"I want to talk to you!" he shouted in my ear.

My backside bumped up against him, at first by accident, the next time deliciously not. "Dance with me."

He laid one hand on my hip and slipped the other around to my stomach, his fingers dangerously splayed and angled downward. Pulling me hard against him, I could tell that he was back in the mood. Thank God. All was not lost.

The band came on again, and I turned and wrapped myself around him. I shivered as he spread his fingers along my lower back. He was so much more than a bargaining tool. I fitted my body up against his, spreading my legs so one of his edged between them. Oh God, finally. Music I could really touch him to. I pressed closer. Oh, yeah. I definitely had his attention. Ay, *Dios*. I had no willpower.

But then the song ended, and Jack had apparently had enough torture. He grabbed me by the hand and pulled me toward the back hallway that led to the restrooms.

"Where are we going?" I asked, stumbling behind him.

His voice came out in a growl. "Somewhere private."

We passed the restrooms and rounded the corner. Dead end. My heart raced when he stopped, pushed me up against the wall, and flattened his palms against the wall on either side of my head. "This isn't a game, Lola. Stop messing with me."

"I'm not—" I started to say, but he moved a finger against my lips.

"Why'd you call me?"

"Because your card was in Emily's—"

"And we're here tonight so Antonio would go out with Reilly—?"

192

"That's how it started—" His finger slid along my lower lip, slipping inside my mouth, the tip of it brushing against my tongue. I caught my breath.

"You didn't want to see me."

Yes, I did! "It's not like you were calling me—"

His jaw tightened, and his hand dropped to his side. In the dim light of the hallway, his fingers managed to find mine and brushed the tips of them. "I've wanted you since I was sixteen years old."

My breath caught in my throat. I stopped myself from grabbing his hand; I knew I had to tread carefully. I had to confess. To tell him that I'd wanted him longer than that. "It's just—I have some pic—" Damn. I couldn't get the words out. I felt my face flush and my knees go weak, and I pressed my palms against the wall to brace myself. All this was just from the touch of his hand and the briefest tease of his lips on the dance floor. Imagine a full-blown kiss. *Ay, Dios.*

He leaned closer, talking low into my lips. "I can't get you out of my head."

I nearly jumped out of my skin when his lips touched mine, soft and warm and moist. "Does it hurt?"

Somehow I managed to whisper, "No."

"Good," he murmured, and then he worked his tongue between my lips. He brought one hand around to the back of my neck and shivers flew up my spine.

He pressed his body up against mine. A quiet moan slipped from me as he took his tongue back—*no!*—and his mouth moved down to my arched neck—*yes!*

My fingers wove through his silky hair as he nudged down the neckline of my top with his lips. If he kept this up, Jack's kisses alone were going to take me into the multiple-orgasm realm. What would happen when he used all the resources at his disposal?

Squeals of tipsy women echoed in the hall. *No!* I knocked the back of my head against the wall just as Coco and her pals tripped down the hall toward us. "Lola!"

Jack buried his face into the crook of my neck "Shit," he murmured into my hair.

I pasted a heavy smile on my face, barely able to keep my eyes focused as she came into view. "Coco."

She looked at us with bleary eyes. "Ah, Jack Callaghan, I presume."

He raised his head, and my skin chilled. "Coco Sandoval," he said, looking royally pissed on top of hot and bothered. "It's been a long time."

He dropped his hand from the wall, and I moved away from him. As frustrated as I was, I was also relieved. Another few minutes, and Jack might have had undressed me right there in the hallway. I was twenty-eight. He was thirty-one. Coco had been right. We needed a bedroom.

I took her by the arm and guided her to the ladies' room, the girls in tow, then made a beeline for our table. A minute later, Jack came up behind me. A quiver shot through me as he put an arm around my waist.

"Where have you been!" Reilly screeched, her lips trembling. "I've been waiting for you. Penne. Um, macaroni. Oh hell." She frowned. "We have to go."

Red alert. I wasn't going anywhere. "It's not even close to two o'clock."

She pulled out her ponytail and fluffed out her hair. "I've been sitting here alone. I—I don't know what happened to—to your—" She heaved a sigh. "—your brother."

I looked around for Antonio. If he'd bailed and left me to pick up the pieces, I'd kill him.

"He went to get a drink," Reilly said.

"How long ago?"

Her bottom lip puffed out, but before she could answer, Jack let go of me and held his hand out to her. "Let's dance, Reilly."

I sat and watched Jack and Reilly do a chaste salsa—if there is such a thing—impressed with how quickly he'd stepped up to the plate for her. His gaze caught mine a few times, and I smiled, batted my eyelashes, let him know that I couldn't stop thinking about him either.

As they wrapped up the dance, Antonio sauntered back to the table, two drinks in hand. *Ah, good man!* He hadn't bailed. He set the drinks down, glared at me, but went to take Jack's place on the dance floor.

An hour and a half, and about a hundred mental cold showers later, Jack and I left Antonio and Reilly with their Denny's waffles.

"I'll follow you home," Jack said, "to make sure you get there safely."

I wasn't going to argue with that. A little while later, I unlocked my front door, dropped my purse on the couch, and turned to face him. "You've got some good moves, Callaghan."

"So do you, Cruz." His lips curved up in a slow smile. "How's the belly button?"

I shrugged, impressively coy. "Waiting for inspection."

His grin widened, then fell when his cell phone rang. He checked the caller ID and shook his head, muttering something under his breath. "I have to take this, Lola."

Who the hell was calling him at almost two o'clock in the morning? "O-*kay.*"

He turned his back to me and flipped open his phone. "What?"

I took a tiny bit of comfort in his tone. He didn't sound happy to get the call, whoever it was. After all, he had my belly button to check out.

Eavesdropping is second nature to me, what with my PI training and my love of *chisme*. He spoke softly, though, and I was distracted by the way his black shirt hung from his shoulders, the clean-shaven skin on the back of his neck, the shape of his legs under his gray pants. He'd grown leaner and stronger and more attractive over the years, and I couldn't wait to experience more of him.

His voice rose slightly, and I thought he said, "Not now, Sarah." Then he lowered his voice again, and no matter how hard I tried, I couldn't make out any more of his conversation. A few seconds later, he ended the call, sliding his phone into his pocket. He turned back to me. "I have to go."

I balked. "You're kidding, right?"

His gaze dragged over me, and I felt desire pulse from him. He raked his hand through his hair, disheveling it in a delicious way, but his jaw pulsed with frustration. "I wish I was."

He came closer, put his hands on either side of my face, and kissed me, long and deep and full of promise. "Right now."

No! I had pent-up lust. I had an orgasm waiting in the wings. "Jack—" I panted as he pulled away. He couldn't leave me in this condition. He *wouldn't*.

"I'll take a rain check on the belly button inspection." And he walked out the door.

Alone in bed a little while later, one question buzzed relentlessly through my mind: Who the *hell* was Sarah?

Chapter 14

woke up the next morning in pain. I sat up, squinted one
eye, and peered at my stomach. "Oh. My. God." My hand
clamped over my mouth. A small area of my skin was pea
green, the shiny silver post the only thing remotely attractive
about my midsection. So much for sexy. Holy shit. I better not
get a heart infection and die. At least not before I lived my
fantasy with Jack Callaghan.

I rolled onto my back, my hand slipping under my pillow as
I fluffed it under my head. My fingers brushed against the slick
surface of—my breathing hitched—the pictures of Jack. Antonio had put them back! But now I had the real McCoy.
What did I need two-dimensional images for?

I pulled the pictures out and looked at them anyway. Really, Jack hadn't changed much. He was broader in the chest
now, more muscular and leaner overall, but he had the same
blue eyes, same chestnut hair, same taunting dimple.

I swallowed. There was no way I could get rid of these photos, because I *didn't* have Jack in the flesh. Sarah had called
and he'd run.

Pushing the disturbing thought out of my mind, I reached for the phone. My first order of business for the day was to find out the truth about tattoos and infections. After some fancy talking, I convinced the receptionist at my doctor's office that I had to speak with the doctor herself. After a short wait, she came on the line. It was a brief conversation, but she confirmed that, in very rare instances, a tattoo could actually cause an infection that could lead to death. It had happened to a student at a local college in just that way.

I thanked the doctor and hung up, but felt less than relieved. My gaze settled on my discolored stomach again. The doctor's theory supported Emily's story, but only worked to heighten my anxiety over my own piercing.

Distraction. That's what I needed, and since Jack wasn't around to be distracted with, I did the next best thing. I threw on a pair of shorts, slipped on a T-shirt, and took Salsa for a low-impact jog around the block. Conquer the pain. I hadn't forgotten about my near-death experience at My Place and watched my back the whole time.

After a long steaming shower I inspected my abrasions from the hit and run. They were healing, and the bruises were starting to fade. My lip was almost back to normal. Just my stomach looked and felt like hell. The things women did for the sake of beauty, fashion, and PI work.

Dressed in lightweight jeans and a sleeveless blouse, I wrapped my hair into a loose bun, making sure a few coppery strands framed my face. Grabbing a jacket for the flower mart, I jammed to pick up Chely, checking the rearview mirror every few minutes. My gut told me it had been Muriel yesterday in Bonatee's building, and it had crossed my mind more than once that she'd followed me there.

Chely bounded out of her front door, climbed breathlessly into the car, and flung a coat into the backseat. "This is so exciting, Lola. A room of flowers. So cool."

I gave her a serious look. "You have to decide today. No more fooling around. The party's in three days."

She fidgeted in her seat during the entire fifteen-minute drive, and I wondered if she was capable of making a decision. Of course, what fourteen-year-old girl, almost fifteen, really knew what she liked? I sure as hell hadn't. Except for Jack. And being a PI.

As I slowed to park in a space in front of the boxy building, a truck barreled past us, horn blaring. I stared after it, but it disappeared, and I dismissed it as something unrelated to my case.

Chely brought my focus back to the *quinceañera*. "What if we go to all this trouble and my mom and I still can't agree?"

Jackets in hand, we climbed the rickety metal staircase that led to the accessory room of the Flower Shoppe. "One of you has to give."

She nodded her head but didn't look convinced. Then she came to a dead stop in the doorway. "Oh," she said, her enthusiasm sagging even more.

I put my hand on her back and propelled her forward. "What now?"

Her forehead crinkled. "It's just, like, this isn't, you know, very *pretty*. Where are the flowers?"

I looked at the familiar room. I'd been coming here since I was seventeen, picking up Abuelita's flower orders. It was no frills—a step below the décor of the huge warehouse stores—with gray metal shelving defining the aisles and boxes stacked high on the shelves. "It's wholesale," I reminded her. "They sell the products, not the atmosphere. We could go to a pretty little florist shop, but it'll cost three times as much."

That got her moving. Tía Marina was nothing if not a tightwad. Chely pulled her shoulders in as she walked, afraid to knock dust from the shelves onto her Cabo Wabo T-shirt.

After several redirects on my part, she spotted a sleek cylindrical vase, heavy on the bottom and about ten inches high.

We picked up black-and-white curling ribbon, confetti to sprinkle on the tables, balloons to decorate the hall, and little mesh gift bags to fill with silver Kisses. She was happy again, and I was relieved that we were moving quickly. Finally, we crossed the warehouse landing outside to the fresh flower room on the opposite side of the building.

"Lola!" Marissa—flower goddess—greeted me as I walked into the room. "I haven't seen you in ages." She gave a wicked smile, enhanced by her spiky black hair and rosy cheeks. "Not that I'm complaining, mind you, but I *love* it when Antonio picks up Abuelita's order."

"Eww." Chely wrinkled her nose and bared her teeth. "Yuck." She leaned in to me and whispered loudly, "Does she, like, *like* Antonio?"

"What's not to like?" Marissa winked. "That man is heaven."

No, *Jack* was heaven. My lips tingled just thinking about his kiss last night.

Chely hopped back and forth on her feet. "Eww, yuck. No he's not. Antonio's my cousin."

"Well, he's not *my* cousin," Marissa said, walking over to one of the center block tables to wrap an order. "And you can tell him I'm waiting for him to call me."

Okay, time to move it along. "We're going to check out the freezer, okay?"

"Sure thing. Holler if you need me." She moved off to help another customer as Chely and I slipped on our jackets. Windows and steel doors separated the work room from the refrigerator. I grabbed hold of the heavy door handle, braced my feet, and put all of my weight into sliding it open. A wall of freezing air hit us as we stepped into the arctic.

"Oh. My. Gosh." Chely's eyes popped open as she stared at

hundreds of buckets full of every type of flower imaginable. "Now this is what I'm talking about."

My teeth chattered, and I pulled my coat tighter around my body. Oh, to have long johns and woolly socks . . .

We tiptoed around puddles of water and up and down the bucket-lined rows until our lips were blue. Finally, after she rejected at least ten suggestions, I snapped. "Come on, Chely! We don't have all day. You don't like the pink roses?"

She hemmed and hawed, studying the rose buckets. "Okay," she finally agreed.

Hallelujah! Although, hadn't she been against pink? Teenagers. Argh!

I picked a bunch of pink buds—wholesale meant we had to buy two dozen—and handed it to her. "Let's go. I'm a Popsicle."

She nodded, her teeth chattering. I grabbed the door handle and pulled. It wouldn't open.

I stomped my feet, trying to send the blood circulating again. Trying again, I put all my weight into it. It didn't budge.

What the hell was I doing wrong? Grab the handle and pull. It should be simple. My heart skittered. Something wasn't right. I pulled again. *Nada.* "Help me, Chely," I said, gritting my teeth and trying again.

Chely's eyelids flew open. "Is it locked? Oh m-my G-God!" She dropped the roses, and we both took hold of the handle.

"On three," I said, my teeth clanking together. "One, t-two, th-th-three!" My toes were going to break off any second. That fueled my determination. I had too many cute sandals to be toeless.

We pulled and heaved, but the door wouldn't open.

"Oh my G-God!" Chely wailed again. "We're g-going to d-die in here. And I n-never even k-kissed a b-boy!"

And I'd kissed Jack only once. I shushed her. "We're n-not going to d-die," I said, but we might lose a couple limbs if someone didn't open the door . . . *now*. I ran to the thick window as fast as my frozen legs would take me and pounded my fists on it.

Marissa had her back to us, still helping the same customer. I peered at them through the foggy glass. Flannel coat, hunched shoulders, steel-colored wiry hair. Muriel!

I was not delusional. I grabbed a bucket, dumped the flowers and water on the ground, and holding it by the handle, swung it with all my might against the window. It bounced off, reverberations shooting up my arms. Was the refrigerator soundproof? Couldn't Marissa hear?

Another customer walked into the warehouse. I banged the window again, waved my icicle arms like an air traffic controller, my movement finally drawing his attention. His reaction was slow, but his eyes finally bugged when he seemed to understand and he raced toward the refrigerator. A second later, we were free. Chely fell into his arms as we both stumbled out into the warmth.

Marissa whirled around. "What happened?"

The man stripped his coat off and wrapped it around Chely.

"Th-the d-door was l-l-locked." I stomped my feet, my mind and body frozen as I looked for the woman in the flannel shirt.

"It can't lock by itself."

"It w-was l-locked." I wheeled my head around. The place was empty. "Where's the l-lady you were h-helping?"

Marissa strode over to examine the refrigerator door. "She left," she said over her shoulder.

I ran on my block feet for the exit.

Marissa followed. "What's going on, Lola?"

"What's her n-name? Why was she h-here?"

"She didn't give me her name. She changed her mind about her order at the last minute."

202

Tires squealed from outside. I made it to the street in time to see the back end of an old red truck race past the building. The license plate was caked with mud. I couldn't make any of it out. Damn.

I stood, rooted to the spot, until I started to thaw and could wiggle my toes again. "Was she an older woman?" I asked as we went back inside. "Pasty skin and a million wrinkles?"

She nodded. "That sounds like her. How'd you know?"

Nerves gripped my gut. I folded my arms and glanced at Chely, who was still shivering and wrapped in a stranger's coat. She'd almost been an innocent casualty, thanks to me. "Just a hunch," I said grimly.

Back at Camacho and Associates, I stood in front of my whiteboard where I'd mapped out all the information I had on Emily Diggs so far. Something wasn't adding up. Even though I suspected Muriel O'Brien was the wrinkled woman in plaid who'd locked Chely and me in the cooler at the florist, I couldn't picture her as Emily's killer—or at least not on her own. And if she was acting on behalf of someone else, I had no idea why.

Muriel only managed businesses owned by someone else. She had no motive for murder. I had to delve deeper to find out who was the puppet master behind Muriel.

I looked through Emily's notebook again. More scattered, random words popped out at me. Her name, *Emily*, written over and over; different letters jotted down in various, meaningless combinations; Jack's name and the phone number to the newspaper; *my lie*; the word *investigation* scribbled out in dark, angry pencil marks; the word *circumstantial*, also crossed out.

Several times there was a series of words: *tattoo, infection in the blood stream, heart failure, death*. What happened to Garrett had been foremost on Emily's mind.

I'd checked with Manny, who'd checked with Seavers, and there was no indication that she'd ever gone to the police with any suspicions about the fatal tattoo. She'd been killed before her suspicion had turned into anything more substantial. The million-dollar question was this: Had she been killed because her suspicions were warranted?

Somebody tapped my shoulder, and instinct kicked in. I wheeled around, throwing up my arms in a self-defense stance.

"Dolores!" Sadie yelped, jumping back.

I relaxed. "Don't do that."

"Touchy, aren't you?"

Damn it if she wasn't right. I was completely on edge. Being targeted for murder can have that effect on a person. "I'm fine."

"What's going on with the case?"

I cocked an eyebrow at her. I didn't feel like sharing with her, even if she did project this I'm-in-charge attitude.

"Nothing's going on," I said. If you didn't count someone trying to turn me into roadkill at My Place, and then into an ice sculpture this morning . . .

"Nothing?"

"Nothing." I eyed Manny, who was hunched over his desk in his office. He was either ignoring us completely or truly oblivious of our presence. My bet was on the former. Superstar PIs were never oblivious.

"I'm free right now. I can lend a hand."

Reilly snickered from her corner.

Sadie shot invisible evil-eye darts at Reilly's back, then made her voice sweet as pie. "We're a team, Dolores. You need to remember that."

Over Sadie's shoulder, I saw Manny look at us. *Ah-ha.* He *was* all-knowing, all-seeing. I knew it.

Sadie studied my whiteboard, her hand on her hip, a picture of perfect posture and perfectly messy hair. "What about that corporation that owns the tattoo shop?" she said after a few minutes. "I could find the principals for you."

Manny walked out of his office and came toward us. "Good idea, but Dolores can do it."

Her voice turned flat. "No," she said, "I can do it." She laid her hand on my shoulder and gave a light scorpion squeeze. "Take help when it's offered, Dolores." Then she lifted her steely gaze to Manny. "You never know when things will suddenly change."

Ice shot through my veins, but I forced a smile. "Okay, thanks."

Sadie's eyes flashed as she went to her computer. She cued up the search screen and began typing rapidly.

Manny turned on his heel and went back to his office.

And I popped an Advil for my pounding head and aching stomach.

I laid my purse on the conveyor belt at the L Street entrance of the domed capitol building and stepped through the metal detector. Ryan Case's office, marked with a green name tag on the wall, was on the fifth floor, off the beaten track. He was low man on the totem pole.

I paced up and down the hallway, psyched myself up, and turned back to Case's door.

A sparring session later might chase away the heebie-jeebies that were taking up residence in my body. I did not like being a target.

I steeled my nerves and burst into Case's suite. A startled assistant popped up from his desk just inside the door. "Can I help you?"

I'd been planning on playing it straight. *My name's Dolores*

Cruz. I'm looking into the death of Emily Diggs—blah, blah, blah. Screw that. I went with my spastic mood. My new piercing gave me the perfect cover story. "I need to see the assemblyman," I said, letting my voice inhabit a strain of the hysteria I felt deep inside.

He shot me a *you've got to be kidding* look before glancing at his day planner. "I don't see an appointment, Miss—"

"I don't have an appointment, but I need to see him." I wagged my finger at him. "I'm a voter, you know."

"What's this regarding?"

"What's this regarding? What's this regarding? Let me show you." I yanked up my shirt to show him my navel piercing. "Just look at this!"

He sputtered, and I glanced down to see what color my stomach had turned to in the last couple of hours. Bluish green with a hint of sickly yellow. Gross. Perfect.

A door opened at the end of a narrow hallway, and a man walked out. His eyes zeroed in on my discolored navel.

I recognized Case from his photo in the *Bee*, although he looked years older now. "Assemblyman," I said. I didn't want security called, so I curbed my hysteria slightly. "Just the person I want to see."

His heavy cheeks pulled his mouth into a perpetual frown, but his eyes lit up. Why not? Here I was, his constituent, in the discolored flesh. "Yes?"

The assistant, looking put-upon now, stepped forward. "She doesn't have an appointment, sir."

I shot him the evil eye. *Back off, buddy.* "I have a right to see my assemblyman," I said. "He works for me, you know." I looked at Case with his saucer cheeks and slicked-back hair. Yuck. But I managed a smile. "It's not an unreasonable request."

"I only have a minute, Miss—"

"Cruz." Damn. It came out without thinking. Rule number—I don't know—five or something: Never give your identity away if you don't have to. I'd been advertising my name all over town. No wonder someone was out to kill me. I'd made myself an easy target. Rookie mistake.

Case just nodded politely. Had his daughter passed on the messages that I'd stopped by his reelection headquarters and that Emily Diggs was dead? There was no way for me to know, but if she had, Case wasn't letting on.

He flashed a well-practiced toothy smile. Career politician. "It's fine," he said to his assistant. "This way," he said to me, leading me into his office. "What can I do for you?"

I went with my hypothesis. Imagining myself as Emily, I launched into a tirade. "Regulations on tattoo parlors. That's what you can do for me," I said. "There needs to be rules that make it safe. Just look at this." I yanked up my shirt again and pointed to my piercing. "Just look at what he did to me."

Case brushed a stray strand of slick hair back into place. His face turned the color of my stomach. "Ms. Cruz, please."

"That tattoo guy said everything would be fine. And look at me now. I know I have an infection! I just know it." I collapsed onto a straight-backed chair that faced his desk. "He's a liar," I sobbed. "I may never be normal again."

He frowned, his cheeks pressing down on the corners of his mouth. "Perhaps a doctor would be better suited to help you deal with this, Ms. Cruz. Or a lawyer. May I suggest the yellow pages?" He started toward the door. "Now, if there's nothing else . . ."

I needed to know if Emily had talked with this man. I went fishing. "A lawyer can't help me. I have a friend that just died because of a tattoo from the exact same tattoo parlor. I was stupid to go there—" The truth. I faked a sob. "Now I might die, too."

207

The sickly greenish-yellowish color drained from his face. "Your friend died of a tattoo?"

"That's right. And nobody did anything." I jumped up and pointed at him. "You have to write a bill or a law or something so it's safer to get tattoos. I can't believe no one's ever asked you about this. Isn't this your *job*?" My voice rose. "There have to be other concerned people. Look at my stomach. Who's going to want me now?" Besides Jack, of course, which was a given. Except he'd left for Sarah. Argh.

"Miss Cruz," Case said, opening the door. "You should see a doctor."

Oh no. I wasn't leaving yet. *Think, think.* "My friend saw a doctor after her son died. He said it was true. It could happen." I covered my face and wailed. "Oh God, I'm going to die!" I gave a big sniff and calmed myself down. "I shouldn't have gone there. Not after poor Garrett—" I looked at the ceiling. "I'm sorry, Emily." I buried my head in my hands. "I'm sorry I didn't believe you." I squinted and peered at him through my lashes, wondering if my sob story would soften his heart any. Or if Emily's name would ring any bells.

He stopped dead in his tracks. "What are you talking about?"

Bingo! "Poor Garrett never saw it coming. One day he's getting a tattoo, two weeks later he's dead." I jabbed my finger in the air again. "That's not right, you know. His mother was so upset." My adrenaline was pumping. I tried to bring it down, to ease my tension.

The color had returned to Case's face, but his tone was guarded now. "His mother?"

"Poor Emily. She knew that tattoo killed Garrett. She *knew*. Why didn't I believe her?" I sank into a chair and shook my head. "But I didn't believe her. I just thought she was grieving and n-now *I'm* going to d-die. Just like Emily and Garrett. Why, oh why was I so stupid?"

208

"The mother's dead?" He swept back another wayward strand of hair.

I nodded, running my fingers under my eyes. "She drowned. So sad."

His Adam's apple slid up and down in his throat as he checked his watch. He walked toward the door. "Miss Cruz, I'm sure you're not going to die. I'd love to be of some assistance, but I haven't taken a position on the body art industry—"

"She said she talked with a man who could help her. A politician, she said. It wasn't you?"

He shook his head. "I'm afraid she must have spoken with someone else. I'm very sorry that Ms. Diggs and her son are dead, but I'm sure it's unrelated to Tattoo Haven."

Ay, Dios. I tried not to let my shock show on my face. He'd called Emily Ms. Diggs *and* said Tattoo Haven—all in one breath, but I hadn't mentioned either by name. He knew the details, so why was he lying?

His face grew hard. Uh-oh. Had he realized his slip?

I jumped up from the chair. Time to end this meeting. "The industry needs regulations," I said. "You can be the first to demand it."

Case's shoulders hunched as he followed me out of his office and into the reception area.

I flashed him my awful-looking navel again before I dashed out the door into the main corridor. "You can save lives, Assemblyman. Think about it."

Chapter 15

maneuvered my car into a spot along the curb in front of Mary Bonatee's house, taking a second to peer up and down the sidewalk. No suspicious characters lurking about. No Muriel. No Case. Thank God.

I stepped along the cracked sidewalk up to the hidden door. My plan was to determine if Emily might have been blackmailing Mary or her father. My pretense in stopping by was to grab some more of Sean's toys to take to him. Poor kid needed familiar things around him.

Bea pulled the door open with a flourish. "Did you find her?" she said with her first breath. Before I could answer, she wagged a long-sleeved arm at me. "The cops—" Her voice cracked with emotion. "—they say she's—she's—dead."

My heart broke for Emily's friend. It was true that it's the people left behind who suffer the most. "I'm so sorry, Bea. I'm doing everything I can to find out what happened."

She lifted her chin, peering at me from under the brim of her cap. "I know you are. That's good," she said, nodding. "That's real good." Her gaze dropped to my hands. "Where's Emily's notebook? Do you still have it?"

"The journal's really helpful, Bea. I still need it." I didn't elaborate that Manny had handed the original over to the police and that I was using a copy.

She didn't respond, but just shuffled back to the sitting room and stared at the muted, flickering television. I stood there feeling like I'd let her down. Bea had really cared about Emily.

I pushed my sunglasses to the top of my head, stepped inside, and closed the door. Cool air washed over me. Air-conditioning. God, I loved it. A moment later, Mary walked down the stairs, looking fresh and crisp. I tried not to pat my hair. The leftover curls from my salsa dancing night gave me a Girls Gone Wild look. Mary, on the other hand, was like a mannequin, her short plastic-looking hair staying put even when she shook her head.

"Hi," I said. Great opening. I blamed my lack of cleverness on my sexual frustration.

"Hi."

Huh—seemed she suffered from the same ailment. Maybe repressed orgasms were an epidemic. God help us, but we'd survive.

I cut right to the chase. "You heard about Emily?"

She nodded, but her mouth stayed shut.

I wasn't in the mood to beat around the bush, not considering how she'd held out on me at our first meeting, so I went for the jugular. Mary Bonatee needed to start talking. "Sean's father," I started.

She stiffened and tried to set her lips in a hard line, but they wavered. "What?"

"Do you know who Sean's father is?"

Mary's shoulders drooped as if she'd suddenly lost the will to fight her conflict. "What does it matter?"

"Everything matters when someone dies violently." I folded

my arms as if I were a disappointed parent. "You neglected to mention that you and Allison Diggs went to school together. You knew Emily before she moved in here."

"I played with Ally, so yes, I knew Emily."

"Why didn't you tell me this last time I was here?"

Mary's deer-in-the-headlights gaze dropped to her twisting hands. She was nervous, sure, but my gut told me she wasn't the enemy. "It didn't seem important."

I wasn't sure it was important either, but it felt more like a lie than an omission. "Did you know Emily and your dad dated?"

She nodded. "It started after my parents got divorced, but it didn't last very long. Sh—she—"

"You think she broke up your parents?" I finished for her.

Mary hesitated, but finally muttered, "Yes."

I studied her—could her blame for Emily have turned to hate? She bit her lip, and a flurry of tears slid down her cheeks. "That's what you meant when you said that thing about parents not understanding the impact they have, right?"

She smeared her tears across her cheeks with her fingertips and nodded. "Sean has my father's eyes. His features. Does he think I'm stupid? That I wouldn't put it together?"

I leaned against the staircase. As gut-wrenching moments went, this was spectacular. She was really hurting. "I'm sure he knew he could trust you to be good to Sean." She stayed silent, so I went on. "Is it possible that Emily could have been blackmailing your father?"

She thought about this, wiping her eyes a final time. "Blackmailing him with what?"

"That's what I'm trying to figure out. Can we go through how Emily came to live here one more time?"

She sighed. "My dad called me at the end of June and said he wanted to let the room to someone. But he *knew* my friend was living here. He had no right to kick her out."

212

"But he did it anyway?"

"Oh yeah. Took her to dinner and broke the news. She ended up moving back in with her parents, and believe me, she did not want to do that."

"Why do you think it was so important to him that Emily move in here?"

Mary shrugged and shook her head. "He said everything depended on it. That I just had to understand."

"But she lived in Sacramento, right? Why'd she need a new place?"

"She used to have some sort of corporate job, but when she was living here, she worked at a café." Mary's brows pinched. "She moved a long time ago, before Sean was born. Took Ally and Garrett and just left. They were in Sacramento still, but I don't know where. Ally called now and then, but she never said much."

Maybe it was her obsession with finding out why Garrett had died that prompted the career change as well as her return to her old stomping ground. I went back to my original question. "Could it have been blackmail?"

She straightened, her own tiger eyes suddenly glowing. "I can't see my dad denying Emily money if she'd asked. Something went down between them, but I think he still cared about her. And if it would have helped Sean . . ."

She trailed off, and I felt for her. She wanted to believe the best about her dad, but at the moment, she didn't know how. I let Mary talk, still looking for that big break—that moment of clarity—but it didn't come. "And your mother?"

"My mom passed away a few years ago."

"Oh, I'm sorry." So much for Emily threatening to tell Bonatee's wife about Sean. "Did you ever tell Emily you knew who Sean's father was?"

She shook her head. "I wanted to, but I—I just couldn't.

213

My dad didn't tell me, so I wasn't going to be the one to bring it up."

So Sean was a gigantic white elephant standing between Mary and her father. "Your dad said you went to kindergarten with Emily's daughter. Does she still call? Do you still talk?"

She looked uncomfortable. Almost guilty. "Sometimes. We drifted apart."

"Why?"

She paused as if she were considering how to answer that. "We have a friend who works at a tattoo place," she finally said. "Ally started getting tattoos, kind of obsessively—then her brother got a few. They all started doing ecstasy and smoking pot. It wasn't my thing, so I stepped back."

Smart girl. "Did Allison know your dad and Emily had an affair?" I asked.

Mary's black hair stayed perfectly in place as she nodded her head. "Oh yeah, she knew. We were both horrified. We used to stay up at night and talk about it." Her eyes darkened. "But she never told me about Sean."

I remembered how Allison had flung herself out of my car in order to see her younger brother. Her words hurtled through my mind. "She shouldn't have kept Sean from his dad," she'd said. That secret had driven a wedge between Emily and her daughter, but *why* Emily kept Sean to herself might always be a mystery. Maybe Lucy had been right and the secret had been fueled by fear that Bonatee would win a custody battle if it came down to it.

I went back to Emily's obsession. "Did she talk about Garrett's death?"

"Not much. She hated how he'd changed. How he'd been influenced by Ally and had started getting tattoos and doing drugs. It seemed better not to talk about it."

214

She'd said the magic word—*tattoos*—and I jumped. "What did you think of his tattoos?"

She frowned. "One was a cross. It was okay. A little big. One was a yin/yang. It wasn't as good. Kind of small, and the black smeared into the white." She thought for a second. "I can't remember the others—Oh! He gave himself one. It was new, I think. I saw it at the funeral. It was on the top of his hand." She shuddered. "It looked awful. Pretty rough."

"How do you know he gave it to himself?"

"Ally told me. This guy we know showed Garrett how to do it. Apparently it's supposed to look like—" She made air quotes with her fingers. "—a 'prison tattoo.'"

"Huh," I said, but inside I cheered. This corroborated Emily's suspicions and what Zod had said. It didn't point a finger at the killer, but with the doctor's statement that a tattoo *could* actually cause a heart infection, it seemed like Emily had been right about Garrett's death. "What did Emily think of the tattoo?"

Mary's eyebrows pinched together as she thought. "I think she blamed Ally for getting Garrett into all that stuff. They never got along, but Garrett was like the final nail in the coffin."

I asked a few more questions, but Mary had nothing else to offer. "Can I take some of Sean's things to him?" I asked, remembering the other reason I'd come.

She nodded. "My roommate came back. I packed Sean's stuff up so she could get settled again."

Ah. Now I noticed two produce boxes sitting off to one side. I chided myself for not spotting them earlier. Notice the details. It's what any good PI did. How many years did I have to have under my belt before I didn't feel like a rookie anymore?

I picked up the box with a baseball bat sticking out the top. Mary followed me outside with the other. "Mary," I said, nudging my box into the back of my car, a sudden thought occurring to me. "Was your dad seeing anyone before Emily showed up?"

Her lips thinned, and she squeezed her eyes shut for a moment. "He's always dated on and off."

"Anyone particular?"

She hesitated for a second, and I thought she was going to clam up. "Maybe. I went to his office a couple weeks ago. He was with someone." Her voice broke. "It seemed like they were—" She hesitated. "—pretty close."

"Do you know who it was?" I asked, probably a bit too eagerly.

"No."

"What were they talking about?"

"I didn't hear much. The woman was sort of crying. He was telling her that it wasn't her fault and that everything would be all right. Then he said that they weren't meant to be together, and she started crying more. That's when I left."

Mary helped me load the boxes with Sean's stuff into my car, and I drove away. My cell phone, barely audible, played "La Bamba" before I'd gotten out of her neighborhood.

I flipped it open. "This is Dolores."

"I got your corporation for you," Sadie said. Her voice was completely professional. I had a feeling Manny wasn't around, since his presence seemed to send her off the deep end.

"Okay."

"Not over the phone. Come into the office, and we'll talk."

It was all about control with her. She wanted to be the boss. "It's not like my phone's bugged, Sadie."

Click. She hung up on me. "Fine," I barked at the phone. "I'm on my way."

Ten minutes later I walked through the banal lobby of Camacho and Associates and into the meeting room. Reilly gave me a dopey, lovesick look. I hadn't had the chance to talk to her since I'd left her at Denny's. *Pobrecita*. I hoped Antonio wouldn't break her heart too badly.

I hurried past her with a quick smile and stood next to Sadie in front of the whiteboard where I'd recorded all my case notes. My nostrils flared when I saw she'd changed the timeline. Damn it. How dare she butt in.

Then I gasped at what she'd added.

- *Ryan Case and George Bonatee, owners of My Place, Just Because, and Tattoo Haven. Corporation name: B.C. Incorporated*
- *Businesses managed by Muriel O'Brien*
- *Todd Case is tattoo artist at Tattoo Haven, son of Ryan Case*

"No, the tattoo guy's name was—" I slapped my hand over my mouth. Todd. Zod. The photograph I'd seen of the Case family in the newspaper appeared in my mind. If the clean-cut kid in the picture was the pierced and tattooed Zod, that was some transformation.

Sadie shuffled and took a step closer. One side of her mouth curved up. "Vital information, right, Sherlock?"

I let the nickname go. "The tattoo guy at Tattoo Haven is Ryan Case's son. Bonatee and Case own the businesses. . . ." My mind reeled back to something Mary had said when I'd first met her. Her roommate's name had been Joanie. As in Case. I'd been so wrapped up with learning about Garrett and the tattoo he'd done on himself that the name hadn't registered. It wasn't just Allison and Zod that knew each other, and it wasn't just the Diggs and the Bonatees that were connected. It looked like the Cases were old friends, too.

My questions were whether or not the assemblyman believed Emily's claim that Garrett died from a heart infection that stemmed from a tattoo, and whether or not he knew that Todd had taught Garrett how to tattoo himself. "Are you sure about this?" I asked, feeling new respect for Emily and the mission I thought she'd been on.

"Positive."

Sadie's smug attitude didn't even bug me at the moment. I was too busy being surprised by the fact that George Bonatee was part owner of the tattoo shop. If Emily had come to him for help, it was like the gingerbread boy asking the wolf to get her across the river. By helping her pursue a case against Tattoo Haven, he'd have implicated himself as a responsible party.

Sadie leaned her backside against the table with her ankles crossed, watching me. "Epiphany?"

"Sort of," I answered. "This helps, thanks."

Sadie frowned, her eyebrows pinched in confusion. She wasn't in the practice of saying thank you to anyone, and I didn't often say it to her. "You're welcome," she murmured, as if she couldn't quite say the words at full volume.

She ambled to the whiteboard and studied it, still looking puzzled. I couldn't take pleasure in flustering her right now. I needed to reflect on how intertwined Bonatee and Case were. I ticked the connections off on my fingers.

1. Bonatee and Case were partners in three small businesses.
2. Case's son showed Garrett how to tattoo himself, the same tattoo that was potentially responsible for Bonatee's ex-lover's son's death. That was big.
3. I mulled. Joanie, Case's daughter, lived in the house Bonatee owned and was friends with Mary, and Todd Case had to be the tattoo guy Mary had referred to.
4. My mind was blank, and I couldn't come up with a fourth connection.

I didn't need another one. Three was enough.

I didn't know what any of it meant yet, but things were starting to make sense. Sort of.

Manny sauntered out of his office, his limp altering the thud of his boots against the carpet. Sadie's body reacted to the sound of his approach, her spine almost crackling as it straightened. She stood tall, all five feet three inches of her.

He leaned back against the conference table, crossing his ankles and posed exactly as Sadie had been a few minutes ago. Her expression grew tight as she turned around to face him. "Boss."

He nodded stiffly at her then turned to me, his gaze slow and steady.

I swallowed, uncomfortable under the scrutiny.

"Fill me in—" He paused, and I thought he sent a coded look toward Sadie. "—*poderosa.*" My eyes crossed. He'd called me "strong woman" just to irk her. These two were ready to do covert battle, and I was a pawn. What the hell was *that* about?

Sadie seethed. She sure as hell didn't know what Manny'd called me, but whatever tone she'd heard in his voice was apparently enough to piss her off. She fixed her steely eyes on him, then at me. "Yes. Come on, detective. Fill *the boss* in."

I should have taken my pleasure in throwing her off balance earlier, because now the tables had turned again, and she wasn't going to be placated by my thanking her. I worked to keep my tone even and explained the latest developments to Manny, ending with the surprise connection between the Case, Diggs, and Bonatee families.

He rubbed his thumb over the cleft in his chin and summarized. "So, presumably, Emily thought her son died as a result of a tattoo given by Todd Case, but most likely cause of death was directly related to the tattoo he gave himself."

I nodded. "Right."

"And the death-by-tattoo thing can really happen?"

"Apparently it can, although it's not common. Most likely there had to have been some underlying heart condition"—just like Bonatee had said Garrett had—"in order for an infection to take hold."

Manny's gaze didn't waver. "So what now?"

"If Emily went to Bonatee for help and *if* she figured out that he and Case owned the tattoo place, she may have tried to appeal to their compassion. If that's the case, she walked into a minefield instead." *Ah!* Another blackmail theory struck. "She obviously wanted somebody held responsible for Garrett's death. Maybe she decided to use Sean as leverage. She could have introduced Bonatee to him and then threatened to take him away if he didn't help her. But if Bonatee didn't want to help her, then Emily was a liability to him."

"We need to tag-team Bonatee and Case," Sadie said. "I'll take one, and Dolores can take the other."

Manny turned to her. "No."

"No?" She tensed, a vein popping on her forehead.

"I said no. Dolores has already established contact. She'll continue her own way."

My cell phone blared from the depths of my purse. I grabbed for it, almost deaf from the suddenly high volume but content to let Sadie and Manny duke out whether or not I needed help. "Hello?"

"Lola?" Jack's voice on the other end of the line threw me off-kilter.

"Jack. Hi." I sensed Manny's attention shift. His intense gaze was on me. I moved to the corner and turned my back on him and Sadie.

"You there? Hello?" Jack said.

"I'm here." Just the sound of his voice shot my blood pressure sky high. If salsa dancing were sex, I'd be completely ruined for any other man.

"You busy?"

"I'm at work."

"I'll be quick, then. Dinner. Tonight. My place."

Be still my heart. Could I wait that long? I turned my head and dropped my voice. "You're going to cook?"

"Yep."

Ooh, I couldn't remember the last time a man cooked for me. "And you're not going to run out on me before dessert?" I asked coyly, only slightly embarrassed at my nerve.

"Dessert is going to be better than the main course, and there's no way I'd miss it," he said, his voice laden with innuendo. "Seven o'clock." And he hung up.

I slipped my phone back in my purse, smiling to myself. I was already counting the minutes.

Reilly spun around on her chair, her eyes saucer wide, as I came back into the main room. She'd been so quiet, I'd forgotten she was there. "He's seriously cooking for you?" she whispered. "And dessert, too? So cool, though not surprising after seeing you two dance last night. Do you think Antonio would make me a meal?"

I bugged my eyes, trying to signal her to stop, but she just kept blabbing. "He sure did warm up to me," she said. "Ordered me extra waffles."

"Reilly," I snapped when I could get a word in. "Not now."

She flicked her gaze to Manny and Sadie, clamped her mouth shut, and zipped her lips before spinning her chair back to face her computer.

Manny's look turned dark and angry, and Sadie's matched it. Neil lumbered into the room from the direction of his lair. He dropped a computer printout on the table. "The ex-wife is definitely dead," he said to me.

221

I thanked Neil for running the check. I hadn't doubted Mary or Bonatee, but I had to be sure. "So she's out as a suspect." That left four likely motives. Did Zod, fearing implication in Garrett's death, kill Emily to silence her, thereby saving his own ass? Or did Case do it for him to protect his son or his business investment or both? Or, if Emily had been blackmailing him, had Bonatee killed her to stop the threat? And finally, if Bonatee was pissed that Emily had kept his son from him, maybe he'd killed her out of revenge and to have custody of Sean.

There were too many questions, I thought, and in my gut I felt like I was still missing something big.

Chapter 16

I stood in my black-and-red sheer demi-bra with matching panties and frowned at the half dozen outfits scattered on my bed. What did I want to project with Jack tonight? Innocent virgin? Sultry temptress? Hmm. If the underwear fit . . .

The phone rang, and I answered with a clipped, "Yes?"

"What kind of greeting is that?" my mother demanded on the other end.

The kind that says I'm in a hurry and don't know what to wear. "Sorry, Mami."

"Are you coming to Abuelita's? Fish tacos tonight."

"Not tonight. I have plans."

Her tone became accusatory. "You have not been here in a week."

"I'll come by tomorrow, Mami. I'm going out to dinner." I braced myself for the inquisition.

"Lunch tomorrow, then," she said.

I pulled the phone away from my ear and stared at it. Had I heard right? She wasn't probing for information? Had the world turned upside down? "Okay."

I hung up, feeling like the universe was a little off balance. Odd, but not my problem tonight. Back to my wardrobe dilemma. I held up a T-shirt, looking at it in the mirror. My lip was as good as healed, and my other abrasions were barely visible at this point. The phone rang again. "I knew you couldn't resist, Mami," I said when I answered it.

Silence.

"Hello?" I said again. Still nothing. So she *could* wait till tomorrow. I pressed the OFF button, dropped the phone, and discarded the shirt. Way too casual—and it said nothing about wanting to be ravished. Which, I wasn't ashamed to admit, I did want. Badly.

I rifled through the closet and pulled out a red sleeveless wraparound dress. I held it at arm's length to take a good look. Hmm. It might work. Just the right combination of erotic and demure—in a *take me* kind of way.

The phone rang again. Jeez, couldn't a girl get dressed in peace?

I pulled it out from under the discarded T-shirt and pressed ON. "Hello?"

"Dolores Cruz."

My heart stopped for a second. The voice was low and raspy. I immediately went on alert. "Speaking."

"Butt out, or next time, you'll end up with more than a few scrapes."

I dropped the dress. "Excuse me?"

"You've been lucky twice. Third time, it'll be over." Hostile and matter-of-fact. Definitely not a *Mister Rogers* voice.

My stomach clenched, and my palms started to sweat. I looked around, half expecting the boogeyman to jump out from behind my bed. "How'd you get this number?"

But the phone went dead.

I took a deep breath. I couldn't even tell if the garbled voice had been a man or woman. How pathetic was that?

But whoever it was had done their job. I was spooked. If

they'd found my unlisted home number, how hard would it be to find my address? Hell, someone had been following me. They probably already knew where I lived.

Pacing the room in my underwear, I tried to control how freaked I was. *Cálmate*, Lola, I told myself. Think. Think. I'd scared someone enough to try to run me over outside My Place and lock me in a florist's refrigerator. Maybe I *was* in the wrong profession. No way did I have a death wish.

But even the mere thought of quitting made my stomach knot. I was Lola, PI. This was my destiny. *Con cuidado*. That would just be my new mantra. I would do everything with extreme care.

I glanced at the clock. Six thirty. Argh! No time to dwell on it. I had a date—the perfect distraction. I was allowed a night off, wasn't I? I just hoped I could turn my mind off.

I slipped into the wraparound red dress and added my stripper shoes—a perfect match, as it turned out. Sultry temptress all the way. I didn't do anything half-assed.

Pulling the front strands of my hair back into a barrette, I left the rest down, running my fingers through it to fluff it out. I put on some fiery red lipstick then added big silver hoop earrings and studied the effect in the mirror. *Perfecta*. Jack wouldn't be able to keep his hands off me. Which was just what I wanted. And needed. *Listo*. I was ready, baby.

"About time." Antonio waited for me by the front door, my car keys in his hand.

"What are you doing?"

"I need your car. No rental yet." He gave me a low whistle and a twisted grin that said he knew what I wanted out of this night with Jack. "Not exactly playing hard to get, eh?"

I punched him in the arm—for a lot of reasons, only one of which was actually related to what he'd said. "You can take my car, but I need it back in the morning."

"Oh, planning an all-nighter, are we?"

I waggled my head. "No, smart guy. Jack can bring me home."

The drive to Jack's place—a loft apartment off J and Sixteenth—was a quick ten minutes. Antonio stopped in front of the building and let me out. I slammed the door, and he rolled down the window. "Don't do anything I wouldn't do, sis."

That left the field wide open. I smiled sweetly. "You mean you have boundaries?"

"Hell yes, I do. And her name is Reilly."

Great. He'd said it. Now I knew for a fact that my friend would have a broken heart. "Reilly's great. You should consider yourself lucky to have her attention."

He peeled out in response. I took a quick look around to make sure no bad guys were lurking, ready to run me over. All clear. I took a deep breath to calm my nerves and focused on the moment.

Jack was waiting for me.

I found his loft on the third floor, an envelope taped just under the peephole of the door. *Lola* was scrawled in thick black marker across the crisp white envelope.

I pulled out a half sheet of paper.

L—
Had to run out last minute to fax an article.
Make yourself at home. I'll be back by 7:15.
—J

I stood there with my hands on my hips, feeling indignant. He'd be here for dessert, but not for the appetizer? What kind of girl did he think I was? And didn't the guy have his own fax-copier-combo machine? What kind of reporter was he?

Still, I couldn't help but look at this as a golden opportunity—an open invitation to nose around. If he knew me better—knew that I'd started my snooping career back when I was a teenager, with him as my subject—he'd have thought twice about leaving me alone in his apartment.

His mistake.

I tried the doorknob. Unlocked—a bold move, especially downtown. "Jack?" I called as I entered, just to be sure. I stood inside the door, peered down the short hallway, and waited. Silence. He wasn't here.

The hallway led into the kitchen. It was a warehouse apartment—sleek and stylish with fifteen-foot ceilings, concrete floors, and a concrete counter between the dining area and the kitchen. It totally fit Jack.

I braced myself for the discovery of dishes stacked in the sink, an overflowing garbage can, crumbs on the counter, and an unswept floor.

His kitchen was spotless.

I pulled open the stainless steel door of the refrigerator and stood back, trying to figure out what it all meant.

It held more food than mine. So he didn't have an aversion to shopping. Good to know, but he was obviously too good to be true. He had to be hiding something.

Then I remembered. Oh yeah. He was hiding Sarah.

I went back to my perusal. A half-empty carton of low-fat milk and the expected bottles of beer lined the door compartment next to bottles of every imaginable condiment: mustard, ketchup, pickles, barbecue sauce, teriyaki sauce, even a raspberry chipotle sauce.

¡Dios mío! Was he a metrosexual? Did I want a metrosexual? What the hell *was* a metrosexual, anyway? And could Abuelo ever accept one in *la familia* Cruz?

I let the refrigerator door close and leaned back against the bar, my head spinning. I was getting way ahead of myself. One night of salsa dancing didn't mean he needed Abuelo's blessing. Anyway, he was Catholic. That was good enough for me.

I looked at the clock—7:05. Ten minutes before he'd be back. Just enough time to have a quick peek at the rest of the loft.

A small blond-wood table with two chairs on either side was centered just off the kitchen. A heavy black vase was in the middle, a spray of lavender roses fanning out of it. I moved on, concentrating on the details of the apartment. A shaggy gray area rug, a black leather couch, two chairs. A TV and stacks of books—John Grisham, classic sci-fi, a slew of nonfiction, and every book Dan Brown had written.

Two guitars—one acoustic, one electric—perched on a double stand in the corner. I vaguely remembered that he'd started playing guitar back in high school. I plucked the steel strings of the acoustic and my pulse kicked up. Who didn't love a musician?

I kept walking, but my heart skittered to a stop when I caught sight of the foot of Jack's bed. A thousand thoughts swerved around in my head at once, beginning and ending with the fact that someone was out to kill me, so what if this was my last night? I should make it a great one.

I had the right underwear on.

A blinding image of the two of us rolling around on his queen-size love nest flashed into my mind, and I felt dizzy. ¡Ay, Dios! Don't make any sudden moves, and slowly, very slowly, turn away from the bed, Lola.

But, of course, I couldn't. If I wanted to do justice to my snooping, which of course I did, I *had* to tackle the bedroom. It was essential, really. Any PI worth her salt would leave no stone unturned. And hadn't I vowed to take extreme care with everything I did?

I took a deep breath, but sidestepped at the last second, making a beeline for the bathroom instead. It was spotless, like everything else. God, he was my dream man. How was I going to resist him?

Skeletons. He had to have something, anything that might help me keep my sanity tonight—I'd wanted him for too long to just lose control. The medicine cabinet. Of course. There were bound to be secrets in there. Advil, deodorant, cologne, toothpaste, condoms, a toothbrush—

My brain screeched to a halt and backtracked. Condoms? I jammed my hands on my hips. Why did he need condoms?

I took the box out to look more closely. Not just condoms. A *jumbo*-size box of condoms. My head started pounding. And it was open. I dropped it, the little compact packages spilling onto the counter. Shit!

As I pushed the packages into a pile and started returning them to the box, I registered the details. TROJAN HER PLEAS-URE CONDOMS. Twenty-four per box.

I froze. Whose pleasure had they assisted, damn it, and how many were missing? The guy was thirty-one, smart, charismatic, and gorgeous. There was no way he lived like a monk, but the thought of Jack touching another woman made my skin crawl, my heart go cold, and my fists clench. He was back in my life. I wanted him touching only me.

Blood pounded in my temples. With obviously no other alternative, I spread the little packets back out onto the counter and hunched over as I counted. Four, six, eight, ten, twelve, fourteen, sixteen, eighteen, nineteen—That was it. Nineteen. Five missing.

I shoved the box back into the medicine cabinet and tried to calm down. Damn. This was bad.

Maybe he hadn't changed. Maybe he was more than willing to go from Sarah to me without missing a beat. No matter how I tried to rationalize living out my fantasy, I was *not* a one-night stand.

Back to the bedroom. A deep brown down comforter draped over the bed. Two pillows lined the head, each encased in beige pillowcases. No frills, no extra pillows, no throws, no evidence that a woman frequented Jack's bed. Hmm.

He had area rugs, a computer, about twenty skinny notepads, everything all neatly ordered. I knelt down and peered under the bed. Not even a scrap of discarded lingerie shoved underneath in a fit of passion.

Five used condoms, I reminded myself.

In need of some perspective, I pulled out my cell phone and punched in a phone number. "What's wrong with Jack?" I demanded when Coco answered.

"Lola? ¿Cómo?"

"Jack Callaghan. What's wrong with him?"

"What are you talking about?"

"Why isn't he married? Shouldn't he at least have a girlfriend?"

"He's not the marrying kind, chica. You should know that."

Did that matter to me? "He's not the same guy he was in high school."

"Okay, so then why are you calling me?"

Good question. "He has—" I lowered my voice, guilty over my snooping. "—an open box of condoms." I paused for emphasis, in case she didn't see the gravity of the situation. "And some have been used."

She sucked in a loud breath. "¡Ay, Dios! Alert the media. Call Cristina. Call Oprah." She gave an exasperated sigh. "Jack's a guy, Lola. And—oh no—he practices safe sex."

Well, when she put it that way . . . Maybe I was overreacting, but I kept talking. "He's a neat freak. He's perfect. He's got to be hiding something."

She groaned. "Where are you, Lola?"

I dropped my voice and sneaked a look around. "I'm at his apartment. I only have a minute."

"What, are you in the bathroom? Do you have the water running so he doesn't hear you on the phone?"

Oh, she was a riot. And not too far off the mark. "Do you think he could be hiding something?"

"How should I know? I haven't talked to the guy since high school. Ask him, why don't you, *loca*."

"What am I supposed to say? Huh? 'Tell me if you're a raving lunatic or a sex addict because you seem too good to be true, and, oh yeah, I found your jumbo box of condoms'?" I sighed. "I'm in trouble."

"What're you wearing?"

I looked at my reflection. One hundred percent temptress, which meant Jack and I would probably have sex tonight. "What if he's a serial killer? Or a compulsive cheater? Or—oh my God—a dog-hater?" Although he *had* fed Salsa some table scraps.

"*Cálmate*, Lola. I only asked what you're wearing."

I groaned. "A fuck-me dress and stripper shoes."

"Uh-oh," she said gravely. Finally, she was realizing the direness of the situation. "Can't you put on a sweater or something? Give yourself a fighting chance."

"I don't know if I want to. That's the problem."

"Focus, Lola. It's too soon. Find a sweater."

"I don't have one. It's a hundred degrees outside."

I sensed her throwing up her hands in defeat. "Good luck, then. Don't say I didn't try to help you."

I curled my lip at the phone. "You've been a huge help, Coco. Remind me to send you a *You're the Wind Beneath My Wings* card."

She laughed. "You won't be able to resist him, so why bother fighting it? You've wanted him forever. Just be thankful he has the raincoats handy."

And she called herself my friend? Where was the support?

I put my phone away and let my gaze drift to the bed again. "Hmm," I sighed. I propped one knee on it and leaned over the bed, just to test it out. Firm mattress. No squeaks. Another perfect score for Jack Callaghan.

I crawled forward, stretching my arm out to touch the pillow. Squishy and delectable and inviting. The air in the room shifted. Every nerve in my body sent off warning signals. I was a good girl. I need a commitment—or at least a few more dates—before I put out. Didn't I? *Didn't I!*

My mother's frantic voice screamed in my head: *Get out of that man's bedroom, Dolores. ¡Ándale!*

The numbers on the alarm clock on the bedside table changed—7:16. Yikes!

I backed up and jumped off the bed, whirled around—and ran smack into Jack.

His arm snaked around to my back, keeping me upright. He looked down at me. His hands skimmed my sides as if they belonged only there. A slow smile curved his lips. "That dress, and you crawling on my bed, should be outlawed."

I started to melt before I remembered the Trojans. This was a man who very likely was pleasuring another woman.

My mind threw up red flags, but my body didn't care. Flutters replaced the coil of nerves in my gut. He liked me, didn't he? We had chemistry. Sarah was probably nobody.

Right. And Antonio and Reilly were getting married next week. I backed away from him and his hands fell back to his sides.

His dimple skimmed his cheek. "I see you're making yourself at home."

I pressed my hand to my chest to calm my racing heart. If I

232

pressed down hard enough, maybe I could will it into submission. "I—I was just—um, I thought I'd—" I sputtered to a stop, unable to come up with a convincing lie.

He took my hand and led me back to the living room. "No harm, no foul. Find anything interesting?"

I opened my mouth to ask him the burning question and get it over with. But I clamped it shut again. I couldn't do it.

Light filtered in from outside. The candles at the table flickered. I suddenly realized that he'd come into his apartment, lit the candles, and *then* come to find me. Not my best being-aware-of-my-surroundings-at-all-times detective moment.

He opened a bottle of Primitivo from Sobon Estate winery and poured a glass, sliding it across the concrete bar to me. I gave no pretense of being a wine connoisseur and took a good long drink without swirling my glass, studying the tint, inhaling the bouquet, or taking a delicate sip to ascertain the sweetness or the body, or whatever it was. Red and good. That was all I needed to know at this point.

I stared out the balcony window at the city below, then moved my gaze to his face. I wanted to close my eyes and touch every inch of him.

"Lola?" I blinked and found Jack giving me a puzzled look. "I asked if you want some more wine."

My eyes drifted to my nearly empty glass. "Oh." I pushed it toward him.

He held the bottle from the bottom, refilling my glass. "Are you all right?"

Hell no. I wanted his lips against mine. I wanted my fantasy of us rolling around on his perfect bed to be real. I gulped. "Fine."

"No, you're not." He leaned against the counter behind him and studied me. "You're distracted. And you're downing that wine like it's tequila."

233

I pulled the glass away from my lips. Yikes! It was half-empty again.

"You better pace yourself."

He was right. Stay in control, Lola. And keep your hands to yourself. "What's for dinner?" I blurted. "Cold cuts?"

There was that funny look again. "You think I'm giving you cold cuts for dinner?"

I arched a brow at him. "Deli meat in the fridge."

He gave me that half grin again as he leaned forward conspiratorially. "You must have missed the secret steak compartment." He picked up tongs and strode out the French doors to the balcony.

I spun my stool around and admired him. What would he do if I walked up behind him, slipped my hands under his crisp button-up shirt, and brushed my palms against his chest? My vision blurred, and I fanned myself—wow, it was hot in here.

I heard Jack's voice somewhere in the distance. "Earth to Lola."

"What? Oh . . ."

He leaned against the counter next to me—how'd he get there?—and tapped the tongs into his open palm. "Where were you?"

I debated telling him the truth—that I'd been fantasizing about him—but went with distraction instead. "So when do we eat?"

His blue eyes smoldered with gray. "You're hungry?"

I blinked, steadying my nerves. "Yep. Remember I told you—I like food."

He put the tongs down and moved in front of me. Then his voice dropped low, a sexy, wicked grin slid onto his face, and my heart skipped a beat. "Do you want to skip straight to dessert?"

Chapter 17

was not averse to skipping the main course and indulging in dessert. My breath grew shallow as he spread my legs with his, edged his body between them, and traced his fingertips up my thighs. Oh my God, he was smooth—or at least very well-practiced.

Condoms. Remember the condoms.

Right. I tried to break the spell by looking away. No dessert before dinner. I needed answers first—and ground rules. Like when Jack was with me, he would be focused only on *my* pleasure.

But he pushed my hair back and brushed his lips against my ear. "I've waited a long time for this, Lola."

I'd waited a long time for this, too. Fourteen years, to be precise. He nibbled my neck, and a flame of heat spiraled through me. I was too weak to withstand his powers, and I gripped the counter behind me to stay upright.

"Mmm." I don't know which of us moaned. Maybe both.

He ran his hands over my sides and up to my rib cage. "Mmmm. How do you say *beautiful* in Spanish?"

I felt the heat of his tongue against my jaw and struggled to keep my eyes open. If I could see, maybe I'd stay alert and in control. *"Bellísima,"* I breathed, trying my damnedest not to moan again. But a lustful sigh slipped out as I shifted my hips on the stool and pressed myself up against him.

He sucked in his breath and froze, then muttered, *"Tu eres bellísima."* His fingers slipped into the V of my neckline as he trailed kisses along my jaw, my collarbone . . .

My eyes fluttered closed. I loved that he spoke Spanish for me, even if his accent wasn't up to par. My breath caught. *¡Dios mío! That* was his flaw! Jack Callaghan wasn't perfect. I wanted him. Now.

I felt for the buttons of his shirt, working to undo them as he gently pulled down the fabric of my dress. The heat of his breath against the swell of my breast sent flames through me.

Then came his lips. Holy Mary Mother of God. Thank you, Victoria's Secret, for the demi-bra—more uncovered flesh to ravish. I shuddered as he ran his tongue over my skin, his fingers lightly touching my nipple through the lace.

"Red and black," he murmured. "I like it."

That was no secret. His jeans could contain only so much. I pressed harder against him, my body screaming for release. Jack was finally going to be mine. Kind of.

He plumped my breasts together with his hands, his tongue going back and forth between them, his thumbs doing a fine assist on my nipples through the thin fabric of my dress. Oh God, I wanted to rip his shirt off, have him throw me over his shoulder and carry me back to that down comforter of his. . . .

Okay, maybe not. I wasn't a cavewoman. But I could wrap my legs around his hips and he could carry me that way.

I ran my fingers through his hair, arching as I took a deep breath—and started coughing. Black smoke billowed in from the balcony.

"Oh shit." He pulled away and snatched the tongs from

where he'd dropped them on the counter and then raced to the barbecue.

My legs snapped together, and I gripped the counter to steady myself. What was it Jack had said last night? Oh yeah. Timing was everything.

Was the burning food a sign? *Get it together, Lola. It's too fast.* An imperfect Spanish accent didn't chase away the skeletons in Jack's closet, and skeletons *are* important, especially when they involve prophylactics.

Taking my glass of wine, I slid off the stool and went out to the balcony. Flames licked at the two steaks from under the grill. He moved them to the side, turning them and letting the fire die down. "They're a little crispier than I'd planned."

"You were distracted." I didn't mean to say it coyly, but it came out that way.

"Yes, I was." He slipped his arms around me again and brushed his lips over my neck. "In a good way."

A timer went off inside. He dropped his forehead against mine for a second. "Hold that thought."

I followed him back inside and stayed a safe distance from him. "I'm starving."

"I am, too." He gave me that wicked smile again, and I knew he wasn't talking about steak.

But he went back to preparing the meal. He pulled dishes of sour cream, butter, and chives from the refrigerator, and we sat down at the table with our steaks and baked potatoes.

I felt his gaze intent on me as I focused on my food and took a bite of steak. I looked up through my eyelashes. "Delicious. You're a talented man." More coy. Obviously, I had a seduction wish. Or I was schizophrenic.

He gave me a cockeyed grin. "You think so?"

I knew so. "What are your secrets, Callaghan?"

He threw his hands up and looked far too innocent. "No secrets."

Oh yeah? Then explain about Sarah and the missing condoms, bub. "Everyone has secrets."

He cut apart his potato and piled on the fixings. "Try me."

Hmm. A free pass for questions. Not an opportunity to waste—or take lightly. I put my knife and fork down. "When was the last time you had a girlfriend?"

"You cut to the chase, Cruz. Suffice it to say it's been a while. Next question."

Evasive. That wasn't going to fly. I was a detective. Redirect. "How long is a while?"

His smile dimmed a little. "About six months."

Six months. The condom box didn't look that old. "What happened to her?"

He folded his arms over his chest. No more smile. "Next question."

So it was classified information. I let it go, but I was no fool. I'd come back to past girlfriends another time. "Ever been married?"

"Nope." His slow smile started to return. "Next question."

"Ever want to?" I mean, really, what was the point in going out with someone if they never wanted a church wedding, reception to follow at a small local Mexican restaurant?

His body relaxed and he picked up his fork. "Someday—" He shrugged. "—with the right woman."

Maybe with a nice Latina in an outlawed red dress? I scolded myself. "Kids?"

His smile grew. "Don't have any."

My eyes rolled. "Well, that's a relief. But do you *want* any, Callaghan?"

"Of course, *Cruz.* Four sounds like a good number."

I sputtered. "Four kids?" I didn't know if there was a right or wrong answer to the *do you want kids* question, but four? ¡Ay, caramba!

He cocked his head. "How many do *you* want?"

"Not four, I'll tell you that," I said, hoping kid quantity was not a deal-breaker.

He smiled. "Numbers are negotiable."

Yay! Not a deal-breaker, then. Moving on. Next question. "Who called you last night?"

"When?"

Was he serious? Salsa dancing at Club Ambrosía, an invitation to come inside my apartment in the middle of the night, and a phone call that had ripped him away. It had been gnawing at my gut, and he was feigning innocence? I narrowed my eyes. No more pussyfooting around. "Who are you sleeping with?"

The glass he was holding jostled, wine sloshing over the side. "What?"

"It's a simple question, Callaghan." Ooh, I was good. Direct, yet flirty at the same time. "Because, you know, if you're sleeping with someone, and then we happen to sleep together—" I picked up my wine glass and pointed at him. "—and I'm not saying we will, but if we did, that means I might as well be sleeping with that other person because whatever diseases she might have, I'll get." I paused for a breath. "Haven't you seen those posters about knowing who your partner's been with?"

He stretched his hand across his forehead and rubbed his temples. "Wow."

"You've practically seen me naked." Okay, I'd been in pj's, so maybe that was a stretch, but I went with it. Not to mention what would have happened if the steaks hadn't caught fire. Hell, my panties were still damp. "Don't tell me you haven't thought about—" I waved my finger between us. "—us."

"Hell yes, I've thought about us. I can't think of anything

239

else." He leaned forward, his expression painfully serious. "I am currently unattached, not sleeping with anyone, single and available." Then he cracked a devilish grin. "But I'm open to offers."

Oh no. He was going to buy a brand-new, *just for Lola's pleasure* box of condoms before I got into his bed. Or at least he was going to *commit* to buying one. I tilted my head and watched him carefully. "So you're not sleeping with anybody?"

He held up two fingers. "Scout's honor."

I arched a brow. I was pretty sure Jack Callaghan had never been a Boy Scout.

"Now it's my turn," he said as he refilled my wineglass. "Time to spill some of your secrets, Lola."

Ooh. He'd let me grill him only so he could have a turn. Sneaky. I kind of liked that. I held my palms up. "I'm an open book. No secrets here."

Now his eyes narrowed. "Why'd you and Sergio break up?"

My shoulders slumped. Man, he was good. He'd managed to ask me the one thing I really hated talking about. My turn to be evasive. I ate a lettuce leaf from the salad bowl, followed by a slice of ruby red tomato.

He watched me as I caught tomato juice dribbling down my lip with my tongue. "Well?" he said finally. Damn. *Great willpower, Jack.* Not even a slip in train of thought.

"It was time," I said. He could be vague; I could be vague.

"What does that mean?"

"Not sure I remember, it was so long ago."

He cocked his head and gave me a *gimme a break* look.

I smiled. "I'll save that story for another time, too. We can have an ex-bashing discussion—how's that sound?"

His left eyelid tightened for an instant. Then he moved on. Thank God. Jack's voice grew casual. "What's new with your case, Detective?"

Ah, a safe topic. And one I welcomed. I jumped at the chance to process my information aloud. "How's this for shocking? George Bonatee and Assemblyman Ryan Case own Tattoo Haven."

He raised his eyebrows, looking puzzled and dazzling at the same time. "Why is that so shocking?"

"Because Zod—"

"The guy who pierced you?"

"Right, the tattoo guy. His real name is Todd, and he's Case's son. He had motive to kill Emily if she was threatening to take her accusations against him to the police, which she apparently hadn't done yet. And then there's Bonatee and Case. They wouldn't have wanted their names dragged through the mud, so they both have motives. Mrs. Case, too," I said, realizing that she might have been willing to kill in order to protect her husband's career and reputation.

I drew in a breath, trying hard to ignore Jack's proximity, the tone of his voice when he'd mentioned my piercing, and the way his fathomless eyes studied me. I hurried on. "And then there's the fact that Bonatee met his son for the first time and maybe wanted custody of him. Of course, that theory holds more water if Emily was blackmailing him, something I haven't been able to prove. And Muriel, of course," I said, adding one last-ditch suspect, "only because she's a whack job and may have been working for the killer. Any one of them could have gotten Emily out of the way."

He considered it. "Yeah," he said. "But look at the facts: Even though Emily may have believed it, there's no concrete proof that the infection was caused by the tattoo. Whatever Emily had was circumstantial."

"Right, but it *can* happen, we know that, and if Emily had the chance to cause enough ruckus, it might have been investigated and then all hell would have broken loose for those

241

families." I ran through it all again in my head, taking another bite of steak.

Jack put his elbows on the table, propping his chin with one hand. "How's your belly button?"

Warmth immediately crept up my neck. Uh-oh. Back to unsafe territory. It wasn't like I could show him with my dress on, but damn it if I wasn't tempted to undo the tie and let the thing fall open right here and now. I could model my navel—and my underwear ensemble. "Great." *Gulp*. "Next question."

He smiled. "Any other leads?"

It was go-for-broke time. "I got a threatening phone call this afternoon."

His fork stopped halfway to his mouth, and his body language shifted from flirtatious to tense. "What do you mean a threatening call?"

Self-explanatory, wasn't it? "The kind that's—you know—threatening."

He gave me a *no shit* look. "Who do you think it was?"

"I don't know. Could have been any of them. Bonatee, Case, Muriel, Mrs. Case, Zod . . ."

"You don't know if it was a man or a woman?"

"I couldn't tell. The voice was disguised."

When Jack started to say something, I forked a piece of steak into my mouth. Death threats were a worse conversation. "Mmmm," I groaned, hoping to change the subject and get back to flirting. "This is amazing."

"Cut it out, Lola. You brought this up. Someone threatened you. What'd they say?"

There went the mood. I put down my fork and leveled my gaze at him. "He, or she, said to butt out, that I wouldn't be so lucky next time." Oh! This was a totally valid reason—besides the lust bubbling inside me—to stay with Jack tonight. I really

242

shouldn't be home alone. And who knew where Antonio was tonight.

He hesitated for a minute, considering me. "You've almost been run over, and now you've been threatened?" I nodded, not liking the accusation in his tone. "Someone killed that lady," he said. "That means they won't have a problem trying for you next."

"I know that."

"Dangerous business you're in."

I put my palms down on the table and spread my fingers. "Uh, no."

"No? It's not dangerous?"

"Well, yeah, it can be dangerous." I curled my lip. "But this is what I do."

"Do you have a gun?" he asked.

Not this again. "No, I don't. Do you?" I waved my steak knife at him before he could interrupt. "What is it with men and guns, anyway? Is it an extension of your manhood, or something?"

He scoffed. "No. And I'm not a detective. I don't need a gun."

"Well, I don't *want* one. I might shoot the wrong person and end up guilt-ridden and in prison." Hadn't I just explained this to Manny?

"How are you going to protect yourself if this guy follows through with his threat?"

I fell back on what was fast becoming my line and made my tone coy again. "My body is my weapon."

"That's the truth."

But the tension didn't ease. "Jack."

"Lola."

I said a quick prayer in my head, hoping he'd give me the response I wanted. "This is a deal-breaker for me. I'll leave right now if you can't accept that I'm a private investigator."

Of course, I had no way to get home. He'd have to drive me.

He took a sip of his wine and leaned back. "I can accept it. But I think I'd prefer it if you, say, worked at the water company. Or maybe a nice state job."

"Is there another *but* in there?"

"Yeah. But I've wanted you for too long to be scared away by your job. I'm not going anywhere."

Be still my fluttering heart. He wanted me, and he wasn't going anywhere.

A few minutes later, I was standing at the sink, rinsing the dishes he'd cleared from the table, when his hands slipped around my waist, his palm flat on my stomach. His finger pressed against the belly button post under my dress, and he breathed against the side of my neck. "I want to see it."

I swallowed, sure he could hear my racing pulse. How my voice stayed steady, I'll never know. "You show me yours, I'll show you mine." I almost slapped my hand over my mouth. ¡Ay, *Dios!* Had I actually just said that?

Apparently, because he immediately backed away, and when I turned around he was unbuttoning his shirt. One by one, like slow torture. Then—*bam*—I was staring at his tanned chest, an enticing spattering of hair calling to be touched. I felt faint.

My knees turned to putty as he moved closer again and gently—but purposefully—pulled on the tie that held my dress together. It fell open.

He looked me up and down; then his eyes seemed to cloud as he looked at my navel. He dropped to one knee, fingering the silver post.

"It's a little b-bruised still," I stammered.

"I like it," he breathed.

I wound my hands through his hair and leaned back against the counter to stay upright. My fantasy, come to life. "I like you—"

His fingers slipped under the narrow elastic of my panties, and I moaned. Oh God, this was so much better than a daydream.

My legs were going to give out any second. With my dress open, my sheer lingerie front and center, and Jack on his knees in front of me, I couldn't hold out much longer.

His warm lips and tongue explored my belly. I wove my fingers deeper through his hair, tilted my head back, and let my eyes flutter closed. This was it. My moment with Jack Callaghan, fourteen years in the making.

My head pounded and my eyes flew open. *No!* It wasn't my head; it was someone at the door. *No interruptions!*

Jack pulled away.

No—no—no—no! Don't stop.

Then I heard the hammering again, followed by a man's voice yelling, "Dolores!"

Manny?

Jack stood up, intertwined his fingers behind his neck, and closed his eyes for a second. "You expecting a visitor?" he said tensely.

"Of course not," I said.

The pounding grew louder. He headed for the door. I hurried after him, fumbling as I tried to rewrap my dress.

He flung open the door, and I froze, not quite reassembled.

Manny looked me up and down, his gaze hitching at the gaping fabric of my dress and my suddenly numb fingers trying to make a knot with the ties. "Dolores," he said, full-on agitation lacing his voice.

I spouted the first sentence my brain could form: "How'd you know I was here?"

Manny gave me a look that said, *Uh, I'm a detective.* Then he took a deep breath, his eyes seemed to soften, and he said, "Your brother's been in a car accident."

Chapter 18

The room started to spin. I reached for the wall. "Wh—what?"

Jack slipped his arm around my waist, holding me steady. "Is he okay?" he demanded.

Manny nodded. "He's in the hospital."

"But his car's in the shop—" Realization hit me. I pressed my hand to my mouth. He'd been in *my* car. "Oh my God."

Jack's grip on me tightened.

"He's okay, right?" I chided myself and answered my own question. "Of course he's okay. He has to be."

Manny stood stiffly by the door. "Some bruised ribs and abrasions. He'll be fine."

"What happened?"

"Hit and run," Manny said. "He never saw it coming."

I twisted and looked up at Jack. I knew he was thinking the same thing I was—the phone call I'd gotten earlier had been more than a threat. It was reality. And now Antonio had been hurt.

"My parents? Are they with him?"

"Yes. I'll take you," Manny said.

"No, I'll take her." There was no mistaking the possessiveness in Jack's voice. He released me and snatched his wallet and keys from a metal box on the kitchen counter.

Suddenly forced to stand on my own, I wobbled on my heels. Manny caught my elbow, but Jack strode to me and slid his arm around my waist again to steady me.

I took a deep breath as Manny stepped back and Jack guided me out the door.

After three hours at the hospital, I was reassured that Antonio was going to be just fine. Jack drove me home and followed me up the stairs. "I'll stay with you," he said as I unlocked the door.

"You don't have to," I said. Any thoughts of seduction I'd had were long gone, but I wanted the comfort of being with him. The threats had taken on a whole new spin, and I was jumpy beyond belief.

"Yeah, I do."

Thank God. "I'm going to change. You can borrow—" What did Jack sleep in?

"I'll find something." He wandered off to Antonio's room as I dropped my purse and headed to mine. It was a disaster. I'd forgotten about the mess I'd left behind before "the date." I ignored it, no small feat, considering I had Magdalena Cruz's compulsive clean genes in me.

I slipped out of my dress and bra and into safe pj's. The photos of Jack were scattered on the dresser. I tucked them away in the drawer. I didn't want to take any chances that he'd see those pictures. Explaining them was a conversation I wasn't ready to have. Pulling my hair up into a ponytail, I went to make sure Jack had found what he needed.

My stomach fluttered when I saw him. He sat on the couch in a plain white T-shirt, a pair of blue drawstring pajama pants that I'd never seen my brother wear, and Antonio's guitar perched on his knee. His head was lowered as his fingers picked out a quiet melody. An Eric Clapton song, I think.

I stretched out on the opposite end of the couch and let my eyes drift closed. Antonio was safe, and I was here with Jack. Things were less than ideal, but I wanted to forget about it for a little while. After a few minutes, the music stopped, and I felt his finger on my silver toe ring. My eyes fluttered open again, and I readjusted my position to distract myself. Exhaustion didn't stop my body from reacting to his touch. Damn, it was hard being a woman. I had zero control over my emotions and hormones.

He lifted my feet onto his lap, laid one hand on top of them, and stretched the other along the back of the couch. "You okay?"

"Considering someone tried to kill Antonio and it should have been me? Nope, not okay." I waited for him to say again that being a PI was too dangerous, that I was in the wrong profession, that it was my fault Antonio was sleeping in a hospital room tonight. I'd heard it from my parents, from Gracie, from my grandparents—why not from Jack, too?

"You have to figure out who's behind all this."

I wiggled my finger in my ear and blinked. "What?"

"You're not safe till you find the killer."

"You're not going to tell me I should quit?"

One side of his mouth pulled up, that enticing dimple appearing. "Nope."

That was it, just "Nope." He might as well have professed his undying love and committed to a lifetime of monogamy with me, I was *that* moved by his response. In one quick motion, I pulled my feet off his legs, sat up, and straddled him. I suddenly didn't care about his secrets.

He ran his hands up my arms. I wound my fingers through his hair, just as I'd done earlier. I couldn't control whoever was trying to kill me, but this moment with Jack? That I could. I *needed* to.

Jack nudged the strap of my top off my shoulder and pressed his lips against my collarbone, then my neck. My body tingled, and I opened my thighs and moved against him.

I yelped, surprised, when his mouth grazed my breast through my top. My back arched, and I grabbed the side of the couch. My arm hit the lamp from the side table, and it crashed to the floor.

"Oh!" I lurched, nearly falling. Jack steadied me. Tears pooled in my eyes. My brother was in the hospital because of me. I didn't want to confuse my need for comfort with what I felt for Jack, and I was so not in control at the moment. Maybe the lamp falling was a sign. Maybe it wasn't the right time for this. "I'm sorry," I said. "I c-can't . . ."

"It's okay, Lola."

I dropped my forehead against his for a second then pulled back when I heard heavy footsteps up the back stairs followed by thunderous pounding at the kitchen door.

"*Dolores! ¿Qué pasó?*"

Oh God. Now the night was complete. It was—what?—one in the morning, and my dad was trying to break down the back door.

"*Nada, Papi,*" I called. "*Estoy bien.*"

"I heard a crash. What is going on in there?"

Reluctantly, I climbed off Jack and hurried through the kitchen, cracking the door open as I wiped away a stray tear. "I'm fine, Papi. Go back to bed."

He tried to peer around me. I let him. There was nothing to see in the kitchen. And he didn't have super vision that could make a right angle turn into the living room. Finally he gave up and leveled a look at me. "*You* go to bed, *mi'ja.* You have a job to quit in a few hours. You will come work at Abuelita's."

My jaw dropped. Oh no. As soon as I woke up in the morning, I was nailing a hit-and-run killer. "I am *not* quitting my job."

My mother marched up the stairs, her finger wagging in front of her. "Oh yes, you are."

"No. I'm not."

She threw her hands up and made a motorboat sound with her lips. "Maybe when the bad man kills us, then you will get some sense, eh?"

I was not going to let her guilt me into quitting. "Maybe," I said, heavy on the sarcasm.

But she had to have the last word. "We will talk tomorrow, Dolores." The *punto* was implied. End of discussion.

Like hell. I was going to be busy. Family castigation could wait.

My father peered around me again, his eyebrows angled together in suspicion. I turned and looked at the empty kitchen then back at him. "What?"

With a frustrated shake of his head, he said, "Nothing." Finally, he turned and followed my mother back into their house, and I went back to Jack.

I knew my parents would be downstairs for the next hour, each with an empty glass pressed against the ceiling. It really was time to find a new place to live. The hell with cheap rent. It wasn't worth it.

Jack was leaning against the door to my bedroom when I found him. "I need to go to sleep," I said. I didn't know if my anxiety would let me, but I had to try. I had a killer to hunt in the morning.

Jack took my hand. "I'm not leaving you alone."

I tried to read him, looking for ulterior motives, but saw only weary concern. "Okay."

He wrapped his arms around me. "Okay."

There was a loud thunk, and the floor vibrated, something pounding against the ceiling downstairs. "*¿Quien está allí, Dolores?*" My mother's muffled voice followed more pounding. "Who is there?"

I pulled away from Jack, giving him an exasperated smile as

I shook my head. "Go to bed, Mami!" I yelled at the floor and stomped my foot. "Go to bed."

Jack led me to my bedroom. We lay down under the quilt, and I curled up next to him. And amazingly, we slept.

A door shut, and I awoke with a start.

The killer! He'd tracked me down.

I bounded out of bed, grabbed the nearest weapon, my high school girl's softball trophy, and slipped into the hallway. The blazing sunlight streaming through the living room windows cleared the bleariness in my brain. The night before flooded back to me. The killer wasn't in my flat. It had to be Jack.

My white-knuckle grip on the trophy relaxed as I went to the kitchen to start a pot of coffee. A slip of paper on the counter next to the morning newspaper caught my eye.

> *Finish the job. I'll call you later.*
> *—J*

I smiled. He'd written me a love note, brought the paper inside, and had faith in me. I didn't need the pro list anymore.

My mind screeched to a halt. ¡Ay, Dios! Today was Thursday. The *quinceañera* was in two days!

The clock came into focus. It was 7:49. I had to haul ass if I was going to catch a killer *and* help finish making the favors and arranging the flowers. After racing through my morning routine, I grabbed a cup of java to go, tucked the *Bee* under my arm, and ran out to the driveway.

Dead stop. I had no car. Shit. Papi had said the driver's side was smashed, but the car was still drivable. After the accident, he'd taken it to the restaurant and left it there. I'd have to get it later.

251

I pulled out my cell and dialed Manny.

He picked me up ten minutes later, greeted me with a barely perceptible nod, and we plowed through the thick morning traffic into downtown. After a few minutes of the silent treatment, he asked, "How's your brother doing?"

"They're discharging him this afternoon. He's going to be fine."

Manny's eyes went back to the road. Apparently that was it for conversation, so I ripped the rubber band off the newspaper and riffled through the sections until I got to the Metro. Jack's latest column was there. Seeing his picture and byline sent a ray of warmth through me. I'd curl up with his words later—after I'd caught a killer.

A few minutes later, Manny parked and stepped out of his truck. He waited for me on the sidewalk, his face grim. He glanced at the paper that was tucked back under my arm but kept silent as we walked toward Assemblyman Case's reelection office.

Mrs. Case had been talking to her daughter but stopped midsentence when she saw us. I wanted to spit at her and yell, *¡Mentirosa! You knew about Emily!*

She snapped her cool gaze at Manny for a split second. "What is it now, Ms. Cruz?"

I was impressed that she remembered my name, but felt no compulsion to sugarcoat things anymore. "How far was your husband willing to go to protect your son Zod from Emily Diggs's accusations?" I rattled off my thoughts out loud. "Or maybe it was all *you*, trying to protect your son and your husband."

If the ice queen was thrown off guard by the questions, it didn't show. She was a pro. "I'm sure I don't know what you are talking about."

"*I'm* sure you do—" I gave her a *gimme a break* look. "—but let me share my theory with you. I think either Zod gave Garrett Diggs a tattoo using poorly sterilized equipment *or* your son showed Garrett how to give himself a"—I made air quotes with my finger—"'prison tattoo.' Either way, it wasn't very hygienic, and it caused a heart infection and he died."

Mrs. Case slammed the stack of papers she'd been holding down on a desk, and her daughter jumped, her eyes wide. *That's right*, I wanted to say, *your mom just might be a murderer.*

"That woman was a slanderous lunatic, and I told her so," Mrs. Case said. "She was always getting involved where she had no business. Affairs with married men, secret children, each with a different father. She was a gold digger." She took a step toward me. "My son was *not* involved in that boy's death," she ground out from between her clenched teeth.

I shrugged. "Maybe not intentionally, and we really can't prove it anyway, but I don't think the voters care too much about that. Your husband's career could be ruined whether Garrett's death happened the way Emily Diggs thought or not."

The arctic shrew ran a palm down her charcoal suit and blinked, slowly, three times. "What do you want, Ms. Cruz?"

"Emily Diggs met with your husband. I believe she told him about Tattoo Haven and Garrett's death with the hopes that he'd do something about it."

Mrs. Case lowered her chin and stared at me through her spidery lashes. "The boy died. I'll say it again. It was tragic, but Todd—" She took a deep breath and brushed her suit down again. "—Todd was not involved. Now, I do have a full schedule today. If there's nothing else—" Then she picked up her stack of papers again and walked away from me.

"Mrs. Case, the story's out there. She contacted a reporter, you know."

She stopped dead in her tracks, flicked an icy look at Manny, and then faced me. "Let the story be told, then. My family has nothing to do with that woman's death."

253

She turned on her heel and passed through to the small office, slamming the door behind her. Before I knew it, a man who looked to be the president of the Young Republicans appeared out of nowhere and ushered us out of the building. With a pointed glare at us, he turned the key in the lock.

Manny took me by the elbow and steered me toward his truck. "Nice job."

Yeah. His sarcasm wasn't lost on me.

My cell phone vibrated from inside my purse. Pulling my elbow from Manny's grip, I dug it out and flipped it open. "Hello?"

"Ms. Cruz?"

"Yes."

"It's Joanie. Case." She whispered.

I perked up and knocked the back of my hand against Manny's arm. "Joanie. What can I do for you?"

"Can we talk?"

Maybe she was going to snitch on her dysfunctional family. "Definitely. Now?"

"I can meet you around the corner in a couple of minutes."

"We'll be right there."

"Uh . . ."

"What is it?"

"That guy you were with makes me nervous."

Yeah, he makes me nervous, too, I thought, darting a glance up at Manny's brooding face. "I'll leave him here, then." The phone went dead, and I dropped it back into my bag. "She wants to talk," I said to Manny.

"Good."

"Alone." I shot him a faint smile. "You make her nervous. Can't imagine why."

His jaw tightened. "I'll wait for you in the truck." He walked off, and I headed in the opposite direction to meet Sporty Spice.

Chapter 19

Waiting for Joanie in the blistering sun, I started to open the paper, just to see the smoldering picture of Jack again. But then the assemblyman's daughter was in front of me. She glanced at the paper before I tucked it back under my arm, Jack's face against my body. I didn't want to share him.

She looked up and down the street. "Can we go somewhere more private?"

Before I had a chance to answer, she started down the street toward the capitol. "Are you all right?" I asked.

"I—I'm not sure." We walked onto the grass, and she stopped behind a huge evergreen, leaning her back against it.

Give up the goods, chica. I knew from my conversation with her brother that she was on Prozac, but she was still seriously on edge. "Maybe I can help?"

"It's just—" She pressed her palms against her eyes, shaking her head. "I didn't know."

"Didn't know what?"

"You think my brother's involved in Garrett's death?"

Poor thing. She was so out of the loop. "I think it's a possibility."

She pressed her palms to her eyes again then shook her head as if she were clearing it of cobwebs. "How?"

"Like I told your mother, Zod may have given the tattoo—or he may have taught Garrett how to give himself one. I've spoken with the woman who manages the bar, and she said Emily Diggs felt that she had enough to go to the police and raise the question."

"Proof? To prosecute him?"

"She kept a journal of everything she discovered. I think she wanted someone held responsible for Garrett's death. She talked to a lawyer, but she died before there was an investigation."

Despite the blistering heat, Joanie's face lost all color. "She talked to a lawyer?"

"Your roommate's father."

She gave me a look like I was speaking pig latin.

"George Bonatee," I said.

Her expression cleared. "Right. It makes sense that Mrs. Diggs would talk to him." She played with the hem of her T-shirt, then looked at me. "So is Zod in trouble?"

Poor girl probably felt guilty for her part in getting him the job in the first place. "If he killed Emily to keep her quiet, he is."

"He doesn't have it in him."

So she didn't think mangy Zod had a violent streak. I inched to the left, trying to follow the minuscule bit of shade the tree offered. Sweat dripped between my cleavage. Lovely. "So Zod never talked about any of this with you? You're not close?"

She shrugged. "Average, I guess. We don't talk a lot. And if he wasn't worried about it . . ." She hesitated and darted a glance at my newspaper. "You told my mom that Mrs. Diggs contacted a reporter?"

I nodded. "After she didn't get anywhere with your father. What makes you so sure Zod didn't kill her?" I asked.

Joanie's eyelids fluttered in the heat, and she scoffed. "Zod wouldn't hurt a fly. He's all talk. Always has been." She glanced around the park before she looked back to me. "What can I do to help him?"

My job is to help bring Emily's killer to justice, muchacha, not help the potential killer get off easy. "I can't help you there. Sorry." I squeezed her arm. "I'm just trying to find out what happened to her." I ran the back of my hand across my forehead, wiping away the sweat. "Are you glad to be rooming with Mary again?"

She nodded, a small frown playing on her lips. "Just moved back in. Kind of freaky knowing the woman who lived there before me died."

"Emily was murdered."

"Right. Murdered."

It sounded so sinister when someone else said it. "But it's better than living with your parents?"

She rolled her eyes. "God, yes. I'd do anything not to be in the Case household. No freedom." She hesitated. "Beatrice is really upset, though. I guess she and Emily became friends."

"You can tell Bea that I'm not going to stop until I find out who killed Emily, and why."

Joanie's gaze was intense and direct. "It wasn't Zod. He wouldn't do that."

I couldn't comfort her, or reassure her that I believed Zod was innocent when I hadn't discovered the truth yet. Instead, I asked, "When was the last time *he* lived with your parents?"

"Oh, Jesus, I don't know. He escaped a long time ago. I don't think he'd take a million dollars to go back."

After last night, I completely understood wanting to get away from nosy parents. "He's got a pretty good gig going since your dad owns Tattoo Haven."

She bared her teeth. "You think he's guilty, don't you?"

My guard went up. Despite how skittish she was around her

257

mother, Joanie clearly didn't want to consider that her brother was involved in Emily's death. I didn't blame her for being upset. If Antonio were under suspicion of murder, hell, I'd defend him to my grave.

It was go-for-broke time. What had Jack's note said? *Finish the job.* That was exactly what I intended to do. Until I found Emily's killer, I wasn't safe—and neither was my family. I needed to push buttons and see what happened. "He has a pretty clear motive. But then, so do your mother and father."

"He didn't do it." Joanie flicked her wrist in front of her face, her shiny gold Rolex knockoff reflecting the sun. "I have to go."

"But—"

"I have to go," she repeated, her tone leaving no room for discussion.

Right. Mama Case was probably ready to unleash some whoop-ass on Joanie for being gone so long. She pushed off on the ball of her foot and jogged across the capitol lawn and back toward her father's reelection office. Despite the short leash Mrs. Case managed to keep her daughter on, Joanie hadn't defended either of her parents. Did that mean she thought *they* were capable of murder? And if so, which one?

An hour later, Reilly and I were sitting in her lime green Volkswagen Beetle in front of Bonatee's office. The bubble car didn't exactly blend in, but I couldn't throw stones with my mangled car still sitting in Abuelita's parking lot.

"This is so boring," Reilly said after twenty minutes.

She was right. This stakeout had been duller than watching paint dry. I grunted noncommittally, slouched down in my seat, and kept staring at the doors to the building. My eyes scanned up and down the street every few seconds.

"Shouldn't we go see how Antonio's doing?" she asked.

"We will. Just a few more minutes." *Come on, I willed.* Something had to happen. I needed a break in this case. Someone needed to make a mistake or act or do *something.*

My prayers were answered fifteen minutes later. A man came from around the back of the building and darted into the middle of the street. I recognized him immediately. George Bonatee.

I aimed the camera I'd borrowed from Neil's stash and clicked. Documentation for my report. It felt so spy-novelish—now, if only it led me somewhere.

I bolted upright when Bonatee slipped into a mint-colored sedan that had come to a halt just ahead of the building. The driver's side was smashed, streaks of dark green and brick red paint marking the crumpled steel. "Reilly!" I nudged her with my elbow. "Start the car!"

Reilly jumped, fumbled with her keys in the ignition, and brought the bug to life. "What? What's going on?"

I strained but couldn't see the driver. "Follow that car."

She gunned it, screeching tires finally catching hold of the asphalt.

"Quietly, Reilly." I caught a glimpse of the car's license plate, committing the number and letters I could see to memory. *SJ3. SJ3. SJ3.* I buckled my seat belt and held on for my life.

"Who is it?" Reilly shrieked, her pudgy hands white-knuckling the steering wheel.

Grappling for breath, I let out the air I'd been holding. "I'd bet my life that that's the car that hit Antonio last night." And smashed the Mustang at My Place. Whoever it was, they had some nerve driving it around. I looked around for a police cruiser. There were none to be found.

Reilly slammed her foot down on the gas pedal. "My Antonio?" The car seemed to recoil for an instant before surging forward. I repeated the partial plate in my head—*SJ3, SJ3*—and dug my cell and a pad of paper out from my purse again. SJ3. I jotted the plate number down, wishing I could see all of it. I dialed the office.

"Camacho and Associates," Sadie said into my ear.

"Sadie. It's Dolores," I said. "I need your help."

"Jesus, Dolores. Relax—"

I took a breath. Screw relaxing. I wanted to nail the bastards—whoever they were—once and for all. "I need you to run a license plate."

"What is it?" She seemed to be talking in slow motion.

I looked at the partial I'd written in my notebook. "SJ3. It's a green—" I peered at the car three lengths ahead of us. "—Mercury, I think. Or maybe a Buick?"

"That's all you have?"

"I can't see the rest. We're too far away."

"Get closer."

Like I wouldn't if I could? "We're trying."

"Fill me in," she said.

Sadie barked, "Back off—" I heard a scuffle, and then Manny's voice came across the line. "What's going on, Dolores?"

I ignored their squabble and told him about the banged-up car that Bonatee had climbed into. "I don't know who's driving. Reilly and I are following him now."

As if on cue, Reilly cranked the wheel to the left, and the car skidded around a corner. Horns blared at us from all directions.

"I'll call you back about the plate."

I snapped my phone shut and dropped it in my lap, grabbing the handle of the door to keep from careening into Reilly. "Manny's on it!" I shouted over the screeching tires and my thudding heart.

"Where'd it go?" she shrieked a second later. "It's gone!"

Sure enough, we'd lost it. There was no green car any-where, smashed front end or not—except for the fluorescent green bubble we were in. "Damn."

"Sorry." Reilly pulled over, her hands shaking as she held them against her cheeks. "How can you do this every day? I'm a wreck!"

I didn't have time to answer. My phone rang. I jumped, grabbed it from my lap, and slammed it against my ear. "Manny, what'd you get?"

A low, raspy voice came over the line. "Are you following me?"

My heart thrashed. It was my threatening phone caller. The same person who was in the car with Bonatee. Or maybe it was Bonatee on the line. "Not anymore," I said, sounding way more calm than I felt. I thought my heart might sponta-neously combust any second.

"Your brother was a mistake. Drop this case, or next time, there won't be any mistakes." And the line went dead.

"Who the hell are you?" I yelled at the phone.

As if answering, the phone rang again. "What?"

"This is how you answer the phone?" My mother. "We have to work on the favors."

Shit. I banged the heel of my hand against my forehead and heaved a frustrated sigh. I couldn't do *quinceañera* busi-ness right now. Reilly needed a pep talk to keep going. The killer had just threatened me again. I didn't have time for mesh bags and chocolate Kisses!

Then I remembered my car parked at the restaurant. If a killer could drive a smashed-up car, why couldn't I? I was the good guy—and I needed my wheels. "I'm on my way, Mami."

Chapter 20

An hour of making party favors turned into two. I silently brainstormed my case the entire time, but wasn't any closer to a plan or an answer than I'd been before I began shoving silver Kisses into the little bags.

I managed to avoid conversation with my mother, however. She was too busy worrying about whether or not to refry her *frijoles* and if we'd have enough guacamole to discuss my job or late-night activities. Finally, with the promise that I'd be at the hall to decorate bright and early Saturday morning—if I lived that long—I left.

Camacho and Associates' gang of three was gathered around the conference table when I made it to the office. Manny's expression was dark. Apprehension settled in my gut. Something was going on.

Neil sat with his back to me, his neck completely sunk inside his shirt. His fingers flew across his laptop computer. I pulled up a chair next to him and sat down, nodding my head in one communal greeting.

"Dolores," Manny grunted. He cleared his throat. "Muriel O'Brien is dead."

I nearly fell off my chair. What happened to buttering a person up before the blow? "You're kidding."

"Died yesterday afternoon."

Yesterday. That meant she couldn't have rammed Antonio last night. Which meant someone else had. I rubbed my temples. Poor Muriel. She'd been nothing more than a puppet, and now she was dead. I came back to the same potential puppet masters I'd been considering from the beginning: Assemblyman Case; Bonatee; the ice queen, Mrs. Case; and Zod.

Neil growled, but the *tap-tap-tap* of his fingers striking the keys never let up. "Cause of death?"

"Mixture of drugs and alcohol," Manny said.

"Accidental?" Neil asked.

Manny closed the folder he'd had open in front of him. "Doubtful. Bottle of codeine next to a bottle of blood pressure meds and cough syrup."

"Just like Emily," I muttered.

Manny nodded. "All washed down with one too many bottles of beer."

A sound came from deep within my throat. Muriel wouldn't touch beer. She'd said it herself—she was a Myers's and Coke broad. I took a deep breath and faced Manny. The bodies were piling up, and it was past time to spill my secrets. "I was almost run down outside My Place on the night I went to see Muriel. And I was locked in a freezer at the florist, although I'm pretty sure it was Muriel who did that, and then my brother was hit while he was in my car—"

Manny and Sadie both slammed their hands down on the conference table at the same time. "What?" she shouted, while he barked, "¿Cómo?"

My eyebrows pulled together as I looked from one to the other. "And then I got a call a while ago saying to drop the case.

263

Or else." I rubbed my temples again. It was so cliché, but it had me on edge. "Muriel ran My Place and Tattoo Haven. I think she was probably working for one of the suspects or was being blackmailed into doing their dirty work." It was the only thing that made sense. "If the killer was feeling threatened . . ." I trailed off, not wanting to say aloud what I was thinking. As long as I kept investigating Emily's death, I was a threat to the killer, and I could be next.

"—murder eliminated that threat." Manny's eyes were black slits. "You will not take any chances, Dolores. *¿Entiendes?*"

Hell yes, I understood. I didn't want to climb the lonely stairway to heaven.

Neil leaned toward me. "What did the broad tell you the night you talked to her?"

Ay, Dios. Neil had spoken a complete sentence. "She said she only drank Myers's. Besides that, nothing substantial. The only thing that was strange was when she said—" I closed my eyes, remembering how Muriel had phrased it. "—'Emily was screwing the wrong people, and she didn't even know it.'"

"Interesting but vague," Manny said. "Anything else?"

"She was hostile. Emily was trying to blame Tattoo Haven for Garrett's death, and Muriel seemed to be taking that a little personally. She took a phone call while I was there." I replayed it in fast forward in my mind. "She was bartering. Negotiating the price of something. I thought she was buying or selling something." Little did I know she'd probably been making a deal with the killer to stalk me and scare me off. "A few minutes later, she completely closed up. Practically chased me out. I spotted her a few times over the next couple of days— like she was tailing me." When they all stared at me, I went on. "Once outside the tattoo place in a red truck, once at the florist, and once at Bonatee's office."

"So you think she was on the killer's payroll," Manny said.

I had no proof, but he was all about developing hypotheses. "I think it's possible."

"And you have no idea who called her that night? She never said a name?"

"No clue." I paused, something tugging at my memory.

"What is it?" Manny asked.

"It's just—I don't know." I thought back to that night at the bar. Whoever had tried to run me over had either followed me or had been in the bar at the same time Antonio and I had been there. "My Place is strange. The people didn't all seem to fit." But I wasn't able to identify a killer from my memory of who had been there that night.

Manny watched me for a moment, drumming the table with his fingers. Finally, he looked at Neil. "Anything on that license plate?"

Neil tapped on the laptop. "Not yet."

"Keep thinking," Manny said to me. "It'll come to you."

God I hoped so, because when Manny adjourned the meeting, the killer had two and I still had zip.

I could feel Manny staring at me as I went over my notes again. He came up next to me. "The first rule for any private investigator is self-preservation, Dolores. You have to take everything seriously and be cautious to the extreme. You got lax on this one."

He was right. Emily, and now Muriel, had been murdered. I could be next. "Do the police have anything new?" I asked, avoiding his scrutiny.

"As of yesterday, no."

Great. So Detective Seavers and I were neck and neck in the race.

Manny left, and I spent the next twenty minutes following

up loose ends by contacting Café Venezia where Emily had worked, and then Sean's teacher. Both phone calls yielded nothing new.

My eyes blurred on my notes, and my head throbbed. I flipped open my cell phone and dialed Just Because.

"This is Dolores Cruz," I said when Tom Phillips answered the phone.

"Yep?"

"I just heard about Muriel. I'm sorry."

He harrumphed on the other end of the line and I got the distinct impression he wasn't wearing black. "At least she called you first," he said.

"What?"

"I heard her on the phone telling someone she was going to call a detective and tell her everything if she didn't get some money—whatever that means. I figured you were the detective and I know the man didn't come through."

The hair on the back of my neck stood on end. Muriel had died before she'd called me. "What do you think she meant?"

"Hell if I know. Said some literaratzi bullshit." Tom hacked a cough, and I held the phone away from my ear. "A woman scorned, or some shit, and something about a lie."

My pulse raced. Muriel had been tangling with a killer and had paid the price. Question was, who was the woman scorned—Emily, or someone else? And what was the lie?

The pieces I'd been trying to connect were still miles apart. I hung up with Tom, more confused than ever. I needed a break. And some perspective. Yoga, I decided. That would clear my mind.

Chapter 21

Khandi glided into the yoga studio, serenity oozing from every pore of her body. Meditative calm—that's what I wanted, but I was too racked with nerves. I closed my eyes and breathed in through my nose, trying to channel some of the teacher's tranquillity.

It didn't work. How could it? Someone wanted me dead, and Jack hadn't called.

"Welcome," she cooed into her headset.

I moved into the first pose, but my mind whirled with death and killers and threats. I was missing something crucial. Damn it, what was it? *Think*.

Khandi moved us through poses. Her lyrical voice sounded tinny through the speakers. Take her out of the yoga studio and plop her in a jungle boat at Disneyland shooting fake hippopotami, and she'd fit right in.

She started in with her typical train-of-thought monologue. "All of us put on different faces, playing different roles throughout the week. Focus on your core, the you beneath the faces."

"Different faces. Okay," I muttered. The woman next to me shot over a *shut up* look. I ignored her and thought about the roles I played in my life: Daughter, sister, friend, PI, Jack Callaghan's almost lover.

I moved to the next position, the muscles in my calves uncoiling. What about Emily Diggs? Mother, activist for her son, George Bonatee's ex-lover, victim. Had she and Bonatee rekindled their affair? A woman scorned, I mused. Bonatee had betrayed Emily a long time ago. Had she held on to that grudge?

"Everyone does it," Khandi cooed.

Emily's killer was certainly playing multiple roles.

My mind worked as I arched my back. I'd been focusing on Zod, but now everything kept leading me back to Bonatee. He'd been involved with Emily. He'd fathered her child. He'd steered her away from filing charges against his tattoo shop, and his buddy's son. He'd been seeing someone else, but was that before or after he moved Emily into his house? Had he called it off with the other woman, hoping to get back with Emily?

Different faces. Different roles.

I thought. And I thought. And I thought.

The revelation hit me so suddenly that I fell out of my pose. "Oh . . . my . . . God," I said.

The woman next to me frowned. "Shh."

I frowned back. "I'm solving a murder here. Do you mind?"

Her spine stiffened, and she scooted away from me.

I went back to my theory, following the threads that wove through my mind. It was a completely different scenario from the one I'd been focusing on, one that didn't have a single thing to do with tattoos.

Jack had told me that people kill for revenge and jealousy. I groaned, half in distress, half in anticipation. Had I been looking in the wrong direction all along? Whether or not Bonatee had taken up with Emily again—if his lover *thought* he had, she

268

could be the woman scorned. I bolted up. *¡Dios mío!* "It's possible." One question remained, however. Who could the scorned woman be?

"Go solve your murder somewhere else," the irritable woman next to me said. Good idea. I'd already grabbed my bag and was halfway to the door. I had to know if my theory still made sense outside the yoga studio and under fluorescent lights. God, I hoped so.

The drive to Camacho and Associates seemed unbelievably long, especially in my smashed-up car. I cursed under my breath, barely resisting the urge to jump the curb and barrel down the sidewalk.

I screeched to a stop in front of the office and crashed through the door. "I have a new theory," I said, bursting into Manny's office, belatedly hoping he wasn't with Isabel on a six-minute rendezvous.

Nope. Empty. Where was he? It was seven fifteen. Didn't superdetectives work around the clock?

It's okay, I told myself. *I'll call him when I'm sure.* I settled myself at the table and hunched over my notes. Ideas went round and round in my mind. The conversation with Tom was front and center. *A woman scorned. A lie.* I looked at the case from every angle and pieced together a hypothetical timeline of events:

- *Emily's son dies.*
- *With no one else to turn to, she contacts George Bonatee, a lawyer, her ex-lover, and the father of her son, for help.*
- *When he hears her story and puts together the connection to his business and his friends, the Cases, he sets Emily up in his rental house so he can keep an eye on her. Or, he really wants to help the mother of his son and sets her up in his rental to get to know her again.*

269

- *Maybe he still loves her, maybe not, but his girlfriend probably freaks when she finds out Emily is back in the picture.*
- *And is even more freaked when she sees Sean. It had taken me all of two seconds to determine that Bonatee was Sean's father, and I didn't know the man. It would have taken his lover a nanosecond.*
- *The woman scorned lures Emily to the boat and manages to kill her. No more obstacle between her and the man she loves.*

"What's going on, Dolores?"

Sadie startled me out of my concentration, and my gaze darted to the clock on the wall—8:35. Where had the last hour and twenty minutes gone? Time flies. "Working my case."

My empty stomach roared. When was the last time I'd eaten? Maybe food would boost my brainpower.

I gathered up my things. "Did Neil come up with anything on that license plate?"

She nodded, looking me up and down like I'd lost my marbles. "Manny was supposed to call you with the information hours ago—" She bared her teeth. "—before he left with—" She paused.

"Nevermind." She handed me a note, her red-lipped frown dissecting her face. "He left this for you."

I made myself breathe evenly. I wasn't going to get angry with her for not giving me the note in the first place. I opened it and read, stunned. "Ryan Case?" I peered at Sadie. "Are you sure?"

"Neil's buddy ran the partial with the make of the car. We cross-referenced the list, and that's the only relevant name that came up."

I immediately started jotting notes and arrows on my whiteboard, erasing and rewriting until it made sense. "So it was borrowed," I murmured.

Sadie came up behind me. "That does show things from a

different perspective, doesn't it?" she said after reading my notes. "Very slick, Dolores. You should definitely call Manny." I heard her take a breath. "Right now."

I had another revelation. She used nicknames for me only when Manny was around. It was for *his* benefit, not mine. What was up with that? "Good idea," I said, digging in my purse for my phone.

I turned my back on her. Two missed calls flashed on the screen. I'd been so gung ho on getting back to the office to review my new theory after I left yoga that I hadn't checked my messages. Stupid.

The first message was from Jack. "Lola, I have a lead on your case. Bonatee owns a boat called *My Lie*. I'm going to the marina to nose around some more. Give me a call."

A surge of warmth spread through me. He *had* called. *And* he was following a lead for me. My lie. The boat was the lie Tom had overheard Muriel talking about! The pieces were starting to fit into place. *I'm right behind you, Callaghan.*

Manny's voice was next. "Your cell phone's not on. *Llámame.*"

"Don't worry, I'll call you," I muttered. *Right after I call Jack.*

I wheeled around, but Sadie had vanished. I checked the time. Nine o'clock. I dialed Jack's number.

His apartment phone rang and rang until finally his machine clicked on. "It's Lola," I said after the beep. "I got your message. Call me back."

I tried his cell phone. Voice mail. I tried Antonio. He didn't answer. "You're supposed to be in bed," I said to the machine. "Have you heard from Jack? Call me."

It was late, would be dark soon, and I wanted to see Jack. But I was no fool. I needed to let someone know where I was going. I looked for Sadie and found her in Manny's office, logged on to his computer. "I'm going on a field trip," I said.

271

She jumped a mile. *Busted.* Unfortunately, I didn't have time to wonder what snooping she was up to.

"I'm going to the marina," I continued. "My friend found George Bonatee's boat." Bonatee said he'd been out of town the day Emily disappeared. He could have been lying, or maybe he'd lent the boat to someone. Someone like his lover.

She logged off the computer and stood up. "I'll go with you—"

"No!" It wasn't like there was a killer there, and Sadie's company would interfere with the way I wanted to greet Jack when I found him. "I'll be fine. I was just letting your know."

She shook her head, her messy blond hair looking tousled and perfect. "It's where the crime took place. You shouldn't go alone. And Manny should meet us there."

"Really, Sadie. Thanks, but no thanks." I headed for my car, but she was hot on my heels. "It's not like the killer's there waiting for me."

"I insist."

Maybe I could make it to my car and lock the doors before she got in. I hurried, nearly breaking into a run. Then I saw my crumpled car. There'd be no quick getaway in it.

I crawled in through the passenger side. Before I was settled in the driver's seat, Sadie was in the car. I stared at her. "I don't need you for this."

Sadie flashed me a mock smile. And buckled up.

Once I realized that she had no intention of getting out, I gave up. I directed my car to the Riverbank Marina, where I hoped to find Jack Callaghan. And if I was really lucky, I'd also find some evidence that would help me solve this case once and for all.

Chapter 22

I stared at the phone after I'd left a third message on Manny's cell. "Why aren't you answering?" I muttered. It was completely out of character for him not to pick up. I threw my phone into the backseat, and then I remembered what Sadie had said. Manny called me before he left with . . . I turned to her. "Who'd Manny leave with?"

She grimaced but kept silent.

Tomb Raider girl. It had to be. And Sadie was acting *un poquito* jealous. Or pissed. Or both.

The sky had turned almost completely black, just a few stars breaking through the thick blanket of darkness. An awkward silence persisted between Sadie and me. "Why were you on Manny's computer?" I finally asked her. Just making conversation.

"None of your business." When I raised an eyebrow at her, she said, "We have history."

Right. I didn't want to touch their history with a ten-foot pole. After another length of silence that lasted almost eight minutes, we reached the marina. A spattering of cars dotted the parking lot, but otherwise the place was deserted. I recognized one of the cars as Jack's Volvo, and my pulse quickened. He was still here somewhere.

A glance at Sadie made me suck in a breath. She held her gun in her hands. Jack had come here to nose around. The marina was the scene of the crime. Take no chances, Manny had said. Good advice. Sadie had been right to come with me.

I dialed my boss again—still no answer—but left a message telling him where Sadie and I were. Just on the off chance that the killer was out there somewhere and—a shiver ran down my spine—we didn't return.

Grabbing the flashlight from my safety kit, I shoved it under my arm. "No gun?" Sadie asked, the pinnacle of calm, her own piece held snugly in her hands. She must have been a Girl Scout, always prepared.

"No. I told you, I'm meeting a friend." But I was all talk. The flashlight doubled as a weapon. And I had handcuffs. I fished them out of my purse and shoved them in the back of my stretchy pants.

I spotted Emily's boxes, the ones I'd taken from Mary's house and hadn't yet given to Sean and his uncle. An aluminum baseball bat stuck out of one of them. I snatched it at the last second and pressed the rear door closed. Yoga pants had no pockets. I debated tossing my keys to Sadie for safekeeping, but opted for under a shrub instead. Better not to risk them being jostled at an inopportune moment.

Even though Jack was out there somewhere, the darkness was ominous. The lapping sound of the river knotted my stomach. Sadie and I stayed in the shadows as we crept along the parking lot to the marina. We picked our way down the wooden planks.

Something creaked behind us.

I spun around. The flashlight dropped. I wielded the bat up over my arms, ready to clobber whoever was sneaking up on us.

274

Mary Bonatee yelped and shrank back. Her black clothes were skintight, shimmered, and hugged her bony body. She looked like a petrified cat burglar in a bad movie.

"What are you doing here?" I whispered, lowering the bat.

Her eyes bugged. "Looking for my dad. I've been sitting in the parking lot, trying to talk myself into going home. Then I saw you."

Bonatee had been with the killer earlier. At least I thought he'd been with the killer. My pulse quickened with agitation. Had they come here? "Why would he be at the marina? You sure he's not at his house or something?"

She shook her head, the whites of her eyes glowing in the beam of my flashlight. "The marina and his boat are his favorite places." Her eyes glistened. "I have to talk to him about Sean."

No more brushing things under the carpet. Good for Mary.

"Why are you here?" she asked.

"Looking for someone."

"Not my dad?"

"No, not your dad." Though it would be a big perk to find whoever he'd been with earlier and lock my handcuffs right around the killer's wrists.

Sadie cleared her throat. "Hate to interrupt, but isn't your man out there somewhere?"

Yes, he certainly was. I handed Mary the flashlight, gripped the bat, and resumed creeping toward the marina. Sadie brought up the rear.

"Did you find something out about Emily?" Mary asked. Her hushed voice trembled.

"Keep going," Sadie barked under her breath, darting a glance behind her and back up toward the parking lot.

I resisted sticking my tongue out at Sadie; then I pried Mary's hand off my arm before she punctured my skin. "I think Zod taught Garrett to give himself a tattoo," I said, deciding I could give Mary a little insight, "and that tattoo may have caused his heart infection."

She sucked in a breath. "And someone killed Emily because of that?"

"Actually, I have another theory about that."

"What?"

"Your father had an affair with Emily."

She rolled her eyes. "Duh."

We followed the wooden planks to a steep staircase leading down to the dock. I went on as if she hadn't spoken. "They had a son together."

"Tell me something I don't know."

"Speed it up, Dolores," Sadie snapped.

I talked faster. "Emily got in touch with him. Your dad said she wanted his help."

Mary covered her ears and squeezed her eyes shut. "If you're going to say my dad killed her . . ."

"No, I don't think he did, but I think he was involved with someone else when Emily came back into his life, and that person might have been slightly scorned."

"Scorned?" Mary stopped; then her eyes grew as she realized what I was saying. "Oh my gosh, really? Scorned enough to kill?"

"You got it." I pulled her into motion again, and a few minutes later the three of us were at water level. We stopped short at the private gate that led to the boat slips, staring at the paint can that held it open. Had Jack done that?

I scanned the area but saw no movement. Nothing, aside from the paint can, seemed unusual. I thought about calling out to him, but a sense of foreboding made me hold my tongue. Something didn't feel right, and I was suddenly grateful that Sadie and her gun were with me.

Mary took a shaky breath. "It looks creepy in the dark."

That was an understatement. I stifled a shiver. "Your dad's boat is called *My Lie?*"

"Yeah. I never understood why he named it that," Mary said.

It *was* odd. I'd been mulling it over since I'd heard Jack's message. My lie. My lie. The letters ran together in my mind, turning and weaving until they blurred together. Was the name of the boat George Bonatee's twisted attempt at irony? What had he lied about? Hiding that he'd fathered Emily's child? No, he'd only just learned about that.

The letters jumbled and reordered themselves. I started and smacked my forehead. *My lie.* It was an anagram for *Emily!* I caught a glimpse into George Bonatee's heart. He was more than a handsome charmer. He was also a tortured romantic. He'd made a mistake by fooling around on Emily. She'd left him, and he hadn't been able to win her back. Heat spread to my cheeks. Despite his errant ways, he'd always loved her. Keeping his love a secret—*that* was his lie.

Mary's shrill whisper broke into my revelation. "I'll wait here."

"Are you okay?" I asked. She looked spooked, her silky skin pasty in the moonlight.

"I—I'm fine. I j-just keep picturing Emily."

"Go call your dad again, Mary. He's probably home now—"

A pop in the distance, like a firecracker, pierced the air. Startled, Mary and I fell back against the gate. Even always-prepared Sadie jumped back, wobbling on the rickety boards of the dock.

"Who's shooting at us?" Mary shrilled.

"No one. It came from the boats."

Mary twisted her arm until she had a vicelike grip around my wrist. "From m-my dad's b-boat?"

I struggled to breathe, feeling like I was choking on air. Jack might be on her dad's boat. I'd come here to meet him, but maybe I'd be saving him instead. I shook Mary loose and choked up on the bat. My fingernails clawed into my palms. If the killer was out there, armed, there wasn't a chance in hell that my body or this bat could fight off bullets. Damn me and my principles.

"Go call the police." I nudged Mary until she moved on her own. "Detective Seavers," I hissed. "Tell him where we are and the name of your dad's boat."

She nodded, her eyes glowing with fear, and then she was running back down the dock, up the rickety stairs. She vanished into the darkness.

I crouched low, adrenaline pumping through me as I scrambled through the gate. Inching forward, my heart thrashed. Sadie's careful steps sounded behind me.

I searched the names of the boats until I found *My Lie*, and we hunkered down to listen.

The sound of voices drifted out on the heavy air. "Listen to me. This is crazy. Turn yourself in."

It was Jack!

I dropped to all fours and crawled along the dock to the ladder, clinging to the bat as if it were Jack himself.

"Dolores," Sadie whispered. "We should wait for the police."

We should, but there was no way I was going to. I knew who Jack was with, and two people had lost their lives already. He was not going to be the third.

I ignored her and crept forward, holding my breath. Would a boat this big rock with my weight? I boarded, moving slowly. It didn't budge. I breathed out a relieved sigh even as my heart slammed against my rib cage.

George Bonatee's voice boomed from belowdeck. I stopped dead in my tracks. "I do care about you, but—"

Someone tapped my shoulder. I swallowed the scream in

my throat and whipped my head around, my fist stopping millimeters from Mary's face. Her face was drawn.

Holy Mary mother of God. My heart was going to explode any second from the pressure. "Why'd you come back?" I mouthed.

The tears pooling in her eyes answered my question. She couldn't leave without knowing the truth. "My dad?" she mouthed.

I nodded, putting my finger to my lips and cocking my head to listen. No sirens yet. Dammit. Of course it took longer than five minutes to get to the river road. All I could hope was that Seavers and his troops would arrive like silent, stealthy, deadly panthers. Until then, we were on our own.

Sadie was unshakable. She crouched across from me, her face like a statue.

Another shout, and spew of words came from the cabin. A woman this time. "Just tell me why. I love you. Since I was little, I've loved you."

Mary inhaled sharply and pressed one hand against her cheek in a moment of clarity. Her eyes bugged, and she rasped in my ear. "My dad and . . . and . . . and Joanie?!"

I nodded. "He's the one that convinced her to move out when Emily needed a place to live," I whispered. I'd had my own moment of clarity when I'd gone over my night at My Place for the fiftieth time. An interracial, May-December couple had sat at one of the tables, their backs to me. I'd bet my life that that couple had been George Bonatee and Joanie Case. It was the perfect meeting place for a clandestine rendezvous—off the beaten track and definitely not the type of place that Bonatee's friends probably frequented. Whether he'd been comforting her, or whether she'd been trying to win him back, I might never know, but things had backfired for Joanie. Killing Emily hadn't made Bonatee come back to her.

The crack of another gunshot cut through the air. My ears rang. We were running out of time!

From the corner of my eye, I saw Mary bolt forward and yank open the door to the cabin.

No! I tried to stop her, catching hold of her ankle. She tripped and tumbled down the short, narrow flight of stairs: The flashlight she'd been carrying bounced down after her.

The next few seconds were a blur. Sadie slithered undercover, and I dashed across the deck and hid behind a lounge chair. The door swung open, and Joanie appeared, her tawny hair disheveled. She wielded a tiny silver gun. She walked briskly across the deck. She peered into the darkness. I shrank into the shadows.

I tried to make eye contact with Sadie, but couldn't quite see her. We had the element of surprise, and I had to trust that Sadie was ready. Joanie turned her back to me, aiming her gun and slowing scanning the deck. Just as I was about to charge, she whipped around, elbows locked, and looked right at my hiding place. I was sure she could hear my heart beating, but I melted back into the darkness and she shifted her gaze.

"Joanie!" Mary screeched. "Stop this."

Joanie screwed her face up. I could almost read her expression. She seemed to realize that she was going to lose control of the situation, and she dashed back to the door. Mary had managed to scramble to the top of the stairs, Jack behind her, but they both froze when they saw Joanie and her shiny silver gun.

"It's too late," she said. She waved the gun, and Mary backed down the stairs again. Jack had no choice but to do the same. Despite his size and strength, he was no match for the little Saturday night special. The bullets would tear apart his insides just the same as anyone else.

Where the hell had Sadie gone? I looked around but didn't see her. I moved silently toward the cabin of the boat. Joanie had to have been the one to try to run me over at the bar, I realized. After she'd killed Emily, it seemed that she'd tried everything, including enlisting Muriel, to stop me from getting too close to the truth.

I heard a splash. Oh God, had Sadie fallen off the boat? My heart plunged into the pit of my stomach. I hoped she could swim, but I couldn't take the time to find out.

With painstaking slowness, I opened the door just enough to sneak a look down the stairs. Joanie's arms flailed, aiming her gun at Mary and Bonatee, then at Jack. ¡Dios mío! Was that blood trickling down Jack's arm?

Random thoughts shot through my head. Fighting crime wasn't like this in the movies. Well, yes, it was, but in the movies I'd look like one of Charlie's Angels in a killer Stella McCartney ensemble instead of yoga pants, "Living la Vida Loca" would be playing in the background, and Jack would be mouthing that he loved me and wanted to father my children—all four of them. I'd have as many little Callaghan kids as he wanted, I decided.

I forced myself to be calm. Jack would be fine. He had to be. I tiptoed to the other side of the door, trying to formulate a plan.

I caught a glimpse of Joanie's arm swinging around until it was trained on Mary. "Why are you here?"

"You and my father?" Mary shrilled. "Y-you killed Emily?"

Joanie choked out a sob. Clearly she was off her meds. Or she'd used them all up on Emily and Muriel. "She was stealing him from me."

Mary scoffed. "You. Killed. Her. Do you understand that? You took her life."

Joanie's voice broke. "She didn't even love him, and he left me for her. You can't understand, Mary. She was going to break his heart again."

I stood, riveted, listening to the story unfold.

"How'd you get her out here?" Mary asked.

281

"Oh God." Bonatee's deep voice oozed with pain. "I let her use the boat. I didn't even ask why."

Joanie interrupted. "I pretended to be George's secretary. Called Emily and told her that he had a surprise for her. She never questioned coming on the boat."

Mary seemed skeptical. "Why? What did she think was going to happen?"

Joanie's sobs turned into awful laughs. "I don't know. And I don't care. She came, and that's all I wanted. Halfway to Discovery Park, I made her take the pills and drink the medicine." She waved her gun in the air, and it was clear that had been her leverage. "And after a while, I pushed her overboard."

Tears rolled down Mary's face. "You're going to burn in hell."

¡Cállate, *Mary! Crazy girl*. Didn't she see the gun? I looked around when I heard a low thud behind me. Sadie, dripping wet, was creeping around to the front of the boat. Thank God. I signaled to her that I was going in—no more waiting.

Joanie's voice drifted up. "I love you."

I opened the door a little wider. Jack stood back against the wall, seething. No dimple for Joanie. He kept his mouth shut. Good man.

"Things change," Bonatee said. His voice dropped to a pleading whisper. "People change."

Joanie waved the gun erratically. "I haven't. You cared about me."

Bonatee sputtered and fought tears. His charming, handsome persona had completely cracked. "But I loved her."

She aimed the gun at him. Her arms drooped, and she started crying big helpless sobs.

Bonatee tried again. "Joanie—"

"Don't." She ran the back of her hand under her nose. "I thought if she was g-gone, you'd c-come back to me. Don't you see, I was trying to protect you."

282

He hung his head, looking forlorn and shaken. But then, with a sudden burst of adrenaline, he lunged toward her. Joanie shrieked, startled, and pulled the trigger.

Bonatee went down like an sack of *masa*, his wounded leg twisted under him.

"Daddy!" Mary screamed, crouching next to him, pressing her palm against his leg. His blood spread like an oil spill.

Bonatee's breath came in labored spurts that were matched by Joanie's desperate heaving cries. "Oh God, no," she sobbed. "No, George."

"Muriel—" he managed through his clenched teeth. "You . . . killed her, too—"

"She was going to tell—"

"You got . . . her . . . involved. She was . . . just a . . . bartender."

Joanie crouched in front of him, wiping away her tears. "She figured it out, George." Her voice dropped to an erratic whisper. "I paid her. But it wasn't enough. She *knew* and she was going to *tell*."

I couldn't tell how aware of her surroundings Joanie was. If I charged in, I could be shot. Or worse, Jack could be. I caught Sadie's eye, waved my finger in the air, and pointed at the door leading belowdeck. *Distraction*, I mouthed.

She nodded as she inched to the side of the door, dripping, her arms bent at the elbow, her big-ass gun aimed at the sky. It was all about timing, and so far, Joanie had the upper hand, what with her hostages.

I tightened my grip on the bat. Hiking up my leg, I hit the door frame with all my might. The force of the blow reverberated up my arms and into my teeth.

"What the hell?" Joanie's voice had regained its edge, her killer instinct surfacing. The gun popped again, and Bonatee let out an anguished cry.

Joanie wailed, and Mary cried, "My dad needs help!"

I took a deep breath, wiped the sweat off my hairline, and held the bat up above my head. Since I couldn't go down to her, I had to get Joanie to come up to me. I brought the bat down, smashing it against the outer cabin wall.

"What *is* that?"

A puddle grew around Sadie's dripping body, but she held her gun at the ready.

The sounds of shuffling footsteps drifted up to me. My stomach whirled, but I managed to choke down the bile that crept up my throat. Catching a glimpse of tawny hair, instinct took over. Heaving my knee up to gain momentum, I swung the bat around, aiming for the middle of the door this time. The crack of Joanie's gun going off and the snap of my bat making contact with the door were simultaneous. My body twisted, and my arms followed through on the swing.

Sadie charged, gun still trained on Joanie as she wobbled on the top step.

I caught Jack's eye and held it for a split second. He nodded, and I knew that he'd finish taking Joanie down.

Joanie's gun dropped and bounced down the stairs. Her arms airplaned as she tried to keep her balance. From the corner of my eye, I saw Jack move. I crow-hopped, hiked up my knee, and kicked her in the sternum. She wobbled, but managed to stay balanced; Jack was up the stairs in a split second and had his arms around her in a death grip. Her arms flailed and she kicked, but he maneuvered her to the ground. With her face down, he straddled her back and clasped her wrists with his good hand.

Mary held the gun by the tips of her fingers. I rushed down, Sadie at my heels, whipped the handcuffs from my pants, and slapped them on Joanie Case.

Finito. It was over.

Chapter 23

Detective Seavers barreled down the dock, gun drawn, following after uniformed officers. About time. They sped onto the boat. A minute later, two officers dragged Joanie back up with them.

Jack came up next. His injured arm hung limp by his side. Guilt flooded me when I saw the blood running down it. "Oh my God." He looked at me. His temple pulsed—whether from pain or anger, I couldn't tell. I didn't care. I whispered, "I'm so sorry."

"Can't say I like the people you hang with, Lola."

Right, like I *hung* with Joanie Case—although I'd actually thought about it. She'd been so nice and had seemed so grounded and had great workout clothes. "I'm not a huge fan of them myself at the moment." Except for Sadie. Tonight I was a *big* fan of hers. She'd stuck by me.

Jack's gaze drifted over my shoulder, and I turned to see what had caught his eye. Manny stood at the end of the dock, talking to a police officer.

Sadie was hurrying over to them. "I especially don't like him," Jack said, his teeth gritted.

I chose to ignore the comment—and the fact that Jack was

practically shooting death rays at Manny. Camacho was my boss. No getting away from that. But his timing certainly sucked.

Jack tried to unbutton his shirt with one hand. "Help me get this off," he said to me.

I undid the buttons and slid the shirt off his good arm first, working the fabric over the injury on his other arm. Even with a bullet wound, he looked good.

He kept silent. Maybe he didn't want to think about why he'd taken a bullet. He clutched the shirt against his arm to stop the blood, grimacing at me.

"Your research is top notch," I said, smiling to fight back the tears that threatened.

"Got me in deep water tonight."

"What happened?" I asked. I was dying to know how Jack had ended up right in the thick of my case.

"I followed the lead on the boat and walked right in on Joanie begging Bonatee to take her back." He gave a sheepish grin and a little shrug. "She saw me, pulled out that gun, and went postal."

A hundred thoughts went through my head, beginning and ending with the fact that Jack had nearly died tonight because of me. "You helped me solve the case," I said. "I wouldn't have come to the marina if you hadn't left me a message and—"

"And I'd probably be fish food," he finished.

I looked up at him, not liking that image. "Funny man."

"I took a bullet. Think you can make me feel better?" he asked. "After I get a Band-Aid and some pain meds." He gave me a little squeeze with his good arm.

"Definitely." I slid my hand up his chest, tangling my fingers in the spattering of hair spread across it. God, he felt good, too. My hands trembled against his skin, and my body went cold, the adrenaline letdown starting. "And now you'll be able to write a killer article about the body art industry, right? And maybe one on psycho killing-mistresses?"

He managed to crack a smile as he leaned against me. "I might need to look at that piercing again to make it really compelling."

Detective Seavers reappeared from belowdeck and stepped onto the dock. He glared at me. "What happened here, Ms. Cruz?"

I shivered. An ambulance wailed in the distance. "We had a little bit of a showdown."

He frowned at me, pulled out a notepad, then turned to Jack. "And you are?"

"Jack Callaghan."

Seavers's sparse hair was moist around his scalp. He looked back at me. "You brought a civilian to help you?"

I held on to Jack. "He was a hostage."

Flashing lights cut through the darkness as the ambulance pulled into the underground parking lot. Seavers, Jack, and I stepped out of the way as the paramedics raced by us and into the boat's cabin. Four minutes later, they came back up. They carted Bonatee off the boat on a body board, a police officer by his side. Mary brought up the rear.

Manny strode across the dock, the uneven clip of his boots tapping against the wooden planks. Sadie, her gray blouse and black slacks stuck to her body, was just behind him.

Manny gave Jack a once-over.

"Camacho," Jack said, his teeth clenched.

"Callaghan." Manny's lips were pulled tight. Then he turned to me. "So it was Joanie Case?"

"Yes."

He lowered his chin. "You take her down?"

I nodded.

"And it almost got her killed," Jack said.

Manny looked at me. "Her life, her choice."

Sadie gave me a look that seemed to say *good choice*. Then she scowled at Manny. I hadn't figured out what was going on

287

with those two, but I was pretty damn sure Sadie wanted to throttle him, and I had a suspicion her anger had to do with that history of theirs that she'd mentioned.

"I'm going to need a statement, Ms. Cruz." Seavers's stern voice cut through me.

Manny gave Seavers a hard look. "Give her a few minutes."

The detective grumbled something under his breath, but he walked away.

Impressive. Camacho had power.

Then he turned his stern look to me. "Didn't I tell you not to investigate alone?"

"Sadie was with me." Whose side was he on, anyway? "And we called you, like, ten times. You didn't pick up your cell phone."

"Personal safety is the number-one rule. You can't solve a case if you're out of the game." He put his hand on my back, letting it linger there for a second. "You have to be careful, *sarge*—" He paused and looked at Sadie, then at Jack. "Dolores."

Jack tensed beside me, possibly from the bullet wound in his arm, but I didn't think so.

Sadie had grown very still. She suddenly turned to me. "Dolores, I have some things I'd like to share with you." She shot a look at Manny before turning back to me. "Next week, when we're back in the office."

Manny scowled, but I smiled and nodded. Had Sadie and I reached some unspoken level of camaraderie? Were we really a team now? The idea made me happier than I thought it would.

But I relegated my curiosity to the back of my mind as she walked away and as Detective Seavers came back toward us.

"Camacho," the detective said. "There's an Angelina Jolie look-alike waiting for you in the parking lot." He handed Manny a folded slip of paper. "Wanted me to give this to you."

288

The hairs on my neck stood up, and I felt my eyebrows raise in surprise. He'd brought his girlfriend *here*—to a crime scene?

The paramedic finally returned and pulled Jack aside to look at his arm as Manny opened the message from *Tomb Raider* girl. I'll be damned if his lips didn't quirk into the tiniest grin.

Okay, I was seriously out of the loop. He had the dark princess, Isabel, waiting in his truck. All that was missing was the ex-wife, and the soap opera would be complete.

A voice came from behind me. "We're taking him to the hospital."

I turned around. It was the paramedic. "What?"

"Mr. Callaghan's arm needs attention."

I forgot about Manny and focused on Jack. He'd taken a bullet for me. Well, not really, but it was still sexy as hell.

Jack wound his good arm around me. "Come with me."

Warmth spread through me, the chill finally gone. I smiled. "I'll be right behind you, Callaghan."

He pulled away and gave me an expressionless look that I couldn't decipher. Without him next to me, the chill was back. I watched as he was led up the dock and into the underground parking garage. It hit me then. I'd done this to him. It was going to take some serious work to make it up. But the man did things to me, so it was work we'd both enjoy.

Manny started down the dock. "Let's go," he said tersely.

He stood to the side and let me go first up the rickety stairs. Yikes. Yoga pants. Formfitting. My ass at his eye level.

I tried to be confident as I marched up. This was not how I wanted my boss looking at me. "What kept you, Manny?" I asked over my shoulder.

I turned around the second my foot hit flat ground.

His smoldering eyes jerked up to my face, and my pulse skittered. "Family business," he said, his voice tight.

I was usually the one with family things going on. "Everything okay?"

"Fine. My wife—"

"Your ex-wife?"

He hesitated, and then ground out, "Never mind."

I tried to be cool and went into detective mode. "Everything doesn't sound all right."

Manny's eyes narrowed. "Not your concern."

"Huh." Okay, then, end of that conversation.

The uneven clip of his boots against the wooden planks thundered in my head. I asked the burning question. "How'd you get that limp?"

He slowed and looked at me. "I was shot."

No kidding. I probably could have guessed that. "Who shot you?" *The spouse?*

He didn't answer.

We finally made it to the parking lot. I did a double take when I saw Isabel. Reilly had been right. She put everyday people to shame, including me and my curves. I'd never seen such perfection. I seriously thought people might go to war over her.

She sashayed toward Manny. "Finally, baby." She kissed him—kissed *Manny*. "You got my note?"

He nodded and gently guided her back. She noticed me. "Oh. Manuel, are you going to introdu—?"

I raised an eyebrow. *Manuel?* Ick.

He hesitated for a beat then said, "Dolores Cruz. Isabel Martinez. Isabel, Dolores."

"*Mucho gusto,*" I said, holding my hand out to shake. Maybe some of her ethereal beauty would rub off on me.

She took it, her perfect red lips parted seductively. She blinked slowly, and for a second made me think I'd said "pleased to meet you" in some alien language instead of in Spanish.

290

"Nice to meet you, too," she finally said. "You work with Manuel?"

"I work *for* him," I said.

She looked at me for an extra-long beat. "Uh-huh. So you know his—"

Manny suddenly grabbed Isabel by the elbow. "Come on," he barked, and steered her to the cab of his machismo truck.

Isabel thought I knew Manny's what? Or who? Something tickled at the back of my brain, but I ignored it. *Focus, Lola.* Jack—the man who'd put his life on the line for me—was in the hospital. He was the only person I wanted to deal with right now.

I saw Sadie waiting at my smashed car. I started toward her. I still had to give Seavers a statement, but I could do that at the hospital.

"Dolores," Manny called.

I stopped and turned around. Dolores. No nickname in front of Isabel. *Good move, boss.* "Yes?"

"*Buen trabajo.*"

My eyes bugged. *Good job?* A full-blown, unsolicited compliment? Holy cow. And all it had taken was two men getting shot and my single-handed apprehension of a killer. Okay, apprehension of a killer with a lot of help, but still . . .

"*Gracias,*" I said. I was filled with pride. "I learned from the best."

He nodded, and I thought I caught the smallest hint of a satisfied smile. He opened the driver's door of his truck and threw a quick glance in Sadie's direction. "You did good," he said when his eyes settled on me again.

Thank God he got into his truck, because I couldn't control the goofy smile that erupted on my face. He pulled away, and I heard his words again in my head. I'd done good.

Chapter 24

The *quinceañera* was going off without a hitch—if you didn't count the cold shoulder I was getting from my family.

Mami glared at me as she walked by, squeezing Tía Marina's hand.

"It's perfect," my mother said to her sister. "Look at her."

I followed their gazes and saw Chely boogying in the center of the dance floor. She was a star.

Antonio sauntered by. His goatee was trimmed, his skin was browned, and his ribs were bandaged under his black guayabera. He gave me half a smile, but his eyes twinkled. He'd forgiven me for endangering his life. The question was, had I forgiven myself?

I really had to figure out a way to keep my business separate from my family.

"My Antonio!"

I turned to see Reilly skipping through the crowd toward him. Her halter dress looked a couple of sizes too small, but her emerald green hair looked fabulous.

Antonio shot me an *I'm going to get you for this* look and

darted off, clutching his ribs, just as Reilly reached me. "Where's he going?" she asked.

I shrugged, not knowing which one of them to root for.

She giggled, then started after him. "Silly boy."

Antonio didn't stand a chance.

I ran my hands down my sides, looking around for Jack. We hadn't had much chance to talk since the marina. He hadn't made it to the Mass this morning. Maybe he'd had second thoughts about us. Maybe there *was* no us. And I'd been willing to bear his passel of kids.

The DJ put on my favorite Juanes song, and I moved my feet, my hands pressing against my stomach. My eyelids fluttered closed. God, Juanes had a great voice. Maybe he could help me forget about everything for just a little while.

My body quivered as someone pressed up against my back, hands slipping around to my stomach. Mmm. I knew that body. "You made it," I breathed.

Everything slowed as I dropped my arms to my sides and turned to face him. The contact between our bodies never broke.

An enticing smile crossed Jack's lips. His hands slid up the sides of my body, finally resting on my lower back. He drew me in closer and edged one of his legs between mine. "I wouldn't have missed it."

I hadn't thought his showing up was a given, but I kept that to myself. "Good." I gently ran my hand over his bandaged arm. I was shameless. I'd take any excuse to touch him. "Don't I get a little thank-you?"

He gave me that *you need a straitjacket* look again. "Thank you for what?"

For what? Was he serious? I pulled back and put my hands on my hips. God, didn't I get any credit? Men. "Um, for saving your life?"

"Here's a little news flash, babe," he said, pulling me close again. "My life wouldn't have been in jeopardy if it weren't for you."

Minor detail. I changed the subject. It was time to set those ground rules. "Who's Sarah?" The question, along with whom he'd used the missing Trojans with, was going to bug me till the day I died—or until I tortured the answer out of him. Which, come to think of it, might be a lot of fun.

I thought I saw him hesitate, but then he smiled. "Nobody."

I grinned coyly. "I'll find out eventually. I'm a detective, after all."

He put one hand on the small of my back, interlaced the fingers of the other hand with mine, and pulled me closer. "Yes, you are. And *bellísima*."

I shuddered as he held me tighter. *La vida* Lola. Secrets or not, it was a good life.